ONEWORLD CLASSICS

Boy

James Hanley

ONEWORLD
CLASSICS

ONEWORLD CLASSICS LTD
London House
243-253 Lower Mortlake Road
Richmond
Surrey TW9 2LL
United Kingdom
www.oneworldclassics.com

This edition first published by Oneworld Classics Limited in 2007
Printed in Great Britain by TJ International, Padstow, Cornwall

ISBN-13: 978-1-84749-006-3
ISBN-10: 1-84749-006-9

The Forest Stewardship Council (FSC) is an international, non-governmental
organization dedicated to promoting responsible management of the world's
forests. FSC operates a system of forest certification and product labelling
that allows consumers to identify wood and wood-based products from well-
managed forests. For more information about the FSC, please visit the website
at www.fsc-uk.org.

Contents

James Hanley (1897–1985)

A young James Hanley

James Hanley's wife Dorothy
(Timmy)

From left to right, Margaret, Gerald and Bridget,
James Hanley's sister, brother and mother

The Liverpool docks (above, photograph by Liam Hanley);
Hanley's London residences: 28 Camden Square, where he lived
from 1964 to 1967 (bottom left) and 51 Lissenden Mansions,
where he lived from 1967 to 1980 (bottom right)

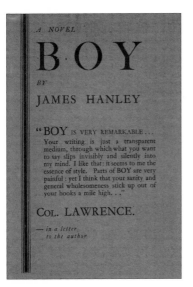

The cover of *Boy* in the 1931 Boriswood edition (top left)
and the "lurid" Paris Obelisk Press edition (top right);
James Hanley in front of his cottage in Llanfechain, Wales (bottom
left) and a letter from Hanley dated 1982 (bottom right)

Introduction by Anthony Burgess

W HEN JAMES HANLEY DIED in November 1985, a year younger
than the century, the *Times* headlined its obituary with
"Neglected Genius of the Novel". Only in England, perhaps,
could such a summation fail to arouse guilt. "Neglected Genius" is
accepted merely as the category to which Hanley belongs: neglect is
so regularly accorded to some of our best writers – Rex Warner and
William Sansom come immediately to mind – that we complacently
acquiesce in it as a necessary aspect of our culture. The geniuses who
are neglected are usually the geniuses who disturb, and we do not
like to be disturbed. The *Times* obituary accurately referred to "the
integrity and disturbingly acute though gloomy vision of his best
books" and prophesied that they "will certainly be remembered in
the chronicle of the century's literature". Chronicled then, though
not read. But there are signs, and this reprint of *Boy* is one of them,
that Hanley is about to be granted a posthumous audience.

One of the causes of neglect in his lifetime was a kind of double
solitariness: he belonged to no literary school, and he cherished the
self-elected condition of a recluse. He was impossible to categorize.
Sean O'Faolain, writing in 1941 in the *Virginia Quarterly Review,* felt
that he belonged to an Anglo-Irish literary movement belied by his firm
declaration that he was not Irish. He had, nevertheless, quirky qualities
unallied to British writing. William Faulkner, another neglected genius
no longer neglected, said that Hanley's work was "not British, not
American, not South African, not Ebury Street, not Chicago. Just
language like a good clean cyclone". Open-air turbulent language,
then, exactly fitted to Hanley's preoccupation with the sea. I remember
reading both *The Ocean* and *Sailor's Song* during the Second World

War. They earned the accolade "Conradian", but Hanley's modernism was full-blooded while Conrad's stood on the Edwardian brink. *Sailor's Song* is about four sailors on a life-raft, and their delirious memories shift from one war to another. It is not easy reading; it offers no concessions to the middlebrow in search of a rattling good yarn. The novel he published in 1943, *No Directions*, was equally uncompromising. It described one night in a tenement in Pimlico during the Blitz; it was deliberately chaotic, with one stream of consciousness merging into another: as the Luftwaffe blitzed London so Hanley blitzed English. It remains one of the best records we have of what it was like to be a civilian under fire. It is, of course, profoundly disturbing.

Like Ernest Hemingway, James Hanley made fiction out of the action he had himself experienced, but Hemingway learnt to live soft out of what had come hard. His toughness became a well-publicized pose, and it was, finally, only the elected toughness of the bullfight aficionado and the big-game hunter. Hanley, reared in Liverpool, ran away to sea at thirteen and sailed around the world. Jumping ship at New Brunswick, he joined the Black Watch Battalion of the Canadian Expeditionary Force. He saw action round Bapaume, was gassed, spent time in hospital and then was discharged. Back in Liverpool, he combined the dirty work of manual labour with the study of the piano and the reading of Russian fiction. The punishment he gave to his fingers, particularly as a deckhand on his frequent sea trips, precluded any chance of his becoming a pianist, but the musical component of his work is, in my judgement, important. He sometimes makes words behave like notes; as with James Joyce, the cultivation of strange rhythms suggests a musical sense working in parallel to the literary. Clearly it was an unusual ear that gave distinction to his first book, *Drift*, which was rejected by seventeen publishers before it reached the hands of the great philologist Eric Partridge, then briefly in the book game. It is significant that Partridge, an outstanding scholar of the spoken word, was almost alone among publishers in seeing, or hearing, its merit. Hanley got five pounds for it; the five hundred copies sold out; the reviews were good. A fine press but low sales – the pattern was established early.

Boy appeared in 1931, at the beginning of a decade of hard work and meagre rewards. Hanley wrote it in ten days and dedicated it to Nancy Cunard, who had given him the typewriter he could not himself afford. It is the grimmest of all his stories, and it essays a frankness then, despite *Ulysses*, very rare in fiction. A boy escapes from a tyrannical father by stowing away on a merchant vessel bound for Alexandria. He is ill-treated and sneered at by the crew, undergoes his sexual initiation in an Egyptian brothel, and then, writhing in the shame of syphilis, is put down like a sick dog by the ship's captain. It came out in a limited edition of 145 copies for subscribers only, but this was followed by a trade edition notable for the asterisks of expurgation: these made the text seem more candid, or scabrous, than it was.

In 1934 a cheap edition was brought out by Boriswood. It had a highly provocative cover – a *danse du ventre*, very nearly naked – and the book had to be withdrawn because of police action. The main voice of middle-class condemnation was that of Sir Hugh Walpole, a once respected popular novelist, knighted for services to what the middle class thought of as literature but now nearly forgotten: "It is so unpleasant and ugly, both in narration and incident, that I wonder the printers did not go on strike while printing it." Walpole was said to have torn up a copy publicly in a London bookshop. *Boy* became a cause célèbre in the fight against Britain's Sedition Act, with E.M. Forster addressing the International Congress of Writers in Paris in 1935 in eloquent endorsement of the book and fierce denunciation of official squeamishness. As for Hanley, he suffered. His mother and sister were catholic and devastated by the scandal of the burning of a hundred copies. The attachment of obscenity to Hanley's reputation, very far from justified, haunted him for the rest of his life. New readers now have an opportunity to be shocked directly, rather than through notoriety. They will undoubtedly be shocked, but the shock will have nothing to do with the titillations of the pornographic.

I have mentioned Hanley's preference for the life of the recluse rather than the contentious and self-promotional bustle of literary London. In the early 1930s he settled in North Wales with his wife Timothy (compare Yeats's wife George). He persuaded John Cowper Powys, at that time living in New York, to make a similar move westward. The two men became friends, and it is Powys's continual celebration of Hanley's genius, both in private letters and in public statements, that best confirms the status of his work. Powys was Celtic enough, and Hanley became an honorary Celt. It became a little too easy for critics commending Hanley's lyricism to find something bardic there and, ineptly, even to speak of the influence of Dylan Thomas. *The Welsh Sonata*, first published in 1954 and the first of his books to be reissued by André Deutsch (in 1978), prompted the critic Victoria Glendinning to find echoes of *Under Milk Wood* in it. There was no possibility of such an influence, since Thomas's "play for voices" was first heard (by myself among others) a year or so after *The Welsh Sonata* was conceived. There is a cognate lyricism, but Hanley lacks Thomas's rather juvenile humour. The fact that both were drawn to writing for radio (and, in Hanley's instance, for television) had more to do with the need for money than a desire to exploit Welsh vocal whimsy.

Hanley grew discouraged by the slim rewards of novel-writing and took to the drama in the 1960s. *Say Nothing* was put on at the Theatre Royal, Stratford East, in 1962, an appropriate venue, since, under Joan Littlewood, that playhouse was to be associated with the non-commercial and avant-garde. *Say Nothing* seemed, to such critics as Kenneth Tynan, to be a venture in the mode of understatement that was altogether contemporary: the names of Beckett and Pinter were invoked. The play was put on in New York and in Helsinki (by the Finnish National Theatre), but it made Hanley no money. Writing for the BBC ensured a firm fee and repeat payments (John Tydeman, head of the BBC's radio drama department, informs me that seventy-nine of his plays in all were broadcast), but Hanley yearned for the stage, a capricious mistress that rejected him. Seeing *Say Nothing* on television in the 1960s, I was, like many viewers, impressed by its power, but it totally lacked the easy charm that one associates with a British dramatic success. Hanley remained uncompromising, stark, too truthful to be comfortable.

He needed, and still needs, worshipful advocates. One of these is the American Frank G. Harrington, who produced a slim study – *James Hanley: A Bold and Unique Solitary* – in May 1987. To this I am indebted for facts, vital and bibliographical, otherwise difficult to track down. Fancifully, one sometimes thinks that one of the preordained functions of literary America is the salvaging of Britain's neglected geniuses. Britain, as I have indicated, prefers to explain neglect as though it were diagnosing a disease, loath to peel off the rubber gloves; America sees the disease in the scantness of the audience and administers the medicine of scholarly rehabilitation. This applies not only to literature. The almost forgotten music of Arnold Bax and Peter Warlock has been promoted by American societies that find no parallel in Britain. We are an ungrateful lot and we glory in our philistinism.

Harrington has had the advantage of reading Hanley's autobiography *Broken Waters*, published in 1937 and long out of print. Hanley admitted, when a reprint was urged in 1983, that he had written it only at the insistence of Chatto & Windus and had regretted it ever since. Harrington finds in the book a humour and optimism doggedly bypassed in the novels. By all accounts, Hanley could be charming, hospitable and, in the manner of seagoing men, happy to yarn the night away with strange tales and bizarre reminiscences. The man himself retained into old age all the physical hardness of his youth. He was slender, handsome, eagle-nosed, blue-eyed, strong. He had powerful affections, not the least of which was for his adopted Wales. He lies in Llanfechain churchyard.

The checklist of the work he left behind is formidable. Typically, the labour of assembling a bibliography was performed far from the motherland, in Vancouver by Linnea Gibbs (one of the few critical studies of his novels was published in Melbourne by Edward Stokes). To André Deutsch is left the heroic task of presenting the best of him to a new audience. What this new audience will make of *Boy* one awaits with interest. If it were a work of our own time, rather than a relic of the 1930s, one could predict praise tempered by an unspoken wish that he had not written it. It would certainly not find itself on the Booker Prize shortlist. Hanley was never that sort of prize material. On the other hand, he remains the kind of novelist whose eligibility for the Nobel Prize has become clear only posthumously. Hanley himself wanted this prize for John Cowper Powys, very reasonably. The fact that a novelist as uncompromising as himself received it – William Faulkner, against all the odds – suggests the deserts of rare merit and scant readership. The Nobel Prize has too often gone to the popular and banal. It was founded, one thinks, essentially for artists like Hanley.

I cannot claim the scholarship of the men and women who have devoted much of their lives to Hanley's rehabilitation. A practising novelist has, regretfully, to disown scholarship. He can bring to a great dead practitioner of his own trade only the tribute of a profound homage and the fellow feeling of the fellow sufferer. For writing fiction is mostly suffering, though, with luck and obduracy, the suffering can sometimes be transmuted into a kind of muted joy. The novelist does not expect financial rewards as a right, though he can be forgiven for resentment at seeing them go to the tawdry and meretricious. Hanley earned little from the art he doggedly practised, but he survived into old age with the satisfaction of knowing that what he had done he had done well. Unlike some of us, desperate at the piled-up bills and the prospect of the knock of eviction, he never compromised. He tried to deliver aesthetic shocks but he never set out to give easy pleasure. *Boy* is a typical expression of his view of the novelist's art. It seems to deny art in being pungent with the horrors of the real world. But it is considerable art all the same.

– Anthony Burgess, 1989

Preface by Liam Hanley

T HE HISTORY OF BOY has been a painful one. The book first appeared in 1931, and, four years and several editions later, the three directors of my father's publishers, Boriswood, found themselves before judge and jury at the Manchester assizes to answer charges of publishing an obscene libel. They and their firm were collectively fined £400 and *Boy* was withdrawn from circulation.

The fact that the case originated in Lancashire seemed to have had its own worrying implications. The KC consulted by Boriswood's solicitors strongly urged a plea of guilty, because an energetic defence before a Lancashire jury would be likely to result in imprisonment. According to a letter from a firm of solicitors to the publishers, such a jury "will probably consider that it is its duty to vindicate at least the honour of Lancashire" in such a case. The publishers took the solicitors' advice and pleaded guilty.

Charges were not brought against my father, but I am sure he suffered more because of the furore that *Boy* created.

Afterwards, my father, a most private and sometimes shy man, became more private than ever. He generally refused to give interviews to journalists and he gave a variety of reasons for this stance. "A book must stand on its own, make its own way," he would often say, but I think he also wanted to avoid questions about *Boy*. So many people have wanted to know about the book, only to have their enquiries frustrated. Overtures from publishers to reissue *Boy* were firmly rejected.

The controversy about *Boy* was equally distasteful to my mother, whose support of my father never faltered in a lifetime that was frequently clouded by harrowing worries over money. The reporting of the case and the letters in the newspapers made life difficult in a small community in Merionethshire in the 1930s. For both of them it remained a threat that lay in the background of their lives.

So deep at times were the wounds inflicted by the case about *Boy* that my father destroyed some of his other work. For instance, the only evidence of *The German Prisoner* (privately published in 1930 with an introduction by Richard Aldington) in the library at home was a pile of covers, into which I inserted my own childish stories. The text and, alas, a drawing by William Roberts, had been torn out. The police were doing much the same thing, as reported in the *Daily Mail* in 1935. They seized ninety-nine copies of *Boy* and twelve copies of *The German Prisoner* and had them destroyed.

There were people who suggested in my father's lifetime, as the *New York Times* hinted in its obituary in 1985, that some of the events in *Boy* might have happened to him when he was a young seaman. I have a taped interview I made with my father in his later years in which he laughs at such suggestions and dismisses them as silly.

Possibly moved by the same need to refute autobiographical inferences, my father referred to *Boy* (without mentioning it by name) in a short reminiscence entitled 'Oddfish', part of the collection of *Don Quixote Drowned* (Macdonald, 1953). Here he describes in the first person how a young seaman overhears a conversation on the bridge of a ship, from which emerges the terrible fate of a young boy, who is undoubtedly the central figure of *Boy*.

In the final paragraphs of 'Oddfish' my father defends the writing of *Boy* as follows: "It took me ten days. Now I realize that it should have taken me much longer than that. So shapeless and crude and overburdened with feelings. And in any case it struck some northerners as something less than normal and some critics as rather odd. I have, however, never been able to believe that a searchlight on a scab was anything less than normal, or anything one might call odd."

The northerners my father refers to are a Lancashire taxi driver, who borrowed the book from a library, and his wife, who read only the blurb and took it to the police at Bury. The police in their turn brought the charge of obscene libel.

It can always be argued that some things in the world should be allowed to rest and that there are others that cannot rest. It has been difficult for me to be sure into which category this novel of my father's should be placed. Flawed though it may be from my father's point of view, it remains a brave novel, and in its totality it is a powerful statement. To exclude it would be to deny the complete voice of my father, which, throughout his life, was always compassionate. For me his strength lay in the fact that he was never cruel with his characters, never distanced, never clever. He gave working men and their wives and children a voice – their voice.

– Liam Hanley, 1990

Boy

1

"FEARON! WHAT IS THE MATTER with you, boy?"

For the third time that morning Mr Jackson, the teacher, had had occasion to call the boy out and chastise him for inattention to his lessons. And now he had caught him out during the history lesson. The boy stood in the middle of the floor, his back to the class, his eyes staring up at the angry face of the teacher, who now fingered his cane with a determination that made the boy really frightened for the first time in his life. Quite often he had had the cane, but had thought little of it. In a few minutes the pain wore off and he forgot the incident until the next occasion. But now there was something other than the thought of the temporary pain inflicted. There was humiliation. He would not have experienced this so much had it not been for the circumstances under which he was suffering. Each time he had stood before the class. The teacher had asked him the same question. To each question he had given the same answer. The other boys in the class appeared to be quite amused by this new entertainment on the part of one of their own class. Mr Jackson towered over the boy.

"What is the matter with you this morning? Each time I look up you are the same, your eyes glaring at the wall opposite. What is the matter? Is there something on the wall that amuses or interests you? Tell me now. You used to be such a good boy. Lately you seem to have gone off your head. I won't stand for it, boy. I'll flog you each time you disobey me, and it appears you are dead set on doing so. Don't try my temper too much."

Fearon stood staring at the teacher, his tongue clinging to the roof of his mouth, fear like a great gust of wind circling about his heart. The teacher had not been satisfied with the explanations he had

3

given for his conduct. He felt that he must get to the bottom of this. It seemed so mysterious. Suddenly he roared into Fearon's ear:

"Well! Are you dumb as well as stubborn? You ignorant boy. Tell me, before I make a thorough example of you before the whole class. I will stand this no longer. The best part of a week wasted and examinations coming on…" To himself the teacher said: "If half the class are like this fellow, the inspector's report won't be any credit to me. Damn the boy anyhow."

"Well! Have you nothing to say? Can't you tell me what is wrong with you?" "There is nothing wrong with me, sir," replied the boy at last. It seemed to have been a great effort on his part to utter even these few words.

"Yes. You said the same thing before, not an hour ago, the same thing yesterday. I think you had better remain behind at dinner time and I will take you to Mr Sweeney's office. Perhaps he will get out of you what I can't. Go back to your seat. I won't punish you again. You are beyond me."

The boy with bent head returned to his seat. He was on the verge of tears. He blushed, the blood mounted to his head. He could not sit still, he continually fidgeted with his fingers, drumming them upon the desk. He dared not look either way. He was filled with a sense of shame. He dared not look up.

"Fearon! Did you hear what I said? Open your book please and get on with your work."

With trembling hands the boy opened his Oxford and Cambridge history book and endeavoured in spite of increasing agitation to study Wat Tyler and his short-lived insurrection.* But his thoughts were chaotic. He could not settle down to the work. He made a pretence at it and some twenty minutes later essayed to look around him in a furtive manner. Everybody seemed occupied. The heads were bent to the books, the teacher was busy making corrections in the exercise books on his desk. A strange silence filled the room, periodically punctuated by the scratch of the teacher's pen as he initialled each book. Once he did cast a glance at the bench where the boy sat, saw that he was not occupying himself with the lesson, but this time decided to save his breath and his energy. The boy was beyond him and that was the end of it. When dinner time came the boys filed out of the benches. Only Fearon and the teacher remained in the room. And now that the others had departed, the room took on a desolate air, it seemed to have grown bigger, whilst to the boy staring before him the walls seemed further off and the teacher himself had become reduced in size. But when his name was called the illusion vanished and Mr Jackson appeared to tower above him more than ever. He called the boy to come right up to his desk. Fearon approached with his head down.

"I said I would take you to the headmaster, but on reflection I have decided not to bother. It appears to me that you are not worth bothering about. When you first came here you were a good boy, attentive to your lessons, and even showed an intelligence superior to the others in the class. But whatever has come over you in the last week I do not know, and have gone beyond wondering about it; I have finished with you. You may do as you like. If you cut a bad figure at the examinations you have yourself and nobody else to blame. You may go home now."

Apparently Fearon had not heard this order, for he still remained standing there, and had even raised his head to look into the teacher's face.

"Are you deaf?" he shouted to the boy.

"No, sir."

"Then go. Get out of my sight. You worry me. You bore me."

The boy burst into tears. They welled from his eyes, poured down his pale cheeks; his two hands shook under the emotion he was experiencing. This was something new for Mr Jackson. And as he stood there looking upon Fearon's face, streaming with tears, a kind of mute appeal in the brown eyes, he felt a change coming over him. Momentarily he was afraid of this change. It seemed as though he would be extending pity to this boy very soon. He said in rather a thick voice:

"Go home. I told you to go away."

The boy never moved. Then the teacher got down from his desk and placed a hand upon his shoulder, saying in almost a whisper:

"Fearon, why can't you be manly like the rest of my boys and tell me what is wrong? There is something troubling you and you are ashamed to say what it is. Listen now! I want you to tell me everything, just as though I were your own father…" On the mention of the word "father" Fearon shuddered, an action which made Mr Jackson bend down and peer into the boy's face. He felt this pity stirring in him. He took Fearon's hand and led him to the front desk, where they both sat down.

"Don't be afraid," began the teacher. "There is only myself here and what you say is only to me. Come now. Be a man like the rest of the boys. Have courage. Be honourable. Out with it. Get it off your chest."

Mr Jackson even smiled, though the boy did not respond. At last he spoke.

"I'm frightened," he began – suddenly paused, and continued: "I don't want to leave school. I don't want to go away. No. No. I don't want to go away."

"Explain everything," urged the teacher.

With difficulty the boy stammered through his explanation. He said that he would be thirteen on the twelfth of March, and that on that date his father was getting him exempt from school. His mother was anxious that he should go to work. She had told him that other boys had had to leave school at that early age in order to help their parents.

"And have you no brothers or sisters older than yourself?" asked Mr Jackson.

"No sir! At least I had one brother and sister. Both died during the war, sir."

"Oh! I see. Well?…"

"I don't want to go away, sir. I don't want to leave the school. But my father and mother are determined to get me away. And I was afraid, sir. I wanted to go in for a scholarship. I wanted to study. I wanted to be a chemist, sir. But it's no use now. I have to leave next week."

"What!" To the teacher it appeared like an ultimatum. "But surely…"

6

"My mother has already been to see Mr Sweeney, sir. She has also been to the Education Committee. I have to go to their office one day next week, and if I pass the examination for them I'll be able to leave school."

"And do you want to pass this exam?" asked Mr Jackson.

"No sir," replied the boy. "I don't."

And receiving this answer Mr Jackson began a long interrogation, asking a hundred and one questions that flustered and worried the boy more than ever. What was his father? Did his mother go out to work? Did his father drink? Were they able to pay their rent? Were they good people, attending to their chapel? Did they go to the pawnshop ever? How old was his father? His mother? Had they lived in the town very long?

And all these questions Fearon endeavoured to answer with the best of his ability, whilst also trying to save his parents and himself from any humiliation, and especially in the case of his parents, he was afraid that the teacher himself might start talking. Already Fearon saw this man as being sympathetic. That was what the boy was afraid of. They did not want any sympathy. Besides he thought it might give the teacher licence to chatter amongst the other teachers about the home life of one of his pupils. He told the teacher that his father was a rigger at the dock. Yes, his father drank, but not heavily. His mother went out to work for the wife of the boss, who superintended the riggers at the Leyland branch in the Huskisson shed. No, his mother had never been in a pawnshop, so far as he knew, though sometimes she was behind with her rent. No. He did not know whether she pawned his father's clothes over weekends. Yes, his mother and father were hard-working and good-living people. In reply to a further question, the boy said that his father had always worked at the docks. Had been a dock man all his life. He was sixty-one years old. His mother he thought was about two years older than him.

Mr Jackson leant his head on his hand and stared at the desk in front of him. He tried to visualize the home life of this boy, and looked into the future and saw this same boy ten years hence. He remembered also that on the word "father" the boy had shuddered. This made him think deeply. Why had he shuddered? "God!" he thought. "Something queer about the Fearon family all right." Suddenly he pulled out his watch and discovered he had a bare half-hour left him for his dinner. He immediately got up, saying as he crossed to his desk: "Very well boy. You may go home now. Try and pay attention to your work in future. It reflects upon this class, and I like to feel proud of my boys. I'll see what can be done about you in the mean time."

Fearon brightened up. He stammered out with a "Thank you, sir. Thank you very much, sir," though Mr Jackson hardly heard it as he was already halfway through the door and rushing down the stone steps. He turned down the street and made for the café he always patronized. Over his coffee and cake he thought the matter out. He tried to look at it from every angle. Then with a sudden shake of the head he dismissed it from his mind. And he knew also that it would never trouble him again. After all, he told himself, what is this affair? One of hundreds, one of thousands, perhaps millions. He smiled. What was the use? None at all. Hopeless. Futile. Finished. There was a time in his career when he would have applied sympathy and energy and sense to such problems, but now things were different. He was tired. He was fed up. It was useless to help, useless to try to help. Fearon was only one more to add to the roll of thousands. Mr Jackson sadly shook his head as he waited for his bill. "No. No," he kept repeating under his breath.

He had been a teacher too long amongst the poor children of the town not to know how useless things were. Not to know that futility laughed at and mocked efforts, human endeavour was like a stricken giant. A trick. That's all life was. A mean trick. Mr Jackson paid his bill and left the café. Again he looked at his watch. He had ten minutes to spare. He went to the garden of the church adjoining the school and sat there staring through the branches of a tree at the ceaseless tide of humanity as it streamed past in the midday hour. He had not sat there but two minutes when the bell commenced to ring and he immediately got up from the bench and walked to the schoolyard. There he assembled his class and marched them up to their room. That afternoon the boys gave him no trouble at all and he felt more hopeful of the coming examination. A visit from the headmaster himself took up twenty minutes of his time, and before Mr Sweeney left, he remarked that Fearon must be sent to his office at four o'clock, that the matter was important. Mrs Fearon had been to see him again. In a few words he explained to Mr Jackson that things weren't so good in the Fearon home. The father it seemed had only just returned to his work at the dock after being on strike for seven months. The boy was to leave the school on the following Friday, should he pass the examination on the morrow.

"Tomorrow?" exclaimed the teacher.

"Yes," replied Mr Sweeney. "He will not attend here tomorrow, but will go down to the Education Offices first thing in the morning." It would not be a long exam, nor indeed a very difficult one. It was a question of summing up just the amount of intelligence the boy had. Yes that was all.

Mr Jackson stood staring at the lank figure of the headmaster as he walked down the long room. Then he turned to his class and announced loudly:

"Turn to page seventy-eight. The Reign of the House of Tudor."

There was a series of shufflings as the pages of the history books were hastily turned over. Then a moment's silence. The boys looked to the teacher. Mr Jackson said in a slow drawling voice: "I want you to read the chapter to yourselves, meditate upon it for twenty minutes, after which I will question each of you in turn. Proceed."

The forest of heads bent as one, there was a series of shufflings and whisperings. Fearon like the rest had opened his book at that period in history which explained the Tudors. To the boy himself it seemed rather flat, boring and uninteresting. Beneath the desk, and hidden between two exercise books, was a volume of Scott called *Rob Roy*. In that moment, the boy felt that *Rob Roy* was much more interesting than the matter contained in the Oxford and Cambridge history book. From time to time he glanced slyly up and around. The other boys were hard at work. He felt ashamed again that he could not concentrate like them. Mr Jackson was busy writing at his own desk. Fearon fell to studying his teacher's well-polished brown boots and wished he had a pair like that himself. He became so absorbed in the boots that he failed to hear Mr Jackson calling to him to pay some attention to his work, adding, "even if you are leaving the school next week."

Immediately the words were uttered, a tide of whisperings swept across the benches; they seemed to fill the whole room, criss-crossing, sweeping up and down. A veritable bubble of sound above which Mr Jackson found it hard to make himself heard. The bubble increased, the whisperings became more noisy, and every head in the class was turned towards the boy Fearon. But he did not return their stares. He merely sat there very quiet, very still, his head resting on his elbows, his eyes glued down on page seventy-eight, though his thoughts were far from that period in history. His mind was elsewhere indeed. He was already sitting in the office in the town before a bespectacled person who reminded him of the undertaker whose factory was situated in the street he lived in. And this bespectacled person was now deluging him with questions which he could not answer. His father appeared on the scene then, and when he heard that his son had failed to pass the examination he had gone wild with rage.

"What! What's that? You couldn't pass a simple little examination like that. God blast you for an ignorant little swine anyhow."

He replied to his father: "I couldn't help it. It wasn't my fault anyway." He stood cowering before his father, who seemed ready to rain down blows upon him, when suddenly a voice brought him back to reality.

"Fearon! You have to see Mr Sweeney before you leave school this afternoon."

"Yes, sir."

"Very well," said Mr Jackson. "But don't stare at me in that manner, boy."

"No, sir. Of course not, sir. I'm sorry."

And the boy tried to concentrate once more upon the history book. Sitting there in the bench, he appeared small, insignificant, for most of the other pupils were bigger, more robust, more hardened to things. The whisperings had ceased, though occasionally a boy turned to glance at him hurriedly, and then as hurriedly return to his lesson when the teacher's eye came his way. The boys were thinking of Fearon and of his approaching departure. When they looked at him their eyes seemed to say: "Well, well! What a surprise. Leaving before you are fourteen. You must be in a bad way all right. Is your mother so very poor that she has to get you out of it? Eh!" Fearon knew already the thoughts they harboured. He felt like bursting into tears again, but a sense of shame flooded him once more and he bore up. He stared at the clock from time to time and wondered when the hand would ever point to four o'clock. Then he would be free. Free from those eyes that searched him, that glare from Mr Jackson, the sea of whisperings, the titters from mouths hidden by cupped hands. Free from everything until tomorrow. Before Fearon was aware of it, the bell was already ringing and a series of wild movements broke out as the boys scrambled to their feet and rushed across desks and chairs to reach the door. When they had passed through, he felt a hand on his arm and, turning, discovered it to be the teacher, who reminded him that he must not go home until he had seen the headmaster. Fearon immediately left the room and commenced the long climb up the stone steps, where at the top he turned to his right and stood shivering outside Mr Sweeney's door. For some time he stood there debating in his mind as to whether he should knock or run away. But somebody inside the office was talking and then a footstep approached the door. Just as he knocked the door opened and a pupil teacher came out with a frown on his red face. Mr Sweeney, catching sight of Fearon, called in a gentle voice: "Come in! Come this way, Fearon."

"Yes, sir. Yes, sir," replied the boy and entered the office. Mr Sweeney closed the door behind him and said: "Sit down in that chair. Yes. There." Fearon sat down. The headmaster drew a chair up near the desk and sat nearly opposite the boy. He did not waste much time, but started off.

"Well! You know you will go to the Education Office in the morning. You know the way. Must be there at nine prompt. Don't be late.

You'll have to wait a long time if you miss the exam. You know where Sir Thomas Street is?"

"Yes, sir," replied Fearon.

"Mr Jackson tells me he has been having a deal of trouble with you this last week. You were such a good boy before. I have never had to have you brought up here for punishment. I'm surprised. What is the reason for all this inattention at lessons? Is something worrying you? Or have you been doing something wrong? I'll bet it's that and you are afraid to speak out!"

"There's nothing wrong with me like you say, sir," said the boy. "And I'm not afraid to speak out. The truth is this, sir. My mother is taking me away from school and I don't want to go. I prefer to stay here, sir. I like school. I am frightened of my father, because I know what he is going to do. He told my mother last night that it was the only possible thing that could be done, sir. And I did not want to go to that kind of work, sir."

"Work?" said Mr Sweeney. "Work! What kind of work?"

"I don't know, sir, though Mother says it's somewhere at the docks. My father works down there in a rigging gang."

"Oh! So that is why they want you away from school. Hmm. I see!"

The headmaster sat silent for a few minutes, stroking his chin, whilst all the while he felt the eyes of this boy full upon him, and when he glanced down at Fearon, he saw that look of appeal in his eye that he could not help but respond to.

"If I could be of any help," began the headmaster. "You see there are so many boys just the same as yourself. And mind you, Fearon, some of these boys have made good in afterlife. They struggled through. They told nobody of their troubles and yet they have pulled through. Still there may be a chance. Let me see. Have you an aptitude for anything? Is there any particular trade or profession you feel you would like to go in for?"

"I wanted to be a chemist, sir. But when I told my mother, she just laughed. Father was worse. He said: 'You'll be just what I want you to be and nothing else.' It's no use, sir. My father is a hot-tempered man and he would not listen to any excuse I made. It's too late now, sir. If I don't pass this examination he'll make an awful fuss. All the other boys are talking about it too."

"Are your people so poor that they have to take you away from a school at thirteen years of age? What difference will twelve months make to them? You can't perform miracles in that time. Your father and mother are without common sense. Is your father working, Fearon?" asked Mr Sweeney.

"Yes, sir. But it's not constant, and he was on strike for over seven months!"

For the first time in his life, Mr Sweeney had a good look at the boy before him. He saw a thin and certainly undersized boy standing no more than five feet in his boots, seated in the chair before him. He had wine-coloured skin, the brownest of brown eyes, large-pupilled, and they reminded the headmaster of the clear waters of the trout stream in Ballinasloe, where once he had spent his boyhood. His hands were thin, almost bloodless, and the fingers tapered to a point, much like those of a woman. His neck was thin. The head, well-shaped, was capped by a great shock of black curled hair. The nose was small, and the nostrils had a habit of quivering somewhat in the manner of a horse. The boy was very poorly dressed. In fact the headmaster saw that the clothes he wore were really his father's, cut down to suit his small and slender frame. He stood staring at this boy, trying to get certain information without further questioning. He thought the eyes themselves, the clothes, the whole being of Fearon, that so resembled a shudder, might give him a clue to his life, at home and in the street, for here was a boy who evidently lived most of his time in the streets. He remembered distinctly now that he had once received a communication from the Chief Constable, or his clerk, requesting information concerning a boy, Arthur Fearon, whose parents had applied for a licence and a belt for him that he might sell newspapers. And as this occurred to Mr Sweeney, his own son came into his mind. The contrast was striking. He tried to imagine just what kind of people the Fearons were. He was certainly of the opinion that in their son they saw nothing else but a moneymaker. Yes. He remembered quite clearly. Nearly two years ago. He would only be just turned eleven. But the application had been refused. He felt a little thrill of satisfaction when he remembered he had been instrumental in getting it turned down. Yes. There was no other way of looking at the problem. This was their son. They had a perfect right to do as they wished with him. And it appeared obvious to Mr Sweeney that they were determined to put him down to dock work. He sighed, for he remembered how many others of his pupils had been dragged from their benches, some willingly, many unwillingly, and sent off down to work amongst men at that tender age. He heaved a sigh of relief when he thought of his own son, now seventeen years of age and graduating for a university. It seemed sad that a boy like Fearon should have to be taken away from school. Although the boy did not know it, an eye had been kept upon him by Mr Jackson, and on two occasions he had said to Mr Sweeney: "That boy Fearon, sir. He seems most brilliant to me. I gave him a paper yesterday afternoon containing some highly complicated problems and he polished them off with consummate ease. I really think he should go in for the Junior City,* sir."

Yes, the headmaster was aware of those two occasions. But his reply had been: "The pity of it is that if the boy wins it, his parents will object to it on grounds of being unable to support him. The fact is, Jackson, people of this nature seem to me to be imbued with one idea only. To take their children away from school the moment there is any danger of their showing intelligence, brilliancy. It's no use, Jackson. I only wish I could do half the things I wished for these boys. There are most deserving cases and my inability to convince the parents, and even in some cases the authorities, leaves me worried and sad."

Mr Sweeney again told himself that all endeavour was useless. That hope was a sin in itself. It was too late to do anything. It was not a question of authorities, he said to himself, of parents, of rule or convention, of economics. It was a question of human nature itself. There was a fundamental rottenness therein. He had seen it long ago. He was not caring about it. He was tired and fed up. It was no use trying to convince anybody. He washed his hands of all things. Boys like Fearon were tumbling over one another. But they had no chance. He recalled the case of a boy named Harrison, who, though his parents were humble working people, had shown quite a flair for mathematics. The boy was sent off to work with riveters in the shipyard. Probably he was still there hotting rivets and would remain a hotting boy all his life. There were even parents who became jealous of their children. Mr Sweeney had interviewed hundreds of parents, he had listened to the humble confessions of hundreds of boys, had learnt to know their secret hopes and longings like no other man had. Yet he himself had to be most careful. Nobody seemed able to escape this huge machine that daily ground people's hopes beneath its wheel. He turned to the boy and said:

"All right Fearon! I'll see what can be done for you. I'll see your mother myself. Will that be all right?"

The boy's face seemed to brighten up at the words and he replied:

"Yes, sir. Thank you, sir. Thank you very much, sir."

Fearon almost ran from the room. But he had no sooner gained the street than this sadness again stole over him. He could not help it, but somehow he knew that all the things his headmaster might say, all the pleadings with his father, would be of little account. Mr Fearon was a stubborn man, one who would have his own way at whatever cost, and the boy visualized the hot words passing between his headmaster and his father. He had heard the same argument before. There had been many arguments as to what should be done with him. As he walked slowly up the street he saw a group of five boys standing beneath a lamp-post. He recognized them immediately. But he did not speak as he passed. Somebody shouted. Somebody laughed loudly. That was all.

The boy reached the door and knocked. His mother opened it. He was going to say something when a hand stretched itself out and, grasping him by the collar, dragged him into the kitchen. It was his father. That huge individual was still dressed in his dungaree trousers and jacket, as he had just returned from his work. In the full light of the kitchen it was possible to get a better view of Fearon's father. There was nothing outstanding in the features. A heavy face wherein were set small grey eyes that had a habit of blinking, whilst the nose was snub and just beneath it sprouted a brown moustache.

Mr Fearon's hair was cut so close that it seemed a miracle the barber ever missed taking his scalp with the hair. He looked like a habitual jailbird. His heavy jaws and huge mouth marked him for what he was, a hard stubborn man, one who had become inured to the ups and downs of everyday existence. One who could pass through ills and storms and epidemics. His hands were huge, very red, with great blue veins running almost to the fingertips. He was a very hairy individual. He dragged his son into the middle of the floor. The table had already been laid for his evening meal. The clock upon the mantelshelf showed just five o'clock. Fearon's mother was sitting crouched in a chair by the fire, her arms folded, and her great back appeared like that of a coal-heaver. She did not move or speak, but just stared into the fire flames. The father said:

"What bloody time d'you think this is to get home from school? You flamer. I know why you were late. Yes I know! Because your mother asked you to go to Mr Dunfey the greengrocer for that nightly and Saturday job. Oh yes, I know…"

"No Dad, it wasn't…"

"Shurrup! Don't talk to me like that. Tell me where you've been. Come on."

He commenced to shake the boy roughly. Fearon's cap had fallen off, his hair tumbled down over his eyes. The father had him by the left shoulder. Getting no reply from his son, Mr Fearon again shook him, this time more violently than ever.

"I was kept in school."

"Liar!" shouted the father. "I'll break every bone in your body if you come that with me."

He flung the boy against the wall and commenced to undo his belt. Seeing this, Fearon backed up against the wall. Meanwhile Mrs Fearon sat like a statue in stone. He saw his father approach him. He was just going to shout something when the buckle end of the belt caught him on the back of his neck. He did not shout. Instinctively, his two small hands went to his face to ward off further blows.

"Why didn't you come straight home when your mother told you to? Eh?"

16

"I did."

The belt descended once again. The boy started to cry now. This had a peculiar effect upon the father, for he immediately flung the belt into a corner and raising his right hand brought it down heavily upon the boy's face.

"Tell the truth. Tell the truth or you won't be able to go to school tomorrow. You undersized young pig. The lip you give."

"Mr Sweeney kept me in. I had to go to his office at four o'clock. I've come home straight from school. Honest I have."

The man felled him with a blow. As the boy dropped he dropped too. Without asking any more questions, he commenced to punch his son, all the while breathing deeply like a horse, the hands ascending and descending, though never a sound came from the boy himself. Fearon's thoughts were elsewhere. He was staring at Mr Jackson's brown boots and wondering if he would ever have such a fine pair himself. The silence began to get on the nerves of the father. He shouted into the boy's ear, almost deafening him:

"I'll really kill you. I will! I will! If you don't tell me why you never came home. I'll do you in. I'm determined on it. You swine."

But Fearon did not speak. Mr Fearon aimed a blow at his head, missed, then dragged himself to his feet. He gave the boy a vicious kick. Then he went to the table and sat down. He commenced his evening meal. Not a sound save the crunching movement of the man's jaws. Even the woman failed to turn round. Once the man at the table muttered: "Like your mother. That's what you are. Another obstinate pig like your mother. But I'll fix you. We'll see. And if you don't pass that exam next week, by God I'll lame you for life. When I was your age, I had to get up and work. I had to rise at five in the morning and drag a milk cart half round the town for a few shillings a week. Here you get a chance of earning over a pound a week and you stick your nose up at it. I'll fix you. You wait. I have had to work hard for my living and I'll bloody well see that you do the same. Want to go into an office. Like the other boys. Who in hell's name are the other boys? And what would you do in an office? Intelligent. Why you can't fasten your braces properly yet. It's work you want and plenty of it. Real hard work. Why you little swine, you even dodged selling the papers when your mother went to all that trouble about you."

For the first time since he had been floored by the huge hand, Fearon spoke.

"It was the police who did that. They wouldn't let me sell papers because I was under age."

Mr Fearon grunted and replied: "You won't get off with the same yarn this time. I have already seen to that. And you'll leave school next Friday. You'll put a pair of long trousers on and a chipping hammer in your belt, and you'll get down to it. God spare me days, why there are young whippersnappers down at the docks not half your age, well, only young kids anyhow, and they work like men. Good lads too. And you don't like it because it's too dirty for you. If you were as keen on keeping yourself clean as those lads are, you'd do well. Now get up the stairs there out of my sight. Go on. Before I send you up on my boot."

The boy rose to his feet and left the kitchen. As soon as he had gone, the mother turned round and said to her husband:

"You needn't go so far next time, you excitable bugger. You'll get run in one of these days the way you treat him."

"What's that? Confound you. Isn't it you who's been nagging into my ear for weeks that he should get off school? Isn't it you that growls at me about this bloody debt and that bloody debt? Aren't you satisfied? What in the name of Christ do you expect me to do at all?"

"I expect you to treat the lad a little better than you do. You're too excitable altogether."

"Well, blast you, you sat there like a sack saying nothing and doing nothing. To hell with it. I wash my hands clean of this kid altogether. Do what you like. But don't come growling at me about money owing. As if it's my fault."

"Your fault! Of course it's your fault. Who kept you all the while you were out on strike? Tell me that. And if I do want the lad off from school it's to help you too. You're not performing miracles mister, not by any means. And whatever job he goes to, he'll have to turn his money up to me, not you. I have a pile of debts to pay that I had to run up while you were running about the place blowing your gas about the worker's rights and revolution. You'd do a sight better if you looked after your home a little better. You never ask me how I'm getting along. Oh no! You couldn't do that. Not you. So long as you fill your belly and can go out night after night guzzling with your pals, nothing else matters. Now don't you say another word about Arthur. He's going to leave school. Of course he is. But it's to help all of us. You're no world wonder, so put that in your pipe."

"You'd aggravate a saint out of heaven. You would that. For the past six weeks you've worried me to death. Can I get Arthur down in Jack Kidney's gang? Can I get him in Tom Johnson's gang? Can I get him with the painters? Well I've told you. He's going to put a hammer in his belt and he's going to do it bloody quick. You're not going to throw up things in my face. I've worked hard all my life. And what about it if I did go on strike? We got what we went out for anyhow. Now I'm not going to sit here listening to your tongue. I'm going out. There's always something wrong in the bloody house."

"Yes, and who starts things, but you? You're always mooching about and picking for a row. If you had done what I asked you there wouldn't have been any need for Arthur leaving school."

"What d'you want me to do in the name of God! You don't expect I'm going to start bumming off the parish or getting relief. Do you! I suppose you do. You're capable of anything."

"Don't I work too? What's the matter with you? You're not keeping anybody here but yourself. I keep myself and soon Arthur will be keeping himself too. Don't be lording it over me about your lousy couple of pounds a week. It soon gets swallowed up in debts. Your debts. You never had much sense anyhow. If you'd taken my advice you would have stayed out in America and made a home for us long ago. No. You were too clever. That's all is wrong with you now."

Mr Fearon jumped up from the table. He shouted:

"Are you going to shut that bloody mouth of yours or do you want it closing for you! Money! Money! It's always money, money, money with you. Well I've kept you all these years and now you say I'm doing nothing. I wish you and the bloody boy were in hell. He's the cause of all the trouble in this place. I'm just sick of things. I've a good mind to go and drown myself."

"Go and drown yourself then. I'm not worrying what you do. All I say is that you go too far with Arthur and one of these days you'll regret it."

"But it was yourself started the whole thing. The lad needn't think he's going to the docks to keep me in my old age. Oh no! I'm good for a few years yet. By God I am. I can do my job as well as any younger fellow today."

"You're a real old boaster that's all you are. Go to the devil anyhow."

"You'd get the last word in if it cost you your life," he shouted into his wife's ear.

"You've always been growling about the lad anyhow," she remarked, to which Mr Fearon replied that it was not so much his concern as hers. It was she who had been egging him on to get the boy to work.

"Well, you're satisfied now, aren't you?' he said as he turned to leave the kitchen. When he had gone out the mother resumed her place by the fire. Mr Fearon had gone upstairs to his room. Whilst standing before the mirror shaving himself, he thought he heard the sounds of sobbing and stopped suddenly. He murmured: "What a little sucker anyhow. Always crying." Then he shouted at the top of his voice that seemed to shake the very landing:

"And don't forget, you're to meet me tomorrow evening at five o'clock outside the dock gates as I'll be waiting to know how you got on."

"Yes, Dad."

Silence. The boy fell asleep. Towards midnight the mother crawled up to her bed. Mr Fearon had already been in bed three hours. He snored and made noises like a pig. In the night the boy woke with a sudden fright. He had been dreaming: "Leave me alone, you!" he shouted.

"God blast this street," said Mr Fearon, suddenly awakened by the shout. "A man can't get a wink of sleep in it."

Mrs Fearon was sound asleep. He looked down at her. He blew out the candle and lay back again. "The whole confounded street'll know about this bloody business," he muttered before he fell asleep again.

2

MR FEARON MET HIS SON outside the dock gate the next evening. He said:

"Well! What did the man say?" Silence. They slowly crossed the road. Again the father spoke to him.

"Well! What did the man say?"

"The man said… said…"

"Open your bloody gills for Christ's sake," shouted Mr Fearon. "What *did he say*? You must be deaf all right. Did you wash yourself this morning?"

"Of course I did," replied the boy.

"Well then what in the name of hell did he say to you? Have you passed all right? That's easy enough to answer."

"The man said that… that…"

"Jesus God," exclaimed the man. "What's wrong with you? Have you done something wrong again?" He looked down at the white face of his son.

"I passed the examination," said Fearon slowly.

Immediately the father changed his attitude. As they passed a herb shop he took the boy in and got him a glass of barm beer, saying: "I'm glad. Your poor mother'll be glad too. You wouldn't believe, Arthur, how much this will mean to us. You might think we're both hard-hearted. Don't ever think it son. Now and again I lose my temper with you, but that's because you're such a stubborn lad when you feel like it. Here! Drink this up. You're all right son. Your mother'll be happy now. But that was a quick examination, wasn't it?"

The boy looked up at him and replied. "No. No. It wasn't. You see it only took an hour and a half. I had to go back in the afternoon. It

21

was then that the gentleman told me I had passed. I will leave school on Friday."

"And are you sorry?" asked Mr Fearon, and there was a queer look in his eye.

"No," was the prompt reply of the boy. They turned up Clio Street, and again Mr Fearon stopped and said to his son: "Are you sure you've passed this examination? You're such a liar, you know."

"Of course I've passed it," replied the boy, and to himself he added, "wish to Heaven I hadn't though." He saw his father looking down at him.

"I'm glad you feel all right about it," continued the father as they went on their way. "The way things are at present it's difficult to get your mother into a good frame of mind. What did she say about it? Anything?"

"I haven't been home yet," said Fearon. "You told me to come right ahead here and meet you. So I came."

"Ay. That's right. I forgot all about it."

They continued their walk home in silence. When they reached the house, Mrs Fearon was standing at the door waiting for them. She said to the boy:

"What were you told the other day about staying away like this? Surely the school never kept you in until now. Why it's nearly six o'clock." The man laughed and pushed the lad into the kitchen, saying to his wife:

"S'orlright. He came to meet me as I told him last night. He's passed the examination so he says, though I won't believe it until I see a letter or something from the teacher. He tells such dirty rotten fibs."

"Oh well, don't start another argument for God's sake. We'll know tomorrow," and the woman commenced to lay the table for the evening meal.

"I spoke to Ned Rafferty about him this morning," began Mr Fearon. "Says if he goes down Friday morning first thing, and doesn't slink behind the other lads, he'll put him on. They have a big job next week on the *Morning Star*. She's lying up for about seven weeks and that means plenty of half-nights. Lets hope he turns out a trump. If he does, I'll be proud of him. It's the best thing in the world for a lad to get out early and earn his bread like a man. When he gets to know a few of the other lads he'll be doing his best to make them jealous. Won't you Arthur?" said Mr Fearon and he turned to look at his son who had taken up his accustomed seat by the window.

"Yes," said Fearon.

"Yes what?" snapped the father.

"Yes, father."

"That's better. I do believe you're sorry you passed the bloody exam. Get up to bed out of it. You make me feel miserable every time I look at you."

"Here, go easy," said Mrs Fearon. "There's a limit to everything. The lad has had no tea yet. Stay here, Arthur, and take no notice of your father. I want you to go on a message into town for me afterwards."

"There you go," growled the husband. "You take the blasted words out of my mouth. You make me look a fool before my own child. No wonder the kid's getting ideas into his head. Both wrangling over him and him not saying a word."

"Oh get your tea for the love of Mike and shut up," said his wife.

As soon as the meal was over Mr Fearon retired to change and dress. At half-past seven he left the house. The boy had already gone for the message, whilst Mrs Fearon, having cleared up the place, was reading the evening paper. "Fancy," she said to herself as she turned a page. "The Government's going to pass a bill regarding schools. Well I never. Interfering gang they are, as if a parent doesn't know what's best for her own child. I don't know. I don't know! We won't be able to call our children our own just now."

Arthur returned then. Mrs Fearon, without turning to look at him, said:

"Leave the message on the dresser there. There's a piece of bread on the enamel plate in the back kitchen. You'd better go to bed now. Goodnight."

"Goodnight," replied the boy.

"Goodnight what, you brazen cur?" shouted Mrs Fearon. "No wonder your father is always getting on to you. You can't speak civil to your own father and mother. I really don't know what children are coming to these days."

"Goodnight, Mother," said the boy. It seemed as though he had had to drag the words out of his mouth. She did not answer him. He closed the door softly behind him and ascended the stairs. Below the mother mused:

"Hmm! He's his father all out. Sly too. Sly isn't the word. Getting the teachers to take pity on him now. As if they can do anything for him. Good Lord, when I come to think of it, these teachers has a neck too. Suggesting this and that for him, as if we don't know what to do ourselves. Seem to think we're all children. And these modern teachers – the huff of them. Yes the huff and importance of them. Bloody kids don't know they're born these days. Why when I was a girl I came out of Dromod when I was only thirteen and did a woman's work for two shillings a week and mighty glad to be earning that."

Suddenly she stopped. There was a sound of a key in the lock. Her husband had returned. Upstairs the boy was still awake. He lay staring towards the window. The room was in utter darkness, and the faintest light came through the window from the gas lamp opposite. He was ruminating on what his parents had said to him. He suddenly muttered:

"I wish I could say what they want me to, but I can't. I wish I could be like the other lads, but I can't. I wish I could stay on at school, but they won't let me. I don't want to go near the docks."

He fell to visualizing his interview with the headmaster, and the advice he had received from him. Then he saw once more Mr Jackson's brown boots, and he wished with all his heart that his parents would let him be a teacher. "It must be fine," he thought, "to be able to wear swell boots like that." His mind was vacant for a moment. Then something new appeared to him. He knitted his brows as though concentrating on the thoughts that now beset him. He was thinking of the talk he had had with the boy who lived at the top of the street. He had met him as he was returning with his mother's message. The boy was a year younger than Fearon. He stopped him under the street lamp.

"Hello, Fearon," he said.

"Hello, Corby," replied Fearon.

"Is it true you're leaving school next Friday?"

A lump appeared in the boy's throat, and now as he recalled the incident, the lump appeared again.

"Yes, I'm leaving on Friday."

"Why? You're not thirteen yet are you?"

"I'll be thirteen in a few days' time," said Fearon. "I don't want to leave at all, but my father and mother are anxious for me to leave. I asked them if I could stay on and they said no."

"That's rotten mean," remarked the boy Corby. "I heard Frankland say in class that your people were very badly off. Now my father is an electrician down at the Dock Board. I'm sure he could get you a job as soon as you're fourteen."

"No use," replied Fearon. "I'll have to be going now as my mother will kick up another row if I'm late getting back." He turned to go, when the other boy put his hand on his arm and said quietly: "Frankland also told me that your mother pawns your dad's suit as well as yours every Monday."

"He's a stinking liar," replied Fearon hotly. "Besides, who is he that he should talk like that? He's no better off than we are, than you are."

"All right," said the boy. "I only heard them talking in class, that's all."

Fearon stirred in the bed. So they had been talking in the class already. Well he wasn't leaving until the next Friday. He'd see some of those fellows before he did leave. He'd report them to the headmaster. He'd tell the whole thing to Mr Jackson. A sense of humiliation and shame descended over him. The last thing he saw before sleep came upon him was the teacher sitting at his desk, and his brightly polished brown boots sticking out from underneath.

3

AT HALF-PAST SIX THE ALARM CLOCK in Fearon's room went off, and the boy was up and dragging on his trousers before it had finished its morning song. The loud voice of his father came up to him from the kitchen.

"Are you up there?"

"Yes," replied the boy in a weak voice. "I'm coming down now."

"Then for the Lord's sake put a move on. Your tea's been poured out twenty minutes now. Shake a leg there. I'm going down with you."

The boy appeared in the kitchen ten minutes later. He had washed in a basin in his room. He was dressed in a brown dungaree jacket and trousers that originally belonged to Mr Fearon, but which his mother had altered to fit his smaller and much slighter frame. The father glared at him as he sat down to table.

"Hurry up! Fancy sitting down to it at this time of the morning. You'll learn in time my lad. Many a morning I've had to go out with an empty belly, so's your mother, and you wouldn't have one too. Are you ready now?"

Fearon gulped the remainder of the tea and put the cup down. He got his hat from the dresser cupboard, and turned towards the door, when Mr Fearon asked him if he had his hammer with him.

"Oh no! I forgot," said the boy and ran into the back kitchen to get it.

"God strike me lucky, you'll have me late as well as yourself. By Christ! You tell me this evening that you were late for that stand and I'll break you up. Come on now." The father turned out the gas and they left the house. All was quiet in the streets. Occasionally they passed other workmen and boys bound for their various destinations.

"Well," began Mr Fearon. "Don't forget to let us know how you get on. I'll be working over in the Hornby. At dinner time you wait outside Farley's cocoa rooms. I'll come along. We'll get a bite of grub together. Don't forget now. I'll be looking out for you."

"Yes, Father."

The boy's father smiled. At last he had conquered. At last he had got the better of his wife for once. Wait till Friday, he thought. Just wait till Friday, and he draws his money. She'll be damn glad she let him go as I wanted. What harm can he take anyhow? He's no better than any other kid who has to work for his living. There's too much coddling of kids these days. Little bits of girls out at six o'clock on mornings colder than this. Little trumps. That's what they are. He turned to his son again.

"Now don't you forget where to go. Don't come telling your mother and me that you couldn't find the stand. We know what you are. You'll dodge anything to get your own way. But it won't come off. You get straight down to the stand. Never mind worrying because you haven't got a button. There will be others there beside you and they are on the same lay. Getting work on the never. Get right in front. The boss scaler knows you and who you are. He can't miss you if you get up to the front. He told me he'd put you on this morning. Well, I have to turn this way. So long."

"So long," replied the boy. He stood for a moment looking after his father. He saw him turn into the dock. Then he hurried along so as not to be late for the stand. In his heart the boy was afraid. He was not known. He was not in the scaler's union. He knew there were many boys out of a job who were members of the union. He was taking the work from them. As he neared the dock gate he became more afraid than ever. Why didn't his parents allow him to stay on at school? He passed through the gates. Here all seemed confusion. Boys and men hurried in groups towards the different sheds. He remembered his father saying that he had to go into no. 5 shed. He made for this shed. When he passed inside he became conscious of hundreds of eyes suddenly turned upon him. He wished the ground beneath his feet would open and swallow him up. He stood there wondering what to do. Looking round, he saw that many of the boys had formed up into a group and now stood waiting to be picked on. Fearon made his way forwards until he was just on the fringe of the crowd. Even then he was aware of murmurings as he approached. A big boy to his left said half-aloud: "Here's one of these bleedin' kids from an office. The suckers. They get their teachers or some other buggers to give them a note to the boss. You watch. This dozy-looking cod'll be put on. You watch Charlie."

Fearon tried his best not to hear. Suddenly to his right a voice was saying: "Hello cocky. Have you come for a job eh? How's your ma? I hope she didn't forget to put your drawers on for you." The blood mantled the boy's forehead. He half-turned to get a glance of the speaker. He discovered that he was a boy his own size and even thinner than himself. He vowed in that moment that he would get to know him. He was not going to be afraid of a kid like that. No bigger and no better than him. There was something wizened and oldish and sly about the boy's features that immediately made Fearon dislike him. He wondered whether he would be picked on. If both of them would be picked and whether they would be sent to the same furnace. There was a sudden bubble of conversation, a buzzing sound. The boss scaler had arrived. He was a big hulking man, with a peak cap pulled down over his right eye. He stared at the assembled crowd of boys. Then he shouted at the top of his voice:

"Only twenty hands wanted. Half you blighters can beat it. I only want twenty."

Immediately on hearing this the crowd pressed forwards, the various expressions upon their faces intimating to the boss scaler just what effect his words had had upon them. Already some of the bigger boys were cursing under their breath, others more experienced and more daring, swearing half-aloud at the man who now began picking out his twenty boys. As soon as Fearon saw what was happening, his whole body grew tense, a wave of fear shot through him and with a wild movement he began to crush his way through the crowd. Other boys seeing this followed his example until it seemed as though the picker-on must be forced back inch by inch and so finally into the dock itself. He roared like a bull:

"Hey! What in the name of Jesus do you bastards think you're on, eh? Tell me that? Back there. Back there, you shower of crimps, or I won't pick a single hand."

Still Fearon pushed forwards. He saw, not the huge figure of the boss scaler, not the mass of bodies that surged with him, but the figure of his father, the frown upon his face. The boy's face was red. His every movement, hampered by the ill-fitting clothes, made him appear a clumsy boy and nothing else. He dropped his chipping hammer, which was immediately kicked along the ground, and in his endeavours to prevent it being shied into the dock he fell. A score of feet trampled over him. Then he rose to his feet. Looking to the far end of the shed he now saw that sixteen boys had been picked. His heart leapt into his mouth. He gave one mad push and the other boys, making way for this, allowed him to be carried on by his own impetus until he almost knocked the man over. This individual suddenly grasped him by the neck and said harshly in his ear:

"Hello wormy. Where the friggin' hell did you come from. Hey?"

Fearon was not afraid. At last he had achieved his object. Nobody could keep him back now. And he was determined not to disappoint his parents. He was determined to get picked on. He looked up into the boss scaler's bloated face. The man was grinning down at him. The other boys edged still closer.

"My name's Fearon. My old fellow told me to come to you. Said he spoke to you about me the other day. Here I am."

The boss scaler laughed. "Here you are, are you?"

Fearon lowered his head as the man suddenly added: "And who the merry hell is your old man? I don't know him from a frog. Fearon! Fearon! Fearon!"

A whistle blew. Instantly the man grabbed Fearon by the shoulder and said roughly. "Right! Get to the top of the shed and join the others. Righto."

He picked three more boys and said to the remainder, "Beat it."

As Fearon made his way up to the top of the shed he felt all those eyes upon him; his ears were full of whisperings, angry murmurings, threats. When he joined the other sixteen, they frowned upon him.

He was a stranger to them. All seemed to be looking closely at his coat. It made him take a look at himself. He could not see anything wrong with it, and he was still wondering what they were staring at, when a boy with a freckled face nudged a companion and said loud enough for all to hear:

"Latest dodge now. Boss scaler's special edition. Well in with his old fellow. Swine's not even in the union. There should be a bloody row about this all right."

The face of Fearon grew redder than ever. His whole body burned with shame, with the thought that he was taking the work from other boys who had more right to it. It made him curse his father inwardly for offering him no advice, no information. "Surely," he said to himself, "he must know how things are. The docks full of boys with union buttons and no work for them. And I'm picked on first go." His ruminating was interrupted by the boss scaler arriving and ordering them on board the SS *Cordovian*.

"Come along! Shake your bloody selves," he shouted.

The boys all hurried off towards the ship which was lying in the Sandon Basin. As they hurried along, Fearon began to take stock of the various boys. Excepting for a few, all appeared to be small in stature like himself. They walked along with a cocksure air, an air of self-assurance. But Fearon felt awkward in his long trousers and ill-fitting dungaree jacket. It was the first time he had ever worn long trousers. He felt slovenly, out of place. Mr Jackson's brown boots blotted the horizon. It seemed he could never forget them. He thought teaching must be a fine job, and teachers splendid fellows. Certainly they were able to buy things they liked. He even knew of teachers who used to give their cast-off clothes to the poorer boys, though there was nothing that would fit him, he was so small. Mr Jackson had once asked him what size he took in shoes. When he told him, the teacher shook his head and said:

"What a pity. I had an old pair of shoes. I thought they would fit you. How is it that you don't get the police boots now?"

"Police boots sir?"

"Yes."

Fearon explained to the teacher that the police had not given him a pair this year because his mother had pawned them. The teacher laughed then.

"She wouldn't be able to pawn any now, Fearon. The police have all the boots stamped now and pawnbrokers won't accept police boots or clothing."

It was then for the first time that the boy had been able to get a view at close quarters of Mr Jackson's brand-new brown boots. Ever since, he had dreamt of having a pair the very same, and it was in this frame of mind that he now made his way towards the ship. He vowed that the first week's wages he earned would buy a pair of brown boots, just like his teacher wore. He knew how to go about things. There were plenty of boys who only gave their parents half of what they really earned. Fearon saw that was the only chance of getting his long-desired brown boots.

They half-ran down the shed. They filed up the gangway. As each one stepped onto the deck, his name was called out and he was handed a tally with his number on it. This he handed in on completing his day's work, and drew again the next morning. Fearon was told off with four other boys to go down the bilges. He had never heard of bilges before and wondered what they were like. He ventured to ask the freckle-faced boy who walked along with him all about them. The boy laughed and showed his blackened teeth.

"You wait. A bilge is a storehouse for all kinds of shite. Phew! The stink. And d'you know," he whispered almost ferociously into Fearon's ear, "us lads don't get a penny extra for going down there, though the bloody boiler-makers are all right. They won't go down unless they get time and a half."

"Oh!" said Fearon, becoming interested, and the freckle-faced one went on: "Ay! Wait till you get down there. I've had some. I always try to dodge that lot, but I'm unlucky this morning. Up to your knees in stinking water. Bailing it out. Bailing it out. Bloody water full of dead rats and God knows what. First time I went down them, I stank for a week. My old lady had to burn my overalls. They were useless."

"What do they pay then?" asked Fearon.

"Same as scaling rates of course," he replied. "Here we are, boyo."

They descended the engine-room ladder. Halfway down the freckle-faced one stopped, and turning to Fearon said: "S'help me. I'm going down the bloody engine room instead of the bilges." They returned up the ladder. As they came into the alloway, the boss scaler met them.

"Hello! Where are you guys bound for?"

"Bilges," said Fearon.

"Put a bloody move on then," replied the man.

The two boys ran right for'ard and descended the long iron ladder into no. 1 hatch. Fearon, looking down suddenly, beheld the cavernous appearance of the 'tween-decks, now emptied of cargo, whilst at the bottom appeared a kind of well, the colour of the water he could not yet discern, though the smell was already in his nostrils. A step above him was the freckle-faced boy, also descending. He shouted below to Fearon: "Hey! Put a bloody move on will yer. You know well the big feller will be round shortly on his tour of inspection. If he finds we haven't yet started work, there'll be a row, I tell you." To which remark Fearon replied:

"All right. Don't get your shirt out mate. He can't eat us anyhow."

They were halfway down the ladder. Fearon, looking down, saw that the colour of the bilge water was green. The smell was even more pronounced. He said, "Phew!" The freckle-faced one laughed then, saying with a grin: "Hell! We haven't even begun yet. D'you know you have to stand in that muck up to your belly?"

Fearon looked up at him.

"You what?" he asked surprisedly. "Do they think we are going to stand in that muck all day?"

"Not all day," said the other boy, smiling. "Only eight hours. You'll get used to it soon."

They continued down the ladder. The freckled one shouted: "Stop! We get in here for our tackle. The buckets and heaving lines are here."

The two boys swung themselves in under the ladder and planted their feet on the iron decks. Their voices echoed volcanic-wise in the huge spaces. Heaps of lumber were lying about, old newspapers containing the remains of meals, pieces of corrugated iron, lengths of rope. Fearon felt sure he heard a rat scuttle across the iron decks. He turned to his companion.

"Better live than dead. You'll pick up any amount of dead rats down there."

Suddenly the freckle-faced one exclaimed: "Well, there should be another boy here with us, and he hasn't arrived yet. Somebody has got to go down there and send the stuff up here on the line. There's only two of us so far. Let's toss up for it. Heads goes down below, tails stays up. As soon as the other feller comes along, which shouldn't be long, we'll stick him down there and let him try his hand at bailing for a while. Well, what's it to be?"

"I haven't a bean," said Fearon, which remark made the other boy grin. His mouth appeared to stretch from ear to ear. He said to Fearon:

"I've a meg* here. Here goes. What is it. Heads or tails?"

"Tails," said Fearon, and again the freckle-faced one laughed, as he turned up heads, saying:

"You down old boy. You down to the shithole first."

He pushed a bailer into Fearon's hands.

"Down you go. I'll send the buckets down on the line. Be careful, be careful. It's a twenty-five foot drop yet, you know."

Slowly Fearon swung himself out onto the ladder and began to descend. Gradually he was lost to sight, for the lower he descended the darker it became. There was a sudden shout up the ladder.

"What about a bloody light. Can't see anything down here."

And the reply roared itself down to the trembling boy on the ladder.

"Damn! Forgot all about it. I'll send you down a lamp right away. Have you any matches?"

"No," came the reply from Fearon, and the other boy said to himself: "What kind of a bugger is this? Hasn't even a meg or a match."

He bent on one of the lamps to the heaving line, having first pushed a few spare matches into the lamp. He lowered it down, shouting as he did so: "Coming down there. Coming down there. Easy she goes."

Fearon stood on the last rung of the ladder. The smell made him sick. Once he nearly fell off the ladder. He called up to the other boy:

"Is it deep?"

"Up to your knees that's all. Look out this lamp doesn't catch you on the napper. Have you got it yet?"

"Not yet," shouted Fearon, and one foot went off the ladder and into the stinking water. He shivered as his foot came in contact with it. Then taking the bull by the horns, he stepped off the ladder and immediately found himself up to his knees in the green slime. He began spitting as though it were an action on which his very life depended. He dropped the bailer into the water. He heard a noise. The lamp was dangling against the ladder. And now he could not hear distinctly what the other was shouting down to him. He reached up and felt for the lamp. He grasped it. He shook the line against the ladder as a signal that he had received it. Then in the darkness he felt inside the lamp for the matches. He found them and struck one upon the back of his pants. Immediately the whole of the pool was discernible. He managed after some difficulty to light the lamp, and hung it upon the rung of the ladder. He called up to the other: "Send a bucket down. Send *two* buckets down."

A minute later he heard them come clattering down the ladder. He unbent them from the line and hung them by their hooks to the bottom ladder rung. Then he set to work. He bailed as though every minute were his last. He felt that he must continue bailing, without resting or ceasing, that he must go on and on, drowning all things in his mind and heart, blotting out the surrounding objects. And as fast as he filled them he bent the line on and called up at the top of his voice: "Heave away. Coming up." Up and down, up and down went the buckets. Fearon, looking at the scene at his feet, said to himself: "Lumme! Looks as if it will take the best part of a year to get all this muck out." A huge grey rat flopped into the bucket. "Ugh!" he exclaimed. "Heave away! Heave away there."

Somebody was coming down the ladder. The steps re-echoed through the cavernous depths. At last Fearon looked up from his task to discover it was his companion. The freckle-faced boy stepped right into the water and made his way to where Fearon was standing, with a bailer in one hand and a bucket in the other.

"The other kid's arrived," he said. "The big feller came along too. Asked me where you were. I said you were sending up the stuff. He says both of us have to go to no. 3 boiler after dinner."

"Said what?" exclaimed Fearon.

"What I said to you," replied the other. "What did you think I said? Knock off work. Wish it were true. I'm fed up already and I'm not on the job a minute yet."

"That's a bit of all right," remarked Fearon. "First they tell you to go down the bilges, and when they find they've made a mistake, they want you to go to where you should have gone at first. A bit of all right I call it. Christ! I'm ringing wet. Look! Soaked right through."

"You'll soon get dry inside the blurry boiler," said the other boy. "I've had some. You might get a cold, but that's not much down these parts. Get me."

The two boys continued to fill the buckets. Once the bucket came down and before it reached the place where Fearon's hand was waiting to grasp it, the knot broke and the bucket itself fell into the water. It made the other boy swear, which in turn made Fearon think hard. He had never heard the like in his life before, and the words were all strange to him.

"Fancy that," said his companion. "Can't send a bloody bucket down properly. I've a good mind to… Hell, I wish I could send the next bucket up to him full of live rats. Wouldn't I laugh if one got down the back of his trousers. Oh boy!"

"Have you been at this kind of work long?" asked Fearon, as he sent his bucket up.

"Nearly two years," replied the other. "How old d'you think I am anyhow?"

"About fourteen," said Fearon.

"Liar, I'm turned sixteen," said the other. "How old are you?"

"Fifteen," said Fearon, and was glad in that moment that he had said it. It was a lie certainly and he knew it. And to himself he said: "Fifteen. Sure! That's my age for the future." He began filling his bucket with the filth.

"S'funny why the big feller wants both of us," he remarked to his companion.

"Well, Lord love me, you know why, don't you?"

"Yes. I do," replied Fearon.

Yes. He knew why, though he would not say so to the freckle-faced boy. They were both small. They were just the kind of boys necessary to get into a boiler. Or even up the back ends. The other boy was grinning again. Fearon asked him the reason for it. He was always suspicious of anybody who grinned continually as this boy did.

"Nothing. Nothing. Not much to grin at here," he said, as he shouted up to haul away on his bucket. Suddenly there was a shout: "LOOK OUT!" but the boy was not quick enough. Fearon, sensing what had happened, dodged away just in time. The bucket of water and slime came right down on top of the freckle-faced boy.

"You sloppy pig!" he roared up the ladder. "You sloppy bastard! Just you wait till I get into those 'tween-decks."

"It's the rotten rope," came the reply down to the boy. "Don't you start saying I can't put a decent knot on a bucket."

"A decent knot on your bloody grandmother!" shouted the other, who was scraping the greenish muck from his coat and trousers with the bailer. This was accompanied by much cursing. He shouted aloud:

"Friggin' sods. They send you down here when a bloody boiler-maker or carpenter or a fitter would refuse, unless he got his extra pay, but we get sweet effay. Anyhow, I am more determined than ever now to get a ship out of it altogether. I'll get out to the States. I have lots of uncles and aunts out there, which is more than I've got here. You bet your boots," he went on. "Anything is better than this. I've had two years of it and what good is it? You get good pay, but look at the muck and heat and cold and everything. Not worth it mate," he concluded.

"And is it that easy to get a ship?" asked Fearon.

"Well, it's easy and it isn't easy, if you get me kid. Besides, a feller can always stow away if he is keen on getting out to the States or Canada."

"Oh!" exclaimed Fearon. And suddenly he appeared rapt in thought.

He looked across at this other boy who was three years his senior. The glance that met his seemed really vicious. "Yes," thought Fearon, "he must be a vicious customer at times."

The boy himself and the work seemed suited to a nicety. There was a sympathy radiating between the vileness of one and the other. Whilst Fearon was making up his mind as to whether it might not be a good thing to follow this boy's example and look for a ship, another accident happened, similar to the one before, but this time it was Fearon who received the contents of a bucket over him. He did not curse and shout like his companion. He quietly began scraping the stuff off his face and hands and clothes, the while the other laughed. "You got your gob full this time all right," said the freckle-faced boy. Fearon did not reply. And the other immediately thinking that Fearon was afraid of the boy in the 'tween-decks, shouted up: "Hey you there! I'll break your... neck. You dopey... You worm... you..."

He pushed Fearon out of the way and began to ascend the ladder. A voice called out:

"It wasn't my fault I tell you. The bucket slipped. Who put the knot on it anyhow?"

"I'll break your neck I tell you," replied the other, still hurrying up the ladder. "Wonder what you take us fellers for. You ought to try your bleedin' hand at bailing that muck up. You wouldn't be so clumsy then, I'll bet. When you've had your share of down there you'll..."

There was a low shout from the boy above:

"Here's Creeping Jesus."

The boy on the ladder stood stock-still, petrified. He tried two or three times to shout to Fearon below that the boss was at the hatch top.

38

Fearon, however, had already sensed there was something wrong. He came up behind his companion.

"S'orlright," whispered the boy in the 'tween-decks. "It's orlright. The bugger's just gone. It's grub time."

Fearon congratulated himself on coming up at the right moment. He felt he had been down the hatch rather a long time. The three boys made their way along the 'tween-decks until they came to no. 3 hatch, which was just behind the engine room. The freckle-faced boy remarked that they might as well ascend by this one, so they would know at what hatch to go next time.

"But we'll be going to the boiler, won't we?" said Fearon.

"Well! I know. D'you think I didn't know what I was talking about? You bloody softy. Down this hatch is the best way to get to the engine room. And as you know you have to go through the engine room to get to the boiler."

Fearon made some kind of reply before he commenced to follow them up the ladder. He felt blinded for an instant as he came onto the deck and into the broad daylight.

"Which way are you goin'?" asked his companion.

"I have to meet my old feller," replied Fearon. "He's working along at the Hornby."

"Oh. Well I'm going across to skinny Lizzie's place. I always go there for my grub. You get the best cup of tea on the dock road at Lizzie's place. Well so long."

Fearon hurried up the shed. It was five minutes past twelve and he had to be back promptly at one o'clock. His father would be waiting for him and he half-ran until he reached the top of the shed. Then he discovered he had a quarter of a mile to go before he would find the Hornby dock. At last he reached it. Crowds of men were standing outside the gates, smoking, chatting together, some were even lying on the floor. These appeared to be old men, and their labours had apparently left them as helpless as babies. The boy could not help but notice the various expressions upon their faces. And noticing them, he felt a sadness in his heart that all these old men should still have to work like young men. He had seen them fighting each other like wolves on winter mornings. He had seen them practically on their knees begging for a day's work. He remembered when he was at school his teacher had always impressed upon the boys that Liverpool was one of the great ports of the world. He hurried past these men until he arrived at the cocoa rooms. There he found his father. The latter came up to him then.

"Hello there! How did you get on, hey?"

"Not so bad," replied the boy, and bent his head as if to survey his sorry self after four hours' standing up to his knees in foulness, in utter darkness.

"You look as if you were waiting to be pitied," said his father. The boy laughed then.

"It's the stink," he said. "Everybody calls me Stinkballs."

"You'll be called worse than that before you die," said his father. "Take no notice of what anybody says, me boy. You're doing a man's work now. You have no need to hang your bloody head. It's nothing to be ashamed of. Let me tell you that. I had to do worse things than that when I was your age."

Fearon thought he had heard sufficient of what his father had done, so he said in rather a quiet way: "I killed two rats this morning. Big grey ones."

"Did you? Well! Well! Have they been tickling your bleedin' legs then?"

They both went inside the dining room. The rough wooden tables were occupied with all manner of men. They had no sooner sat down together than a man at the next table suddenly exclaimed loudly: "Ugh!" and after a pause: "PHEW!" He turned to the table where the boy sat with his father. He glared at the boy. The father noticed this and immediately got up saying:

"What's wrong with you mate?"

The man laughed and replied: "I don't like a… with my dinner."

"What d'you mean?" growled Fearon's father. "What's wrong? We're not interfering with you, are we, eh?"

The man laughed again. He said very slowly: "You interfere with my digestion."

"Think you're bloody clever, son. Don't you now."

Just as there were hopes raised in the breasts of the other occupants that a real good stand-up fight would begin, a large lady came from behind the counter and said to Mr Fearon:

"S'orlright mister. Jus' take this little lad outside will yer. He stinks the bloody place out. Where's he bin?"

Fearon senior saw it was useless to carry on, so he hustled the boy outside. He then advised the boy to get a drink of barm beer and a bun at Parry's. He himself would get a glass of ale at the Darby.

"I mustn't half stink," said the boy to himself, as he crossed the road in the direction of the herb shop. "No bloody wonder my mate is fed up with it. So am I. Fancy. I should really be at school. Gee! They were great boots that Mr Jackson used to wear." He reached the other side and walked up Raleigh Street. In the herb shop they served him with a glass of barm beer and a Bath bun, though the two assistants retired to a back room until the boy made his departure. Fearon was not slow to notice this. He felt more ashamed, more useless, more clumsy and dirty and hopeless than ever. He even swore that one day he would get even with his parents for sending him just where he didn't want to go. He made his way back to the ship. "Wish they were dead, I do," he murmured.

4

THE FRECKLE-FACED BOY, whose name was Jackson, was waiting for Fearon as soon as he stepped on the deck at one o'clock. Fearon saw him standing by the saloon door. He went up to him.

"Has the big feller been along yet?"

"No, I'm waiting here until he shows up. You can do what you like. This chicken doesn't start until he is told off to his job. Savvy, boy?"

Fearon laughed and stood up against the door alongside Jackson. They had not been standing there long before the person mentioned put in an appearance. As soon as he saw the two boys standing there, he scowled and said:

"Well, what about it?"

Jackson grinned.

"Get down the bloody engine room you pair of kites," he growled, and the two boys went off towards the companion ladder. The boss scaler shouted after them: "Don't forget what number boiler I sent you to. And no card-playing inside there either, or both of you'll get the kick from this firm and damned quick too." He watched them disappear down the ladder. Going down the ladder to the engine room, Fearon asked his mate if they were both to go into the same boiler, to which question Jackson replied with an emphatic "Yes". "Good," thought Fearon. "This fellow's not bad, though I only know him five minutes." He stopped halfway down the ladder to rearrange his trousers. His clothes were soaked with water and slime from the bilges.

"We won't half stink when we come out at five o'clock," remarked Jackson as they stepped onto terra firma. The two of them passed through the engine room and into the stokehold. They could already hear a faint tapping. The noise made Fearon put his hand to his back pocket suddenly, and he exclaimed:

"Hell! I've lost my hammer somewhere."

"Christ! You haven't dropped it into the bilge have you?"

Which was exactly the thing that the boy had done. He told Jackson he had.

"Can't you win one from one of the other fellows?" asked Jackson, who began to feel sorry for this new boy. Although he had not revealed anything to Fearon, he was well aware that something was going to happen that afternoon to the new boy. Things did always happen to new fellows. He had once been a new kid himself and he had had the experience. Nor did he ever wish to remember it. He would very much have liked to have warned Fearon, but he knew that no good could come from that, for if any of the others found out, he would be in the same boat himself and perhaps end up worse off than Fearon himself. The two boys reached the boiler. Fearon hesitated. But Jackson said immediately he saw what was taking place in the new boy's mind:

"Don't worry mate. It's all right. You'll get used to it. It's hot sometimes. But you won't feel any heat with those clothes sopping wet. Are you going first or shall I?"

"I don't care," replied Fearon. He seemed a puny thing indeed as he looked at the huge black hulk that was the boiler. One of the boilers of this huge tramp steamer. He espied the small manhole through which the scalers had to crawl. Jackson watched the expression upon his face. Then he said:

"All right then. You go first. Here y'are. I'll give you a leg up."

He bent down and waited until Fearon was ready to climb upon his back. Already Fearon had become aware of this great heat, and now as he stood wondering, the boy beneath, realizing he was hesitating, began to get fed up, for he knew that at any minute the big guy, as they called the boss scaler, might come along. If he were to be sacked there would be a fearful row at home. If Fearon only knew this other's home life was worse than his. He said in a low voice:

"Come on mate. I don't want to stand here all bloody day waiting for you. What are you frightened of? The bloody boiler won't bite you. It won't kill you. You'll come out all right at five o'clock or my name's not Jackson. Tom Jackson. By the way what is your name anyhow?"

"Fearon," replied the other. "Arthur Fearon."

Jackson laughed and replied: "Well come on Arthur. I can't wait all day. The bleedin' boss'll be around any minute now. Hurry up there."

At last he felt the boy's weight upon his back. Fearon stood for a moment. His face was right up against the small manhole now. Inside it seemed very hot, the darkness was almost impenetrable, and he asked:

"What about a light? It's as dark as hell."

"Oh, Christ! Get in first. We can easy fix up a light. My back's getting weaker and weaker holding you all the time. Are you right?"

"Right," said Fearon, and his small form disappeared into the darkness. With an agility born of experience, the other immediately followed him. As soon as Fearon touched the iron floor of the boiler, he screamed out:

"God! It's red hot. I'll get burnt to death here."

"Shurrup!" growled the other. "You won't die. Have you got any matches?"

The whole inside of the boiler appeared to be filling with steam from the boys' wet clothing. The stench became terrific and Jackson was holding his nose when Fearon struck the match. They glared around. Then Jackson took a tallow candle from his pocket, and having lighted it, began to look around for some niche in which to stick it. But no such niche was to be found, and finally Fearon said he had a matchbox in his pocket. Was that any use to him?

"Give us it," said the other. In a few minutes they had the thing settled. Fearon remembered his hammer and nudged his companion.

"Well, I can't give you mine, can I? Why didn't you go and win one as I told you?"

"But where? I didn't see any knocking about."

"Go and pinch something to make a noise with anyhow. You'll find something in the stokehold surely."

But Fearon appeared to be afraid of leaving the boiler. And now the boy Jackson began to hate him. Who was this kid anyhow, he asked himself, who wanted helping at every hand's turn? Besides he didn't believe he was fifteen. He thought he might have escaped from an industrial school, or some such place where boys are sent for sagging school. "I wonder," said Jackson. "I wonder who sent him down here. He doesn't look as if he were ever at any kind of work. God stiffen him. When I think of it. Holding him up for nearly a quarter of an hour outside the boiler, and now he expects me to go and win a hammer for him. He's backed the wrong horse anyhow. I'll get no hammer for him or anybody else. I have my own bit of grind to do without helping other buggers who come down here and get taken on with a note from the office or through getting well in with the boss scaler."

Jackson was a member of the Union and hated all those who refused to join it. He was quite a zealot in that respect. He turned to where Fearon was lying on his belly by the manhole door. He knew Fearon was lying down because he was frightened. Finally Jackson in desperation called out to him in the half-darkness:

"WELL mate. What you going to do about it? Somebody's got to start hammering or else there'll be a row. Here!" he said suddenly and flung his own hammer almost in Fearon's face. Fearon picked it up and wormed his way to the side of the boiler. Here the side was thick with salt. He commenced to chip this salt. Jackson came over to him and said that he was going to win a hammer himself. He was to keep on hammering until he, Jackson, came back. "All right," said Fearon, and his whole body trembled. And the other boy, aware of this sudden shivering, began to hate him more than ever. He shouted into his ear angrily:

"God blast you mate! You're afraid to go and win a hammer for yourself, and now when I give you my own, and offer to get one off somebody else, you're too bleedin' frightened to be left alone. Who the dickens sent you down here, anyhow? Where do you live? What's your old man? A Sunday school teacher? Is your ma all right? Perhaps she doesn't know you're down here? Well, holy hell! are you actually shedding 'em?" (For Fearon had commenced to cry.) He tried to rise

46

to his feet but could not. He felt ill. The heat, stench, the filth and horror of it all revolted him, and he wanted to scream out:

"Take me away! Take me away! I don't want to come back here ever again."

Something moved Jackson. He had never been so stirred in his life. He bent down and put his hand on the other's back saying:

"Beats me mate. Beats me hollow. You shouldn't have come down here at all. I tell you what. Tomorrow you go down to Mr Sloan. He's the hotting man. I'm sure you could get a job with the riveting gang. I'm sure you could. Cheer up mate. It'll soon be five o'clock. Here, give us that hammer. Now you get down in that far corner where nobody can see you, and I'll do all the tapping that's necessary. For the rest of the afternoon anyhow."

Fearon crawled into the furthest corner and stretched himself out. In two minutes he fell asleep. Suddenly the tapping from the neighbouring boilers ceased. Jackson listened intently. Then he heard four distinct taps on the next boiler. This was a signal. He immediately decided that he would have nothing to do with the arrangement he had heard made that afternoon in the cocoa rooms. He made up his mind to leave the boiler and hide somewhere till the ceremony was over. For the gang of scalers had decided to initiate Fearon into their gang. Jackson listened again. He felt sure Fearon was fast asleep. Slowly he wormed his way across the hot floor of the foul-smelling cavern until he reached the manhole. Now a faint glimmer of light showed him that one of the hurricane lamps was lit and standing on the floor by the opposite boiler. Already he could hear the voices of other boys and knew that six of them were leaving their boilers and making for the spot where the lamp stood. He wanted to hide behind his own boiler until all was over. He was afraid he might be seen. If he was, he would be thrown to the floor himself. He managed to work his way out, and dropped to the floor. He crawled slowly round the boiler. Then he sat down on the iron deck and waited. And whilst he waited he listened intently. He was sure that the voice he now heard was that of a fellow, Davies by name. Then when the voice was heard exclaiming: "Do you know Shacklady?" Jackson knew this was Davies. He sat still.

47

"Know Shacklady! Sure I do," replied one of the boys.

"Know Fearon?"

"The new kid. Sure we all know him. Didn't he get picked on this morning? First time he was ever on a stand I'll bet. Looked as if his mammy had dressed him before he came out. Hell, why everybody was talking about him."

Jackson suddenly recollected the incident. There had been a large number of boys on the stand that morning. When the boss scaler put Fearon on, there were titters and murmurs and angry swearing amongst the others.

"Well what about him anyhow?" he heard another boy say.

Davies laughed.

"Well, we're going to prove him this afternoon."

"Yes." This in chorus, though not loud enough for anybody working in the engine room to hear.

"Sure," replied Davies.

Jackson knew they were alongside the boiler where Fearon was sleeping.

"Oh Crimes," exclaimed one of them. "We'll have to get inside there if we are to do anything."

"Five can't get in there, you soft cod," said one of the boys. "We'll have to bring him out of it. Who'll volunteer to go in and razz him out?"

"I will," said one.

"I will too," said another.

"Wait!" said Davies, "everybody can't go in."

Then he added suddenly: "Look out! I'll fish the sod out myself."

He was inside the boiler before the other boys had time to count ten. Davies was sixteen years of age and had been a scaler for nearly three years. He was thoroughly used to clambering in and out of manholes as well as bailing out bilges and other dirty jobs for which boys were always required by the various shipping companies. The mortality rate amongst these scavengers of civilization was never inquired into by any of the companies concerned, though sometimes a boy was burnt to death or suffocated in a boiler, or drowned in the foul water at the bottom of the ship. In such cases a collection was made for the parents,

48

and once one of the companies actually paid the mother of a boy some compensation. The Union, now being in alliance with the ship-owners, could not very well see eye to eye with the average wants and desires of boys. The boys remained boys all their lives and for ever. They accepted a black mark upon the brow, their eyes became black too, their hands, rather than those of children, which many of them were, resembled those of farm labourers. There was a saying amongst the boys: "Once a scaler, always a scaler." Davies was known all along the length of docks. He was a boy very old in the head. There was something vicious in his nature that seemed entirely suited to his calling in life. And when one looked at his small closely set eyes, one realized immediately the make-up of this boy. He was feared by all the other boys on the dock. He was known locally as a bully, being brutal, dirty and even beastly.

The waiting boys now saw a head emerge. It was Fearon. Two pairs of hands shot forwards and grabbed the boy's shoulders. Slowly they hauled his body out and laid it upon the floor. Not a sound came from him. They thought he was naturally asleep from the heat, though actually Fearon was in a semi-conscious state. Davies crawled out and dropped noiselessly to the floor.

"This way," he whispered to the others.

They all made their way behind no. 4 boiler. One of them carried the hurricane lamp in his hand. The scene resembled one from the *Inferno* of Dante.

All this time Jackson had been sitting like a statue, uttering no sound. He began to regret leaving the boiler now. Supposing somebody came along. Supposing the boss lad came down to see how things were going? Supposing one of the engineers passed through and discovered what was going on? He felt that the only safe thing to do was to make his way back to his own boiler and resume his work. No sound being heard, the people in the neighbourhood of the boilers, knowing that a gang of scalers were at work, would wonder at the sudden and prolonged silence. Jackson rose to his feet, and made his way silently to his boiler. He climbed up, squeezed through, and crawled along on his belly until he could reach the hammer that Fearon had left lying there. He picked it up and held it ready in his hand in case of emergency. He was secure now. If he heard anybody coming he would immediately set up a row and so disarm any suspicion as to what was happening. Shielding himself he was also shielding the others, though he did not think of this latter fact. He thought only of himself. They could do as they liked with the new boy. He was going to look after himself. It was nothing of his doing. He would have no hand in it. He hated Davies like poison and the older boy knew it. They had once or twice fought on the dock road over such incidents as this, but always Davies emerged the victor. Still, Jackson was not afraid. He had courage, and though only fifteen years of age, could take his stand like any man. It made him a valued member of the gang. They could rely on him to take their part in all kinds of disputes.

Meanwhile the other boys, having secured Fearon, retired into the darkness, leaving one boy on the lookout for the boss lad, who generally looked them up every hour to see that there was no slacking in the work. If he caught a boy slacking he generally had him sacked that same evening and he was never given work on the stand again. Jackson, lying up against the manhole now, could hear the others talking. He was full of a desire to join these others just to see how the new boy took his medicine. He had never been so surprised before. Fearon was a queer chap, he thought. He heard a voice saying:

"Kiddin' us he's asleep, the bum. No wonder they sent him to work that boiler with Jackson. They knew who they were sending him with."

Jackson immediately cocked his ears on hearing his name mentioned. He crawled out of the boiler and made his way round until he had a good point of vantage and could see all the proceedings without being seen. He himself had been through the mill as all new boys went through it, but now looking ahead of him he felt certain that he had never seen anything like this in his life before. The five boys were grouped about Fearon, whose feet they had tied together with a piece of yarn. His coat and vest and shirt had been taken off. At his head, though he could not see it, lay a jar of shale oil. One of the boys was fingering a white bag containing a powder that looked like crushed lime. They were all grinning down at the new boy. Now he opened his eyes and the leader of the gang immediately said:

"Wow, boys! He's woke up at last. Now we can proceed."

The boys drew nearer, so reducing the size of the circle, and Jackson, watching, found it difficult to see what was going on. He was content to look through Hughes' legs. Hughes was seventeen years of age and known as "The Hump".

"Are we ready?" he asked suddenly, and as suddenly there was a scuffle. The lookout boy had suddenly whispered from his end of the boiler:

"Boss lad. Douse it."

Then silence and order again, for as quickly the boy had whispered:

"Jake! Boss lad gone. Coast clear. Listen again."

Jackson huddled himself into a peculiar position. Then Hughes said: "Well! We'll begin now. Where is the prisoner, gentlemen?"

"Here!" said the others in chorus, though the whole thing was a whisper that could not carry further than the boiler where they were standing. Suddenly one of the boys asked: "Who's in one and two?"

"Never mind him," replied the leader. "There was only one lad sent for the two boilers. Why worry? The others are waiting. Now Mr Bloody Fearon. You are about to be initiated into the order of Scalers and Muck-wallopers. Savvy?"

There was a sudden shout, a second scuffling and all the boys had flown back to their boilers in a twinkling, and a second later a veritable barrage of tapping was going on. The boy in Fearon's boiler crawled further in than ever, leaving a trail of spittle behind him on the hot floor. The heat was stifling. A sudden silence. Then four short taps. Jackson worked his way to the entrance again and pushed his head out. Not a sound. Then from no. 5 boiler another four taps was heard. The scalers were signalling to each other through the hammer taps. "Something on now all right," said Jackson half-aloud, and withdrew back into his boiler. But somebody had heard him. It was Hughes. He was actually standing beneath the boiler where Jackson was lying. How he had got there Jackson could not understand, and he heard Hughes say: "Of course there's something on, you loony. Didn't you know? We're going to prove that new kid now. Are you coming out too?"

"No," said Jackson and disappeared once more.

A boy came up to Hughes.

"Hello," he said.

"Hello!" replied the other. "All ready now. Can't muck about here all day."

The other, who had a harelip, said: "Come this way." They grouped together again. Now Hughes tied Fearon's hands. Suddenly the boy began kicking out in an endeavour to free himself. He did not realize what he was in for. He remembered that he was shivering when he entered the boiler. Then the heat had made him sick. Finally he had fallen asleep. What were these other fellows doing here? Why wasn't he at work in his boiler with Jackson? He appeared bewildered. He heard the biggest of the boys say:

"Well! When does the act commence?"

"Don't be in a bloody hurry mate."

And the harelipped one added: "You might be on your back yourself in a jiffy, so shut your gob." An order the boy quickly carried out.

"Now," began Hughes, "we proceed to receive into the Ancient Order of Honoured Scalers and Muck-wallopers a new member. Name: Arthur Fearon. Age: fifteen. Fearon, answer all the questions put to you."

Hughes bent down towards the boy upon the deck, for the circle had suddenly become a semicircle. All the others now knelt facing Hughes.

"Have you ever had your trousers pulled in a boiler?"

"Let me go!" said Fearon. He wanted to scream there and then, but something about the atmosphere of the place made him afraid. Also, he had sense enough to know that the quicker he answered the questions the better for himself. He was not afraid of the punishment coming to him, as much as the thought they might all be caught and subsequently sacked. He dared not return home and say he had been sacked. He knew his father would murder him. So he decided to answer the questions as best he could. He said:

"No." The other boys laughed then.

"Next question," said the harelipped one. "Have you ever seen your sister washing herself in the bath?"

This question made Fearon laugh, for they had no bath and he had no sister. Hughes scowled at him and then prodded him with his boot saying:

"Well?"

"No."

"He's a little liar," said one of the boys.

"Shut your snout up," said the harelipped one, and Hughes turned his attention once more to the boy upon the floor.

"Have you ever seen your mother when she wasn't so well there?"

"No," replied Fearon.

"Have you ever seen a fly?"*

"Hundreds," replied Fearon promptly.

"I didn't mean one of those flies," replied the harelipped one, when Hughes shut him up with another question:

"Arthur Fearon. Stand up."

Then he remembered the boy was tied. In a flash they had untied his arms and feet. The boy struggled to his feet. Hughes led him to the end of the line and said:

"Each boy you pass will expect you to bow to him."

Fearon laughed. This sudden laugh angered Hughes for he threw Fearon heavily on his back and said in a low voice:

"NOW!"

Immediately they tore his shoes off. Then they covered his body with the shale oil, afterwards sprinkling the itchy cotton all over him. After that they stood two on one side and three on the other and the streams crossed each other.

"He's soft," they said in chorus. "He's loony. He's a little tit. That's what he is. Ha! Ha! Ha!"

Fearon's face was flushed and he wondered when the end was going to come. It came in the form of a voice shouting:

"Douse it!"

Fearon lay upon the floor of the boiler whilst Jackson was speaking into his ear. He could not remember how he had made his way back there. He gasped like a fish. Then he seemed as though he were choking and Jackson became thoroughly frightened then.

"What's the matter? They didn't make you swallow the damn stuff, did they? That's what they did with me though. You'll be all right in a minute or two. We'll be knocking off soon. Nearly half-past four now. While you were being worked on I skipped into the stokehold, where the brass clock is. Which way d'you go home?" he asked.

Fearon did not reply. He could not. His heart was full. His brain seemed burning. He knew he could not stand this kind of work and was determined never to go near the docks again. He hated his parents now. More than ever he hated them. Fearon thought: "No. They didn't make me swallow the stuff. But they made me do something else."

His one desire was to fly from the place and never put his foot in a boiler again. He began talking in a slow, drawling way:

"Jackson! Is the riveting a good job?"

"Sure thing. I was a hotting lad for a month, then I went handing for the holder-up."

"Oh! I would sooner try my hand at that than continue at this. It's awful."

He visualized the possibility of going into the riveting gang. Certainly there was something more interesting in that than scraping dirty salt from a boiler and walking up to your knees in muddy water in the bilges. He had once brought the dinner down to his father who was working on an oil tanker in the Canada Dock. The boy was interested even then in watching the men putting the rivets into the ship. He stood for a long time watching the boy at the heating fire. He watched the working of the bellows until the whiteness of the rivet told him it was ready for the holder-up. In all the things which he had noticed aboard the ship, this seemed the first job that, to him, had any definite purpose or plan. He realized this more than ever when on another occasion he had watched a moulder at work in the company's foundry that was situated just opposite the Canada Graving Dock. It was a shafting job for a big passenger liner. Fearon knew the moulder as he was a friend of his father. He had been allowed inside the shop by the foreman, who was also a friend and an old shipmate of Mr Fearon. In this moulder the boy Fearon saw for the first time in his life the work of a creator. A man who did his job. A man who created something with his hands and so many throbs of thought. A moulder. Standing before the terrible heat of the fire, he thought things.

Fancy! All the rivets that lad must have heated. Hundreds and hundreds of them. Thousands and thousands of them. And the lad had handed each one of them white-hot to the holder-up. Heard the heavy strokes of the hammer that wielded by the man above deck drove them into place. So many rivets heated and hammered into place. He said to himself that that hotting lad could go singing along the deck at the end of the day's work and shout:

"See all those rivets. They were heated by me."

Lying on his stomach in the boiler, the boy reviewed these things. What he really longed for was to do something that he liked and to do it so well that he too could say at the finish of it: "See that! Mine. That's what I made. That's what I did. With my hands."

By the very acts of his hands he would add strength to a ship. A strength of purpose. And such a purpose could not be felt or experienced or realized, only imagined. Only through time and experience would that purpose reveal the richness within itself. For the ship ploughing the charted and uncharted wastes of waters relied upon the very rivets the boy had heated. Relied upon the security with which the holder-up and hammer man had placed them. Fearon's mind had not yet achieved that degree when the smallest idea in reception suffers an expansion within the mind, enlarging the vision behind the idea. He merely realized that as fast as the rivets were heated, a boy rushed forwards with them, held securely though lightly between a pair of long tongs. That swiftly, as though time itself were golden, the holder-up had snatched it from the tongs. That in a moment it had been struck home and became a part of the ship itself.

These thoughts careered through Fearon's mind, whilst all the while he was dimly conscious of the other boy's presence. Knew his mind was occupied with the clock and the hour. He would be glad too when the whistle for knock-off sounded. The whistle would mean goodbye for a time to the dirt and noise, the heat and cold, the filthiness of it all. Fearon shivered every time he thought of the morning's work in the bilges. He tried to think of Friday, which meant wages and some money for himself. Goodbye to work for a whole weekend. But Friday appeared centuries off. He shut the idea from his mind. Jackson had to shake him before he realized that the hour had struck. He was like a big dead rat. He could hardly stand on his feet when he descended from the boiler. The other boy took his arm and helped him along the stokehold. He half-carried Fearon up the engine-room ladder. Jackson, smiling behind his dirt, exclaimed excitedly:

"God love me! That's the longest day I ever spent in a ship's boiler. I'll bet you're not half glad to get out of it too. Never mind, mate. You do as I told you. Try and get into the riveting gang. It's good pay too. Here we are."

They emerged into the alloway. They walked along and gave their numbers to the man at the head of the gangway. Fearon almost fell into the dock when he walked down the gangway. A dock policeman, who was standing at the foot of the gangway, thought the boy was ill and half-ran to catch him in his arms. Jackson said it was all right. He had had a headache in the boiler. He was going to take him home. He knew where he lived. The policeman said:

"Damn it! He doesn't half stink. All right, sonny. Take him home out of it."

Halfway up Raleigh Street, Fearon stopped and said to his companion:

"S'all right, mate. Thank you. I'll get home all right. So long."

"So long, Fearon, lad," replied Jackson and was soon swallowed up in the darkness.

All the way home Fearon was crying. He continually murmured:

"I can't. I can't. No. It's no use. I can't do it. Oh God, if they'd only let me go back to school. Gee! It must be great having a teacher for a father."

When he arrived in the house his father was sitting at the table waiting for him. He smiled and said: "Well! How goes it. How did you get on?"

Fearon sat down in his accustomed seat and replied:

"Fed up."

"What!" – and even Mrs Fearon turned round from her sewing when she heard her husband shout.

"Fed up," said Fearon once more. "I'm soaked. I'm covered with muck. My skin's all singed. I'm sick. My head's buzzing round. Oh Mother! It's awful, awful!"

He burst into tears.

"At it again, you bloody bastard," said the father rising from the table and crossing to his son. "What's wrong now?"

"Fed up," said Fearon, and there was utter weariness and sadness in his voice. As he said this he raised his hands to his head to ward off the blow his father aimed at him.

"Dad!" he screamed. "Dad! Kill me. I won't go back. I won't. I won't go back, Mother! Let me go anywhere except there. Oh Dad. Dad. Dad. Dad!"

He felt himself seized in his father's arms, lifted into the air and suddenly flung down again. He landed heavily on the back of his head and lay still.

"You excitable pig," roared his wife. "One of these days you'll pay for your damned temper." She crossed to her son and bent over him. He was very white. He sighed.

"Arthur!" she murmured. "Arthur," and stroked his shock head of hair with her large rough hand.

"Leave him alone," said her husband. "He's all right. He'll get over it, don't you worry. He's letting on, that's all. I'm just bloody well fed up with him. Twice now he's chucked a job after the trouble I've gone to get one for him. Stuck-up conceited little bastard. Wants to be a teacher, no less. Many a boy would jump at the job he went to this morning. And all the worry I had getting it for him."

"You weren't much better yourself years ago," said his wife.

Mr Fearon laughed. "At least I was a man," he said. "Before I was fifteen I shipped on a full-rigged ship and rounded the Cape. God love me! Lads want wrapping up in cotton wool these days all right and no mistake. He gives me the pip. The bloomin' pip. Anyhow I've finished with him. I wash my hands of him altogether. Let him clear out of my sight. I won't let him in this house again." He looked at his watch. "Well, I'm going to bed. Goodnight. By Christ! Fancy that though. Chucking his job. Blast him. I have to get out all right. Bed. Work. Work. Bed!"

The woman waited until he had climbed the stairs. Then she went to her son.

"Arthur!" she exclaimed. "Arthur are you hurt, son? God! One of these days your father'll swing for that temper of his." She shook the boy. His eyes opened.

"Mother, will you give me a drink of water and let me go to bed."

Immediately she lifted him up in her strong arms and carried him to the old armchair by the fire. She sat him back in it, then ran to the back kitchen for a cupful of water. He drank it greedily while she stroked his hair with her trembling hands.

"Arthur! Arthur!" she said again and again.

The boy remained silent. He did not look at his mother now. He had turned his head and was looking towards the window as though he were expecting at any minute that somebody would jump through it into the kitchen.

"Arthur son!" she exclaimed, "what are you staring at? Tell me!"

"Nothing," he replied. It was impossible to note the differing expression upon his face. Suddenly he said to his mother:

"I'm sick of the job. Sick of it."

"What d'you mean Arthur?" asked the mother.

"I'm fed up," he replied. "Fed up! Fed up!"

Mrs Fearon sighed. "Well!… but listen Arthur, what other job is there that you can go to? Besides, the money is good. Many a boy would jump at such a job. Of course, I'm not asking you to stay there. I had nothing to do with it. Honest I didn't. But times are hard and I suppose every boy should be glad to work for his parents. I had a hard job rearing you Arthur. You were never strong."

"I'm not going back there," said the boy. "Father can do and say what he likes, but I'm not going back to that job."

"What are you going to do then?" asked Mrs Fearon.

"Go to sea," he replied, to which remark the mother replied suddenly:

"To sea! Your father'll never hear of it. He doesn't want any of his children to make the same mistake as he did. Just you see what he'll say."

"Then why is he always talking about what *he* did when he was young?"

The mother laughed. "Your father was always a bit of a boaster, and is still. Why the men he works with are always joking and making fun of him."

"And will he prevent me from going to sea then?"

The boy looked at his mother, who returned his scrutinizing stare as though carefully weighing her reply.

"How do I know, son? If you want to go to sea, then go. I won't be stopping you. I shouldn't think you'd get a ship anyway, because there are too many men out of work at the present time."

The colour was gradually returning to the boy's face. He rose from his chair and threw his arms around his mother's neck.

"Mother!" he exclaimed. "I want to go to sea. I do really want to go away."

"Why?" she asked and raised her lips to his. He kissed her and replied:

"I want to go to help you. That is why. Another reason is that I don't like my present job. I hate it. Hate it. Hate it. The job is dirty and the lads as dirty as the job. Ugh! In the bilges today…"

"Good God Arthur," said Mrs Fearon, "don't think I had any hand in sending you down to work amongst those rascals. Oh! I know all about them, I have heard things! – not today only, but for years. I blame your father and nobody else for this."

Fearon looked at her closely and asked:

"Not yourself then?"

Surprise was apparent upon the mother's face.

"Not me! Lord Almighty no!"

"But you were the first to want to get me away from school. I have had two chances of going in for a scholarship spoilt through either you or Dad. I wanted to be a teacher. Look at the fine money they get. Good job. I didn't want to leave school. Why did you take me away from it? I want to know. NOW."

Amazement sat upon the woman's face. She had never expected such an outburst. Yet she was only too conscious that it was partly through her that he had been got away from the school.

The necessity of the action was her only defence. She took his face in her two hands.

"Son," she said. "I had to take you away. I thought you would have understood by now. Mustn't it be plain to you that things are bad with us? Many another boy has had to do the same thing as you have. It couldn't be helped. Your father's money is little use here, Arthur. Besides, very soon they'll be getting rid of him." She paused for her breath.

"And all these other boys you speak about," said the boy. "Did they want to leave school? Is it fair, Mother?"

"Arthur," said the mother. "One thing the dock has done for you anyhow. It has made you old in the head."

A silence fell between them. Having weighed up in her mind all that her son had said, she felt somehow that her husband was right. The boys these days were nesh,* afraid to work, ashamed to dirty themselves. The more she meditated upon this point the more she realized that nobody was to blame for his being taken from school. He was no different from any other boy. Thousands of boys. She turned upon him suddenly.

"Well! I'm not going to have anything to do with it. As soon as your father comes in you must talk to him. I'll have *nothing* whatever to do with the thing at all."

A sudden anger filled the boy's heart. His reply was like a shot from a gun:

"You will be glad to have my money of course. Won't you now?" And then he saw that this remark had hurt his mother. He was suddenly ashamed of himself.

"Oh well, Mother. Don't worry. It's all right. I want to go to sea. I want to earn money for you. I know how we are placed. Every boy does, who has to go down to the docks to work. Don't you believe me, Mother?" he asked, and there was appeal in the tone in which he said it.

"Of course I do," she replied. "See your dad. If I were better off I would never have taken you away from school. If all mothers were better off they would be able to allow their children to choose the jobs they liked best."

"I'm going out now," he said.

The mother did not reply. She did not stir from where she sat. The door closed with a bang. She got up and walked to the rear entrance of the houses and stood looking up and down the entry for some time, expecting to see some neighbour or other with whom she might pass an odd hour to relieve the monotony of her life. Mr Fearon meanwhile had got up and come into the kitchen. As soon as his wife put her head into the place he asked:

"Where is Arthur?"

"He's gone out," she said. The husband grinned at her.

"He won't get back here again anyhow," said Mr Fearon. "Chucking his bloody job like that, after all the trouble I had to get it for him."

"Nobody ever said he'd chucked it," said the mother.

"Aw! Cut that," said the husband. "Sure, isn't it the truth that he'll never go back to it? He won't. He'll slouch around now. But out of here he's gone. Good! Let him do whatever he likes. He won't come back here again."

He went upstairs to bed again. The following morning the boy had not returned. It was a much altered Mr Fearon who heard the news from his wife.

"What? Not back. Out all night. Done it. That's bloody well done it then. He's finished here."

The man went off to work in a depressed frame of mind. "Boys," he said to himself, "are a bloody confounded nuisance. But by God I'll search that worm out. I'll hunt him out wherever he's hiding. He won't get the best of me. Oh no! He thinks he's clever. But I'm as clever as ever he was. The sly young bugger."

Evening came. But the boy was still absent. Over the tea table Mr Fearon remarked that he might have taken a jump.

"I had a horrible dream about him last night," said the mother.

"Dream!" exclaimed Mr Fearon. "Dream!"

She did not reply, but watched how ravenously he wolfed his food.

"I knew it would all end up like this," she said angrily. He saw the flash in her eyes. "Yes, I could see it coming. I am afraid for Arthur. There was nothing wrong with the boy. And what did he say yesterday? Fed up. Fed up. That's what he said. But you with your hasty temper couldn't see the boy's viewpoint. I'm not surprised that he's gone. I won't be surprised if he doesn't return. You blame me for taking him away from school. But why did I? Why did I? You know quite well, though I'll tell you again all the same. When you were laid up that time I had to do something. You weren't getting any insurance or sick pay. How in the name of Almighty God d'you think I managed? You never once asked me, did you? Well Arthur's few shillings a week at the dairy was helping us a lot. And last year when you went on strike, he helped us then. He even worked nights and Saturdays, and him a bit of a kid, twelve years old. Why do you continually blame me for things you caused yourself?"

Mr Fearon was thinking. He looked at his wife and said slowly:

"Don't let's argue. If I did anything it was with the best intention in the world. I only wanted to help you, Mary. Just to help you. I'm sorry if I lost my temper with you last night. Sorry if I hit him. I was only thinking of you."

He looked pleadingly towards her, and she knew she could say no more.

"Oh well! Let's not talk about it any more. I'm worried about Arthur. Will you try and find him?"

"I will," he replied. "He might have taken a jump. You never know."

"The boy's had no food since last night. I'm sure of that," she said.

"Don't worry. He might have done the wisest thing in the world," he said.

"But now," said Mrs Fearon, "but now... Oh I don't want him to go away. No! No! Find him. Bring him back here. Bring Arthur back to me. I won't rest. I won't sleep. I want him." There were tears in her eyes now. "Poor lad. Poor Arthur," she murmured again and again.

Her husband left the house. "A confounded nuisance. That's what boys are. A confounded bloody nuisance."

5

FEARON STOLE SILENTLY ALONG the deserted deck of the SS *Hernian*. The ship was due to sail on the night's tide. The decks were littered with lumber. The shore gangs had just gone ashore. He had lain in the rope locker all day waiting for this chance. Silently he descended a companion ladder until he found himself near the starboard allo-way. At the furthest end a cluster was hanging from the deckhead. The engine-room entrance, however, was in complete darkness. He walked quickly now. The steady hum of the engines drowned the noise he made with his hobnailed boots. It was hot and stuffy as he neared the iron door. He stopped, looked round. Nobody in sight. He disappeared through the door. Slowly he descended the great iron ladder. When he reached the first landing he stopped, and listened again. "There must be somebody on duty below," he thought, and later added: "Of course there is. They always leave a man on watch." He continued his descent. At last he stood on the floor of the engine room. He started to shiver from fear, and agonizing thoughts seized him. Should he go home or not? He visualized his parents anxiously awaiting his return, saw his evening meal laid out upon the table. He stood there contemplating, torn between the two thoughts. In a sudden moment he made his decision. He had begun. He would see it through to the end. But he must be so careful. He knew of youths who had tried to stow away to America, and had been discovered, returned to shore and heavily fined and imprisoned. A ship's engine room and stokehold were not strange things to him now. He knew in which direction he must walk to reach the coal bunker. He had been turning the plan over in his mind all that day, and he had decided to hide himself in the bunkers. There was least chance of being discovered there. He had read of a boy who had stowed away in the ship's bunkers and had been smothered to death by a heavy fall of coal. But he was determined. After all, he told himself, anything was better than working inside a hot boiler, or standing up to one's knees in a bilge tank. He must watch himself. It was not a question of getting his own back upon his parents, nor a question of getting a free passage out to America. There were other, more important things. He had to be on guard against many forms of death, against discovery, and in this latter he was inviting hunger and fear, perpetual darkness and terror to be his companions. He knew that if discovered, he would be arrested and put ashore at the first port. He made his way slowly behind the boilers, walked on until he reached the port bunker. There was a sliding steel door, a sort of manhole. It was only partly open. To endeavour to open it still further was impossible and, in addition, it might bring a load of coal down on top of him. It was quite dark. The air seemed clammy, and great draughts were continually criss-crossing whilst he stood there, his one small hand resting on the door. He felt all along the opening. He would crawl through. Again he remained quite still and listened. He thought he heard the sound of voices coming from the engine room. His heart seemed to bound into his mouth. He must hurry. Suddenly he said to himself:

"I'll squeeze through this opening. It's the only thing I can do."

And suiting the action to the word, he gradually forced his way through the hole. He was now in contact with a huge mass of coal. He felt like a pygmy standing in front of a mountain. Though this was a mountain he could not see, but only feel. He began to crawl up and up. Several times great lumps of coal went slithering past him, and he held his breath, at the same time stopping his ears with his fingers, his heart palpitating wildly. Fear had laid hold of him. He stretched himself and lay quietly, his whole body taut, his face turned away from the coal itself. He felt hungry already. He had no watch. He wondered what time it might be. Then he turned over on his back and began to think of home. He started to cry. He heard nothing, saw nothing, and somehow he felt he was nothing. There was that great mountain of coal and his puny self. He knew that coal was the food of a ship, and that but for this, the ship could not travel. Suddenly he thought, "Now when she's about five days out, God Almighty, what shall I do?"

Suddenly there was a low rumbling noise and he stopped his ears with his fingers. He was afraid to move. Somehow that noise continued on in his brain. He slid down the pile of coal and came to rest at the bottom. Then he opened his eyes. Still the same darkness, the same sense of desolation, the all-pursuing fear, the continual draughts criss-crossing. He began to cry again. Then he fell asleep. Twice he awoke with a start. Imagining somebody was focusing a light upon his terror-stricken face, he murmured:

"Oh God! What did I do it for? Why didn't I remain at home? I'm a damned coward, afraid of a few belts from my father."

Then he realized something. The whole floor beneath his feet appeared to be moving, or being moved by a force greater than itself. In addition, the coal commenced to slither down towards the bottom of the mountain. The air was no longer stuffy, the draughts pouring through the hole were greater. Then he knew that the ship was under way. He had no matches, no food, nothing. He crouched against the coal, shivering violently. From time to time he murmured: "Mother! Oh Mother!" He did not know the time, where the ship was, how long she had left. Did not know whether he would be discovered or not. Slowly it dawned upon him that discovery was now a necessary thing. He would die if he remained there for the run across. Again, if the ship experienced rough weather he ran the risk of being crushed to death. And yet fear held him. For he did not know at what moment to reveal himself. He must not give himself away until the Irish coast had been passed. Experience had taught him that a boat of her tonnage never cleared the land for nearly sixty-five hours. But he could not imagine how long he had been in that impenetrable darkness. Besides, he told himself, he had been asleep two or three times. If only he had brought his watch with him. What a fool he was not to think of bringing it with him, as well as some food. What a fool never to have remembered a box of matches. He swore.

He lay back and opened his eyes wide to the darkness. In imagination he saw his mother bending over him and tending to his wants. Saw his father talking to him *like* a father, encouraging him to better efforts. The boy's heart throbbed. Again a fit of sobbing seized him, and once more it drugged him for sleep. His two hands covered his face, he sobbed convulsively in his sleep like a child. The darkness itself seemed to lift him up, to bear him unto itself until he became a part of it. A lump of coal slid down past the sleeping boy. A huge rat scurried across the pile. Darkness. Silence.

6

THE STEEL DOOR had been raised. A trimmer was shovelling for dear life. The roar of the engines drowned the curses of the firemen. A heavy head swell made her pitch like a wild and snorting horse. Up and up as though the shock of foam itself spirited her head out of the waters, and then down again overwhelmingly into their trough. Suddenly a trimmer shouted:

"Christ! A dead stowaway! A stowaway! Dead! Help here!"

He closed and opened his mouth like a fish, unable to believe that the body which had rolled down to his feet was a real human being. "God," he murmured.

Two firemen flung down their slices and ran across to where the petrified trimmer was standing, his mouth agape.

"Get out of the bloody way," they both said in unison.

They lifted up the body of the boy and ran with it into the glaring light of the open furnace door of number five.

"A boy. A mere kid!"

"Dead?" queried the other.

"Don't know," said the first fireman hoarsely. "Call the second. Quickly."

He laid the boy down. Then he ran to his can. Came back and dashed its contents into the boy's face. Rubbed his arms. Finally he took off his trousers and started to massage his legs.

The second mate came along. "Hello!" he exclaimed gruffly. "What's this? New kind of fish?"

"A boy," replied the fireman. "One of the trimmers discovered him. Must have been hiding in the coal."

"Run him up to the ship's hospital aft. Then inform the second steward. Here you," he added to the second fireman. "Inform Carruthers I want him."

The first fireman lifted the boy across his shoulder and walked to the ladder. Very slowly he made his way to the top. When he reached the entrance he stopped. Then he laid the boy down on the big rope mat. He stood looking down at him with a pitying glance.

"Poor kid," he said to himself. "Another of them. That's seven in as many trips. What's the world coming to at all when kids like this one have to do such things?" He was a generous-hearted man, and had sons of his own, though he had vowed that none of them would ever set foot aboard a ship.

"A dog's life and nothing more," he had said again and again.

Seeing this boy lying at his feet made him think of his own two sons. They were in good jobs ashore and were likely to remain there if he knew anything.

Suddenly a voice hailed him. "Oh! This is the kid!"

The fireman looked up to find the second steward standing at his side.

"That's him. The poor little bugger's all out. Near dead."

"Lift him up and follow me," said the steward, and he lifted the boy upon his shoulder once more. They walked down the long alloway towards the crew's hospital near the wheelhouse aft.

It was quite dark outside the hospital. The afterdeck looked desolation itself. Far astern one just discerned the erratic wake of the ship, and abeam the mountainous seas. A single star gleamed above. All around the wide waste of waters rose and fell, rose and fell with a steady rhythm and roar. Through this fury and magnificence the *Hernian* steadily ploughed her way. The Chief Engineer was at the moment studying the day's run, which the fourth engineer had just brought into him.

"Hmm!" exclaimed the Chief and puckered his brows.

Meanwhile the fireman had laid the boy down on the deck and covered him with a blanket. The steward had discovered that the electric bulb was missing and had hastened amidships to procure one.

He returned quickly.

"In there," he said to the fireman.

"In where?" asked the astounded fireman, for in the darkness he had not been aware of the steward's approach.

"IN THERE!" roared the steward.

"All right! Don't get your confounded shirt out about it," he growled.

The steward had switched on the light. The ship's hospital contained four beds. In the top bunk just beneath the light the fireman placed the boy.

"That'll do," said the steward, and the fireman returned to his work, glad of the slight breather after the heat below. As soon as the door closed, the steward forced some brandy down the boy's throat. He waited. It might have been twenty minutes or half an hour. At length some signs of life were apparent in the boy, for his body moved slightly. Immediately the steward poured another drop of brandy down his throat. The boy's eyes opened. He blinked. Then stared for a time at the deckhead studded with rivets above him. Surprise and wonder sat upon his face.

The steward spoke to him:

"Are you awake, boy?" Then again:

"Are you awake, boy?"

The boy's eyes slowly closed, then opened again. He tried to move his head, but it appeared painful to do so. His eyes now widened and scanned the surrounding objects. Again the steward spoke to him.

Then the boy spoke.

"Where am I?"

"This is the *Hernian*," replied the steward. "You were discovered in the coal bunkers, half-dead at that. What made you do such a foolish thing? You might have been killed by a fall of coal. Anyway you'll have to appear before the Captain in the morning. See what he'll have to say about it."

The steward was also a married man with one son. And as he looked at this boy he said to himself: "Well! I don't know. Here's a boy, seems quite a respectable one too, doing a trick like that. In the bunkers too. Good God!"

The boy was trying to raise himself up on the pillow. The steward assisted him. Sitting up, he appeared to the steward much younger than he had originally thought him, so that it occurred to him to ask the boy a good many questions. But the boy interrupted him by asking quite a few himself.

"Is this ship called the *Hernian*?"

"Yes."

"Where is she going to?"

"Alexandria first stop, after that, God knows where."

"Does she carry passengers?"

"No. You're the only one at present," and the steward essayed a smile.

For the first time the boy too smiled. The steward had by his effort broken down the hitherto impossible barrier that appeared to exist between them. All the coldness, darkness, fear, rats, hunger and terror seemed to have been blown away by that single smile.

The steward now placed his hand behind the boy's head to support him. Again he gave the boy a drink from the bottle. Then he leant back as though to get a better focus upon this boy, who had dared a horrible death in order to get away to sea. At the back of the steward's mind one single thought held sway: "No boy," he told himself, "would do such a thing unless quite desperate. Perhaps his home life was bad. Perhaps he had run away from school, or even the police."

"How old are you?" he ventured to ask him.

"Fifteen," replied the boy, adding: "I am hungry. Could you get me something to eat? And how long have I been aboard this ship? Where are we?"

The steward laughed. "You'll be all right in a jiffy. The skipper's not a bad sort, and I do believe we sailed a hand short this time. Now I'll go and see if there's anything worth scrounging from the galley. Lie still. And don't utter a sound until I return."

As soon as the door closed the boy burst into tears. Why had he done such a thing? And how did he know the steward was speaking the truth? The Captain might even put him ashore. If only he knew how far out they were! Had they passed the Irish coast? How long ago? What were his father and mother thinking of him now?

All these thoughts became cataract. All the brightness and hope that the steward's smile had brought into being now departed, and he was aware of the fact that he was cold, hungry, miserable, lonely.

Suddenly the door opened and the steward came in with a plate of dry hash and a cup of hot tea.

"Here," he said. "Can you sit up? Try and get this down. You'll be all right. Ever been away to sea before?"

"No," replied the boy.

"Well, all the more reason why you must gollop this up, as if you get sick with nothing in your belly you'll know about it pretty quickly. Now." And he handed the plate of hash and the cup of tea to the boy. He stood on the edge of the lower bunk and leant over until his face was near to the boy's own. He watched him as he drank and ate of the sea fare. He noted that he was a nice-looking boy. He liked his wine-dark skin, the fine eyes, the delicateness of the features, the slight down upon his face, the slender white hands like those of a girl.

Suddenly he leant over and said:

"Boy! Kiss me."

For a moment the boy was astounded. He did not understand. His thoughts were at the moment centred on his stomach, so that this sudden request on the part of the steward left him wondering. A sudden wave of fear shot across his heart and he reached over and kissed the man full on the lips. It was then that he noticed that the steward's breath smelt of drink. In addition, he discovered that the man had not shaved. And with the first realization, all the other things that went to make up the steward as a man became manifest. His eyes were bloodshot, his was a straggling moustache, his face was bloated, and his neck a violent red. But the smell of his breath was the one thing that engraved itself upon the feelings of the boy. He laid down the plate and cup upon the bed and looked at the man.

"Thank you," he said. "I can't eat any more."

The steward looked into the cup and at the plate. His reply was like a shot from a gun:

71

"What's wrong with the bloody stuff? What's the matter with you, you bloody worm?"

All the fear returned again. The boy's face paled, his hands trembled. He suddenly screamed, then shouted:

"Take me to the Captain!"

The steward smiled. He crossed to the door, opened it and looked out. Darkness, the incessant pounding of the propellers, the wild orchestra of wind and waters.

He turned to look at the boy. His was the face of a ghost.

The steward put his hand on the switch and instantly the room was in darkness. The next moment the boy felt a hand stealing amongst the bedclothes. A single blanket covered him. He was afraid to cry out. Like one hypnotized he lay still. Then he felt this hand loosening his clothes. He tried to think, but could not, and suddenly the weight of the man was upon him. He clenched his hands, murmuring:

"Get off. Get off, you dirty beast."

He uttered no further sounds for the man's mouth had completely covered his own. And this mouth sucked rather than kissed him. The boy's whole being revolted, but he was powerless. The steward continued to suck at the boy's mouth. The boy felt sick, the smell of beer and whisky was in his nostrils, and he imagined a horde of worms were creeping slimily about his face. He gave a sudden jump, for the man had rubbed his unshaven chin across his cheek.

"Hey, kid," whispered the steward, "say nothing. I'll see you all right. God's truth I will. I have a boy of my own, I have."

And his two hands began pawing at the boy.

Somehow this man had made that room all powerful, the filling of it with himself alone. Outside the seas heaved a frenzied poem about her poop, so that each time she pitched the poop appeared to be lifted shock out of the water by a gigantic hand. In that moment the roar of the engines in the after wheelhouse drowned even the roars of the waters and the wind. But for the boy the only sound was the incessant grunting of this man on top of him, like that of a well-filled sow.

"Here, you dirty bastard!" the boy managed to speak into his ear. "Let me go. D'you hear? Let me go. Let me go."

"Shut your mouth," growled the man. "I'll make your life a hell on this packet if you say anything. D'you hear me?"

There was a sudden shout outside the door:

"Hey Hughes! Wanted for'ard. Hurry up."

When he had gone the boy moved. The air still seemed to be full of his presence, his voice, his breath, his heavy breathings, his huge and powerful hands. He raised himself up. He tried to climb out of the bunk, reached forwards, then fell to the floor. He managed to reach the switch. The room was flooded with light. He looked all around. He seemed to be covered with slime himself.

"The dirty bugger," said the boy. "The dirty filthy swine."

Another voice was heard outside the door. The boy was standing staring at his clothes, distraught, when the door was thrown open, and a huge man wearing a sou'wester and gumboots called out:

"OUTSIDE, YOU."

7

O N THE FOLLOWING MORNING, immediately after inspection by the Chief Officer, Chief Engineer and Chief Steward, the ship was deemed clean and in accordance with the traditions for order and cleanliness as obtaining amongst the fleet of cargo steamers owned by Morrell and Company. At half-past nine the Captain's Tiger* came down to the boatswain with a message:

"The boy discovered in the bunkers must appear before the skipper at ten o'clock. He must be clean, and," added the steward, "he must be given his breakfast."

The boatswain frowned. "The bloody kid's had his breakfast. I saw to that. Hey!" he suddenly called out, and from behind the door of the boatswain's room, the boy Arthur Fearon appeared.

"You must get ready to go and see the old man at ten o'clock," said the boatswain.

"Yes, sir," replied the boy.

"All right, steward," said the boatswain, "I'll look after it all right. I'll send him up with the diver of my watch."

The boy stared after the steward. Then he turned to the burly-looking individual called the boatswain, and asked in rather a timid manner:

"Will there be much of a row, sir?"

"How the hell do I know, boy?" replied the boatswain.

"You might make a good captain's boy," he continued. "D'you know what a captain's boy is?" he asked.

"No, sir."

"You soon will," he said, laughing.

At ten o'clock prompt the boy was taken up onto the bridge by the diver of the port watch, named Donavon. When they reached the Captain's door, the boy trembled visibly. This made the man smile and he said in a low voice:

"Hell! He won't bite you. Where in the name of Christ did you spring from anyhow? You're like a little girl, so help me…"

He knocked boldly upon the cabin door.

"Come in."

The boy had never heard such a voice before. It was volcanic, it boomed, it thundered. It made him almost ill to imagine the appearance of its owner. Both man and boy entered the cabin. The Captain was lying on his settee. He looked from one to the other of them. He was unshaven, he too seemed to have spent the last few days imbibing strong drink. He suddenly spoke:

"All right, man. You may go."

The door closed. The boy stared at the Captain.

"Sit down," said the Captain, and the boy sat down. Already the man had sensed the fear consuming this boy and he endeavoured to allay this.

"We won't kill you," he said slowly, and then drawled, "not yet."

The boy made as if to speak, but the apparent seriousness of the situation now dawning upon him held him in check. His mouth opened and closed like a gasping fish. The Captain continued to take his measure of the boy, betraying neither surprise nor interest in the strange arrival. In his thirty-four years of ploughing the seven seas he had experienced many such cases as the one now before him, though the stowaways, all boys, were quite individual. Each had his own special reason for stowing away. The Captain was fully aware of the habits, the feelings and hopes and desires of boys of the age when school is rid of them and the outer world entirely hostile to their hopes.

Suddenly he sat up and said:

"Tell me, boy. How old are you?"

"Fifteen, sir," replied Fearon.

"Why did you do this thing? Don't you know you were endangering other people as well as yourself? Saddling busy men like myself with responsibilities. Now then, why did you hide in the bunkers? Be truthful. Out with it now!" He rose to his feet and immediately his importance increased in the boy's mind, even as his stature seemed to increase. He towered over the shivering lad.

"Well, sir, it was like this, sir… I…"

"Come on! Open your damned mouth. Nobody is going to murder you."

Fearon was on the verge of tears. Some courage came to him. Slowly and very clearly he explained the whole of the situation to the Captain. His home life, his work at the docks, his desire to be something more than a labourer, the attitude of his parents, their poverty and inability to do anything for him. The man listened attentively to his story, and every now and then shut his eyes, as though this very act helped him to absorb all what was being said, and to examine it minutely.

"You know the penalty for stowing away on a liner, I suppose?"

"No, sir."

The boy spoke truth. He did not know. Nor was he acquainted with the law, the shipping company's methods. He knew nothing. He was only a boy. He was something suddenly flung into this new world of men. Helplessness, blindness, aimlessness. So he had flung himself among them. What would they do with him? If only his father could see him now! How he would laugh and taunt him for his neshness. Yes, he was afraid. But then his father had been cruel to him at times. And yet, as he looked into this man's eyes he thought he saw kindness mirrored there. Only kindness. The Captain was speaking:

"Well! What have you to say for yourself, boy? What is going to be done? We can't have you on our hands. I have to make out my reports. The company does not make a rule of giving free trips to stowaways. Well!"

"I can work, sir," said the boy, and he looked full in the man's face.

The Captain smiled inwardly at this reply. They all could work. He had seen some of them before today.

"I don't know what can be done," continued the Captain. "There are no hands short aboard. But that we have passed the Fastnet* long since, I would go so far as lowering a boat and sending you

77

ashore. You must make yourself generally useful in some way or other. When we arrive at Alexandria I'll have you sent ashore to the Consul. You may even get imprisonment. By the way, what is your father?"

"A labourer, sir," said Fearon.

"Have you brothers or sisters?"

"No, sir."

"Tell me now, and look straight at me in doing so. Just why did you do such a thing as stow away in a ship's bunker? You might have been suffocated or crushed to death."

There was a trace of kindness in the tone of the man's voice, but if he thought it any help towards getting the boy to reveal the truth of the matter he was much mistaken. On the contrary, the question sealed up the boy's mind. He was like an idiot now, standing there, fiddling with the bottom of his dirty brown jacket.

"I don't know, sir. Honestly I don't know, sir," he replied clearly.

The Captain leant towards the bulkhead. He pressed a button, then sat back and waited. A strange silence filled the room.

There came a knock at the door.

"Come in."

The steward entered. The Captain pointed a finger towards the boy, saying:

"Take this boy to the boatswain, and see if he can use him for anything. If not, take him down to Mr Grierson. Failing that, send him along to the galley. There must be something aboard that he can turn his hand to."

"Right, sir," said the steward, and turning to the boy said: "Come along."

Fearon followed the steward. They walked along the bridge deck, passed down the companion ladder, and walked amidships until they came to another companion ladder. They passed down this to find themselves on a kind of well deck. They passed right for'ard. Two or three men were sitting on no. 1 hatch. A chorus of remarks heralded their arrival. Then both man and boy passed up the alloway. The steward knocked at the door of the boatswain's room.

"Hello! Hello there! What the bloody hell's wrong now?" came the voice of the boatswain. The gruff voice of this bulky person frightened the boy. The door opened. The boatswain had just come out of his bunk. He was due on deck at twelve noon. It was now nearly eleven.

"Christ!" he exclaimed. "What a ship. What a ship! A confounded man can't get a damn wink of sleep here. What the hell do you people want?"

"We've come down from the Captain's room. Can you use this boy?"

A smile wreathed the large features of the boatswain, and he said surlily:

"Can I use him. Well! Well! I can use a brownie any time," and he laughed aloud.

The boy stood there, wondering what his destiny was going to be.

"Cut the joke," replied the steward. "Can you fix him up in either of the watches?"

"No, I can't!" shouted the boatswain. "Take him to hell out of here. Losing my bloody sleep. God stiffen these blasted boys!" and with a volley of oaths he returned to his room and slammed the door. Meanwhile quite a small crowd composed of members of the dogwatch and daymen had gathered at the alloway entrance. The steward caught the boy by the shoulder and pushed him through this gaping and inquisitive crowd, saying as he passed:

"Beat it, you pack of bums. What d'you think it is? A bloody exhibition?"

The boy looked up into the steward's face. It was not the same man. Realizing this, he asked the man at his side a question or two: What did they intend to do with him? Would they put him ashore?

The only answer he got was a slight grunt, and when the boy repeated the question, the steward shouted: "How in Christ's name do I know?"

"Here," he said, and pulled back the boy. They were standing outside the galley now. The odour of half-cooked food came to the boy's nostrils, making him feel not hungry but physically sick. A kind of revulsion passed through him.

The cook came to the door of the galley. "Hello," he exclaimed. "What you got there?"

"This is the kid who was found in the blurry bunkers last night. I've come down from the skipper's cabin just now. Went to see the boatswain for'ard. He's a growling devil anyhow. Look here. The old man says can you fix this kid up at anything? Can he do anything for you in the galley? Do you want an assistant mess steward? Say the word, cook, old man."

"Is this it?" asked the cook, and he came out of the galley to get a better view of the stowaway. The boy stood facing him. His wits were scattered. The whole affair had overwhelmed him. He did not understand. Already he had been butted from one end of the ship to the other. And he said to himself:

"Supposing the cook doesn't want me? Supposing the second engineer doesn't want me?"

"How old are you, lad?" asked the cook.

"Fifteen, sir."

"Have you ever washed pans and things? Peeled spuds, eh?"

"Yes, sir," replied Fearon.

The cook turned to the steward. "I could do with a help, as the mess steward has gone sick. Will you tell the old man I can use him then?"

"Righto," said the steward. "I'll leave him in your hands then?"

"Certainly," replied the cook. "I'll look after this nipper all right."

They both watched the steward walk along the deck and mount the port companion ladder. Then the cook turned round to look at the boy. He studied him closely for some minutes before venturing a word. Then he said:

"Boy!" He paused, whilst Fearon looked up at the man questioningly.

"Yes, sir."

"See now. I'll show you your room. You'll sleep in the bunk below mine. You'll rise at five o'clock each morning and clean out the galley in readiness for me when I come on at six o'clock sharp. You'll get the burgoo all ready for me in the pan, you'll fill that big tank full of water from the pump outside. Then you'll commence to peel a barrel of potatoes. After that you'll clean fish and get vegetables ready. It will be nearly breakfast time for the engineers. As the steward is laid up with a dose,* you'll go into the mess room and lay table for seven men. You'll serve their meals, clean out their rooms, mine as well. If you have a slack hour or so, the boatswain might want you, or Mr Grierson might want something doing. I'm afraid, sonny, that you have placed yourself in a bit of a mess, for as things stand at present, you aren't even a member of the crew. You'll just be used, as the saying is. Come along now. I can't afford to waste much time, as I have to get back to see to the next meal for the watches going on."

He placed a hand on the boy's shoulder and together they entered the starboard alloway. A little way down on the right, the cook's room was situated.

"This way," said the cook, and the boy entered the room with him.

The boy stared around the room. There were two bunks against the wall. Opposite stood a settee, once red plush, but now just one layer of grease and dirt. The cook very rarely slept in his bunk, mostly using the settee. It saved getting undressed and dressed. When any of the sailors or firemen drew attention to his unshaven state, or his dirty appearance generally, he met them with the excuse that he could not do it. Had no time. "I have to work nearly eighteen hours a day to look after you bums, and if you want me to look like a chef at the Ritz you must either get my pay raised for me, or else you must get me another assistant." The men would just laugh, and the incident ended. When drunk, conditions were even worse, for often the cook had to be hauled out of his room to get the fires going, in order that the early watches could get their breakfasts.

With all this state of affairs the Captain was rarely acquainted. Indeed that gentleman found much of his time occupied with the reading of popular novels, when not actually on the bridge, and that was rare too, except during heavy fogs, bad weather, or for fifteen minutes daily at noon, when with his three companion officers, he endeavoured to gauge the position of his ship. And it was bound to follow that he would not be actively interested in the welfare of an ordinary stowaway. He left a matter like that in the hands of his steward. At the moment he was standing leaning over the log in the chart house, though the log itself had no interest for him at the moment. His ship was due at Alexandria in five days' time. There would be a lot of work for him to do on arrival there. The Consul must be seen on many matters, not the least one of which was that concerning the position of the boy discovered in the bunkers. It was whilst he was considering this question of putting the boy ashore that a message came up to him from the boatswain. The Captain dismissed the steward, closed the door of the chart room and then read:

Lookout man Joseph Parr has died of a seizure.
E. Antiss. Boatswain.

"Damn!" exclaimed the Captain.

He flung down the note, put on his coat and hat and hurried for'ard. In the fo'c'sle the man was lying just where he had fallen. His mouth was all covered with blood. He knelt down and felt his pulse. Then turned to the first mate:

"Mr Nolan, how long ago is it since this occurred?"

"I've just come down myself, Mr Wood. I was sleeping in my room when the bosun came hurrying to me to tell me Parr had had a fit. He must have died almost immediately."

"Um! I see. Very well. Inform one of the quartermasters at once. Get his belongings together. Arrange for a burial at five p.m. It is now nearing twelve."

"Very good, sir."

The Captain left the fo'c'sle and returned to his chart room. And as he closed the door with a bang he emitted a further and more emphatic "Damn!"

The quartermaster whom the first mate was searching for was discovered washing his clothes in the men's lavatory. He was called out at once.

"Duggan!! You might get a length of canvas from the storeroom. Then go down and ask Mr Grierson if he will get his storekeeper to give you two or three fire bars. Have you got any yarn in your room?"

"Yes, sir."

"Good! That man Parr has just expired. I don't understand how he passed the doctor in a state like that."

"Is he dead, sir?" asked the bewildered quartermaster.

"He is."

"Very good, sir. I'll see to it."

"We are burying him at five o'clock. At least that is Mr Wood's order."

"All correct, sir."

The first mate returned to his room, cursing the bosun for disturbing his afternoon sleep. He himself had to be on the bridge at four sharp.

The quartermaster procured the canvas, yarn, fire bars. The ship's lamp room was situated on the starboard side aft. To this room three of the sailors off watch carried the body of their mate. The door closed on it. The body was left safely in the hands of the quartermaster. He began his task with misgiving. He could not help glancing from time to time at the blood-soaked features of the lookout man. He had liked the chap himself, and had often, when ashore, had a drink or two with him. Now as he sat measuring off his canvas, he could not help staring at the still figure who so soon was to be lowered away to the deep waters.

"Poor fellow! Dear me! What a bloody life!"

For some time he talked to himself. Then there was no sound save the steady plying of the needle. At a quarter to four the body had been sewn up and was carried by two sailors to the after hatch. There it was laid down and secured with a rope lashing to the hatch combing, in case a sea should rob the crew of twenty minutes' idleness, and the Captain of the opportunity of referring to his Bible, a thing he liked to do on almost every occasion. He even had the men assembled for'ard on a Sunday whilst he read to them a page or two from the great book.

All this time the boy and the cook were sitting in the latter's room, whilst the cook explained just what work he would have to do. It was during a momentary lapse in the instructions, when the cook was filling his pipe, that word came of the death of the port-watch lookout man.

"Oh Christ!" was all the remark the cook made. He sat silent then for some minutes. Then raised his eyes to look across at the boy.

"Well, boy," he began, "I'm afraid you've let yourself in for something more than you bargained for." He spat on the floor with decided emphasis.

The boy looked at him. He at the boy. He went on in the same tone of voice:

"You boys expect to be treated like chickens, and the truth is the whole lot of you are nuisances. Damned nuisances. Look at yourself. You get aboard here, are nearly smothered in coal, and when found you create more disturbance than anybody. The whole ship is wondering where you came from, why you came, and when you're going to clear out. The skipper of a ship has no time for dealings with boys like you. And why have I shown you some consideration? Because I was a boy myself once, though I never did a trick like that, and because I have three sons older than you. Well, boy, you'll have to show a leg and shift yourself aboard this ship, as the saying goes. Now I've told you almost everything. Is there anything you want advice on?"

"Will I get any pay for this work?" the boy asked.

"Pay! Pay! Who mentioned pay? Why, boy, the company can't afford to pay you. You have your board and bed aboard this ship and you have to work for it. As soon as we get to Alex, the skipper'll put you ashore. You'll be shut up for a few days in a jail, I suppose, like all the rest of them. Then they'll pack you off home aboard the first boat sailing. Now do you understand?"

The utter bewilderment upon Fearon's face made it obvious that he did not. He continued to stare at the cook.

"Pay! Pay!" repeated the cook. "Christ Almighty! I like that I do. S'help me I do. Pay! Ha, ha, ha!"

"Here," he added suddenly, "you'd better come along now and get a bite of grub. Do you feel sick yet?"

"Sick!" The boy paused. "Oh no. No. I don't feel sick. I'm all right. I'm all right."

They both returned to the galley. The cook gave him a plateful of soup, and two slices of bread.

"Sit down there and eat that, and consider yourself lucky. When I was a boy your age..." but the remainder of the sentence was inaudible to the boy, who began to eat and enjoy the food put before him. And whilst he ate his thoughts were of home. How they would miss him! He visualized their distress. And they had always looked upon him as being nesh. Well, they would know now as to whether he was nesh or not. Perhaps they thought him dead, lying dangerously injured in hospital, staying with some relative or other. The last thought in Fearon's mind was that his parents should think of but one thing in connection with his disappearance. The sea. But Mr Fearon only thought once and then correctly. He fully expected to have a letter from his son from some odd corner of the world. The boy finished the meal, and handed the plate and cup to the cook, saying:

"Thank you. I was hungry and enjoyed it."

The cook smiled and replied:

"Well then, perhaps you'll feel in form for a little work. Now there's all these pans to be washed and hung up. Those spuds there must be peeled tonight, all ready for the morning. Then the deck must be swilled down. Do you understand?"

It was at that moment that a heavy head swell bore down upon the *Hernian*. The ship commenced to pitch heavily, the wind rose, which made the cook remark, "I'm afraid we're in for some dirty weather tonight."

The boy had turned his face away from the hot fire and was now staring across the waste of waters. It seemed to him as though the ship was being ripped to pieces. Already the ratlines had broken loose, and the incessant rattle of them against the stays and mast revealed to him that a wind from the south-west can be at times a terrible affair, destroying everything in its path. At home he had been out many a windy day. But he could not recall such a wind as this. He said to the cook: "What a wind, cook."

Again the cook laughed, saying as he revealed his horselike teeth: "Well! I told you. It'll be a dirty, bloody night all right, and perhaps you won't run away to sea again in a hurry. Now, my lad would never think of stowing away like that. Not that I don't admire your pluck. I like you for it. But there's that son of mine. He's interested in engines. He wouldn't go to sea if he was paid twenty pounds a week."

Fearon sat thinking. "Well," he said to himself, "that's all right. But if he were in my place he would have to do something." And he recollected the hard living at home, the continual poverty, the disinterestedness of his parents in his welfare. Reviewing these things, he realized there was not another thing he could have done. Not a single thing. It had to be, he told himself. It was his only way of escape from a monotonous existence. And now there were men on board this ship, all of whom had sympathized with him after their own fashion. They had in effect said to him: "You little fool. Why did you do such a thing? The sea is only for those content to live a dog's life and nothing more than that."

But there was a thought lying at the back of his mind. There was something he wanted to say and would not say it. Yet he knew that on the saying of it, it might help the men to understand the only reason he had for stowing away. He was by turns glad, and by turns angry at the result of his decision. What did they intend to do with him? One man had told him that he was virtually at the beck and call of any member of the crew. Was that true? He pondered upon it. So far as he had visualized his position, he was due to perform quite a hundred tasks, and yet he would receive no pay for that. He was disappointed to learn that the ship would touch no western port, for the one idea in his head was to desert in America or Canada, and so work his way gradually towards a new life. He would write home to his parents. He would say to them: "Well, Father and Mother, I have done the thing I much wanted to do. I have succeeded. I intend to work hard and to save up. In the end I will be helping you both." Dreams, he thought.

When he retired to his bunk that night he lay awake for some time, turning over these thoughts in his mind. And at one o'clock in the morning (he remembered it quite clearly, for one bell had struck), the cook had wakened him up. The cook had asked him certain things, suggested certain things. Fearon was a boy whose life had been spent amongst the roughest of men at the docks and yards. He lay quietly, listening to the pleading of this man. Then he jumped out of bed, picked up a clothes brush, hit the cook across the head with it, and finally had fled from the cabin. He rushed along to the first mate's room, distracted and on the verge of tears almost, and knocked at the door.

The mate was playing a game of patience. He turned and shouted: "Come in!"

The door opened and the boy Fearon appeared. He glowered at the newcomer.

"Well!" he growled. "What's the matter with you now?"

For a moment it seemed as though the boy did not know, for he was content to stand stupidly staring at the officer, the while that individual scratched his head in bewilderment. He reached out a long arm, dragged the boy across to him, and said very slowly:

"Where's your tongue, boy? Answer me. Now."

"I'm sorry, sir," began Fearon, "to give you all this trouble. But I thought you would be the best person to go to. I wish to complain about the cook in whose room I am at present sleeping. I have been told off to help him in the galley as well as act as mess steward for the engineers. He interfered with me. I am frightened to go back to that room."

The officer looked the boy full in the eye. Then he said somewhat heatedly:

"Is the cook drunk?"

"I don't know, sir," replied Fearon.

"Show me to the room, boy," said the mate, rising to his feet and putting on his coat and cap. The pair walked amidships until they reached the alloway where the cook's room was situated. The mate pulled the boy by the arm. They stopped, and the boy looked up at the officer.

"Tell me just what he wanted to do to you," said the mate, and there was kindness and sympathy in the tone of his voice. It was like warmth to Fearon to hear this loud-voiced man talk in such a way to him. But he could not speak out what was in his mind. Instead he replied stammeringly:

"I can't tell you that, sir."

They reached the room. The door was standing ajar. The mate knocked boldly.

"Hello! Hello! Who the bloody hell is that now?"

"Open this door, Mr Cook, please," said the mate authoritatively.

There was a muffled cursing within the room. A second later the door opened. The cook was standing in the middle of the room in his singlet and drawers. The mate stepped into the room, pulling the boy after him. The door closed.

"What is wrong with you, man?" began the mate. "This boy has been complaining to me about something you tried to do to him. Explain yourself."

The cook stared at the mate, then at the boy, at whom he frowned.

"Do, sir? I done nothing to him. Nothing at all. I never even opened my mouth to him."

"Yes, you did," interrupted Fearon. "You asked me to undress and get into your bunk. I fell asleep twice and you woke me up again." He turned to the mate and added, "That's the honest truth, sir."

"Come with me," said the mate, and taking Fearon's arm they both left the room, the cook still standing in the middle of the floor, amazement written all over his face. "The blasted little twim," he muttered as he climbed back to his bunk. He stretched himself, reached out a hand, and switched off the light. The room went black immediately. The open porthole was right over the cook's bed. He could hear the incessant swirl of the waters. The moaning of the wind.

"The blasted little twim," he repeated.

8

IN THE PORT ALLOWAY of the *Hernian*, the rooms were situated as follows. First lavatory, boy's room, lamp room, carpenter's room, then boatswain's room, storeroom and baker's shop. That night Fearon slept in the boy's room. This room generally accommodated two ordinary seamen, but three months previous the company had decided to effect certain economies, and had dispensed with the boys. This room being vacant, it was on the mate's suggestion that the boy became its occupant. Fearon was glad of this. It prevented interference from the men, meant his having his full sleep, and also certain privacies. The boy rigged up his bunk and settled down to sleep. He dreamt. There were seven men in this dream. The second engineer, the steward, the cook, the boatswain, the Captain's steward, the post-watch diver and the leading greaser. They talked with him and of him. They talked about him to each other. He heard all their whisperings. They were plotting against him. Because he was a boy. There were no other boys aboard. Only him. He caught fragments of conversations:

"When I was a boy… Jesus Christ! I had to work before the mast on a schooner. If I did the least thing wrong I got my arse tanned with a bloody rope's end. Yes… when I was a boy…"

"These bloody boys are a confounded nuisance. Why shouldn't they work? Why shouldn't they do all the dirty work? That's what they're on board ship for. The little sods. Why in my time… Now I remember my first trip, we rounded the Horn in a bloody hurricane. I had to go aloft with two of the seamen. I was like a little girl in those days, with silky skin and slender hands. Those two buggers tried to do me one all right when we were perched aloft. And d'you know, ever since I recall those days, I hate boys. God damn my soul, I hate boys. Why? Just because I was a bloody boy myself."

"This bloody kid gives me the pip. In any ship excepting this, well he'd be used as a brownie. Strike me pink. Boys these days are becoming old in the head, developing cuteness. The little bastards. I was seventeen years in the *Niobe* as seaman-gunner. Why every man jack aboard had his own brownie. Why can't it be the same in these ships? That's what I say. Why can't it?"

"Bleedin' boy comes on board. Probably run away from home, robbed somebody. Never know. Won't stop at murder these days. Stuck in bloody bunkers. Gets pulled out. Nearly dead. Everybody sympathizing with him. Up before Captain. Comes to me. Yes. Will work for me. Help me in galley. Fed the sod. Fed him well. Said that night, 'Drop 'em down.' Bloody kid whingin'. Runs to mate. Crying. For his mammy I suppose. Such lads these days. Stupid little mucker. Like a girl."

"Lad comes to me crying, who am I? Man of course. Crying like hell. Will I do this and that. Where is she bound? When will she reach port? Will he get paid for working on board? What will they do with him? Should string all lads up like monkeys with brass balls, I say to myself, but not to him. Bloody cringing wimp. A man's a man and a boy's a boy, and sometimes a man's a bloody user. User. Know the word. Use him."

"Boys are little devils. Want tamin' they bloody well do. I know. I know. Had five sons of my own I had and know damn well they never did and never will do me a bit of good. Scoundrels. Buggers don't know what sea life is. Was a boy in a four-masted barque in the Nineties. Had to work. Holystone decks with belly not much filled and cold as hell getting to Nova Scotia. Had to put up with things. On bloody knees in early morning with a piece of stone in my hand, making ladders look new. Bent down all the while. Even snot freezing on the end of your nose, so cold it was. Sailors coming along and kicking you in the rump, putting hands where they shouldn't be. Did I kick? No. Couldn't. Had no right to. Just a boy. Well, am a man now and hate these bloody boys. Know what they're like now I do. Use the buggers for all you're worth."

A beam swell had set up, thunderous seas continued to crash broadside on, the tons of water crashing to the iron decks. One of these seas struck the deck just abaft the boy's room. In a second or two his door had been staved in and the water poured in. Four and a half feet of it, but fortunately the boy was sleeping in the top bunk, and still slept. Before retiring, he had screwed down the deadlight. He began talking in his sleep. Like the speech of the men he dreamt of, it was fragmentary and without coherency.

"Oh Mother! Oh Dad! If you could see me now. With these men. I like all except these seven."

There was a slight pause, then he rambled off again:

"Boys have hard times at sea. Wish to God I was not a boy. Had never been a boy. Wish I had been born a man right away. Boatswain hates me, he does. Five o'clock in the morning calls you and says, 'Show a leg, you sucker. Get on bloody deck and take kinks out of the bleedin' hose. Get my breakfast from the galley!' Hate him. Hate him."

He was awakened at half-past five by the cook who ordered him to set to work at once in the galley. Fearon was only now beginning to feel sick. His head seemed light, his inside he felt was almost near bursting point. When he reached the galley the cook was smoking his cheap shag. He had neither washed nor dressed. He leant over his favourite stew pan. When he heard the boy, he shouted out:

"Come on, sissy. Get a move on you. Men are waiting for that burgoo. The whole ship's talking about you, you confounded whimperer."

Fearon dragged himself into the hot galley. The heat, the smell of the tobacco, of the cooking food, almost made him vomit. He collapsed on the iron seat.

"Hello!" exclaimed the cook. "What's up now? Been using two hands, have you? Shake yourself together. The men are more important than you. Damn men out half the night working. Waiting for their grub. I won't stop them coming along and tickling your ribs for you."

He began to laugh. The boy looked at him with an almost glassy stare. Suddenly he leant forwards and vomited all over the clean floor. The cook made a rush at him.

"Strike me! I swilled that floor last night. Get out against the bulwarks and do your bloody stuff there. Idea! Seasick, I suppose. What the hell did you come away for? I wonder. You should have stayed at home with your mammy," and the cook again burst into loud laughter.

The boy struggled to his feet, and lurched out of the galley. With an effort he kept his feet, and just managed to escape catching his head on the iron pump handle. The ship was rolling badly. He slithered from one side of the alloway to the other. He fell and moaned pitiably. The steady hum of the engines, the smell exuding from the engine-room entrance made him vomit again. Just then the boatswain happened to be returning to his room from the bridge. He roared out as soon as he caught sight of Fearon:

"Get your broom, boy! Get it quickly and clean that bloody mess up. Hurry up now before you peg out on the way to the storeroom." He disappeared inside his own room, and the boy could hear him laughing.

The carpenter was dining with the bosun that morning. The latter remarked:

"A peculiar kid that! What's the matter with him this morning? He seems to be a bit crazy."

The boatswain laughed again. "I wish you meant it," he said. "D'you know," he continued, "when Mr Fell told me three months ago that they were discontinuing boys, well I was glad about it. For in my opinion a boy is quite useless aboard a ship. I don't know about a passenger ship, but these boats anyhow. Last boy I had looking after me came from one of those training ships. A real cut-throat and robber. I must tell you about Peter Larrigan sometime."

The carpenter said slowly:

"They're much better than a woman any time."

The Captain in conference with the Chief Officer had remarked upon the death of the lookout man. The mate said his place would have to be filled.

"Quite obvious," said the Captain sarcastically. "What about placing this boy on deck? I have already wired to the owners and informed them that I had a stowaway on board. I am waiting for a message from them advising me on the matter."

Just then the wireless operator knocked at the door. He handed in a message he had received from the Liverpool office. The Captain read:

"Cancel order for placing stowaway ashore in civil authorities' hands, Alexandria. Boy to be signed on as ordinary seaman."

"There you are," said the Captain, "just what I had in mind myself. That boy can be sent up here to me immediately and I will have him sign as OS. It will save me a lot of trouble getting a spare man in port, and incidentally all the fuss with the officials ashore. Right you are."

"Very good, sir." The mate left the cabin and went in search of the boy. He discovered Fearon on his knees in the engineer's mess room, his head lolling about like that of an idiot and every second threatening to fall off his shoulders into the bucket.

"What's the matter, boy?" he asked.

"Sick, sir," replied Fearon looking up from his task.

"Come! Come! You'll soon get over that, my boy. Captain Wood wishes to see you. Hurry up now. Straighten yourself up quickly and get to his room. You know the officer's house on the bridge?"

"Yes sir! Very good, sir!"

When the officer left the mess room the boy rose to his feet. His face was ashen, his hands trembled. He longed for nothing so much as a rest. If only he could lie down somewhere. Anywhere. Why had he ever come away? How sick and sorry he was. Yet he thought of his home life and the determination to make good only strengthened itself. He made his way slowly up to the bridge. The Captain answered his knock with a gruff "Come in."

"Oh!" he exclaimed. "Sit down there a second. Let me see. Your name is?…"

"Fearon, sir! Arthur Fearon."

"Yes," said the Captain. "Fearon. Fearon." He took a long look at the boy.

"Well, Fearon, we are a man short on this ship through losing our lookout man. I had already advised the company of your being discovered on board and was awaiting orders as to what to do with you when we reached port. I now have their reply. You will be signed on as an ordinary seaman. You will have the articles read to you. Your pay will be three pounds ten per month. You will report to the boatswain immediately, who, I understand, will fix you up."

"Yes, sir," said Fearon.

The Captain then read out the ship's articles to the boy. Afterwards he had the boy sign his papers as being a member of the crew for a period not exceeding six months. This done, the Captain placed the papers in a drawer. He turned round and said to the boy:

"I think somehow you will make a good sailor. I hope you fulfil that promise. You do not look a bad sort of boy at all, and I hope you will do well in whatever task is set you."

The boy blushed, his skin seemed to tingle, his heart leapt. Something was happening, he told himself. Something was happening at last. And now that he came to think about the whole affair, the Captain seemed to be the best of the men on board, and not that kind of man he had imagined him to be.

He sat staring at Captain Wood, his two hands clasped together in his lap, twirling his thumbs. He liked that Captain, he told himself. Suddenly it occurred to him to open his heart wide to this man. This man who appeared so gentle and so kind, like a father, though certainly not like his own father. He was so different from all the others and he inspired confidence. The more this man looked at him the more he felt he must burst out with all that was seeking utterance in his heart and mind. And then he said:

"Thank you, sir. I want to make good. I want to be something. I will do anything, work hard, have courage and hope if I can make good. My father and mother are poor people. They had to take me away from school before leaving age. I went to work at the docks and I did not like the work nor the boys with whom I had to work every day. Always my father was tormenting me. In the end I could stand it no longer, and one morning I did not go to work. I came home. My father did not speak a word to me. He knew already what was wrong. I did not speak either. He picked me up in his arms and threw me to the floor. Then I left home. Here I am on board your ship. I know I very nearly lost my life when that coal came down like that, but I was not afraid, sir. I wanted to show my parents, especially my father, that I was not nesh. He always made jokes out of me. Called me a girl. I am not a girl. It is just that I like to work with good people. I hated the boys and the men in the shops and yards. I was fed up. Fed up. But now that I've got a job I am prepared to do my best. Thank you, sir."

"All right, boy," said the Captain curtly, "go below and report to the boatswain."

His turning to some papers on his desk was an indication that he had finished with Fearon. Before he reported to the boatswain, Fearon went into his own room, there to sit down for a few minutes and think the thing over. He felt happy at last. So his rash act had ended up in his having got a job. The very thing he wanted. Well, he would show them now. All of them. He was not afraid of work. It was only that he had been frightened of what they might do to him when the ship reached Alexandria. Now he would be able to write home to his father and tell him that he had struck out on his own and had succeeded. He did not look upon it as a triumph, so much as a means of helping his mother. He loved his mother. He knew that she had had a hard life. He meant to help her, and by so doing, to reveal to his father that there were good qualities in him after all. Sitting on top of his bunk, these thoughts running riot in his mind, he suddenly decided that he would write a letter home that night, a long letter.

"God! I'm so happy now," he said as he left the room and walked for'ard to the boatswain's room to report himself. The boatswain was standing by his locker filling a glass from out a bottle of whisky when Fearon knocked. He had already heard from the mate that the boy was to be put in either his or his mate's watch as an ordinary seaman until the completion of the voyage. But although he was aware of this he did not reveal himself to the boy. He called out:

"Well! What is it? Who is that?"

"Fearon, sir," replied the boy.

"Oh!" There was a pause and the voice called again: "Come in! Come in!"

Fearon entered the room. The boatswain looked closely at him. Then said:

"Yes? Did you want anything? Is there something the matter with you again?"

For a moment the boy did not seem to understand, but stood there looking at this bearded person, until he was brought to his senses by hearing the man say:

"Well! What the bloody hell do you want?" He found himself then. That question was like a blow on the head to Fearon.

"Captain Wood told me to come down and report to you, sir," he said.

"Oh!" Pause. "I see." Pause. "Um!"

He fingered his glass and the boy saw his brows knit as though he were passing through the torment of indecision. Suddenly he laughed:

"I see," he said quietly. "Well, you'll be in my watch." Pause. Then:

"Oh no, of course you won't. You'll be on daywork. Of course. What am I thinking about? All the boys aboard these ships go on daywork. You're lucky, boy. Indeed you are. These ships ceased to carry ordinary seamen three months or more ago. Here's what you have to do. You'll be called at a quarter to five every morning. You'll immediately go to the second steward and draw my day's rations. Then you'll get my breakfast from the galley. The carpenter and lamp-trimmer eat in my room with me. You'll clean up and put your crockery away. Then you'll clean out and polish up my room. After that you'll clean up and polish the carpenter's and lamp-trimmer's rooms. Then your own. All the brass in this alloway must be polished before ten o'clock in the morning. After that you'll report to me on deck. There you will help the watch in any work they may be engaged on. Mostly you'll be cleaning winches, and chipping paint off the bulwarks. At half-past eleven you'll go and clean yourself up and get dinner from the galley. You'll have your own from what we leave. You strap up and report on deck again. At five o'clock you'll go to the galley for teas. Strap up again. Clean out room. My room only. Always make the beds first thing in the morning. After that you're free. Perhaps the mate might tell you to get on the bridge and learn to steer. Do you know the compass yet? Can you put an eye splice* in a piece of rope – a piece of wire? Can you rig up a boatswain's chair? Do you know how to paint? Can you take the kink out of a canvas hose? Never mind. You'll learn all these things bloody quick. Can you remember all that now?" he grinned at the boy.

"Yes, sir," replied Fearon.

"Very well. Cut along to the lamp-trimmer's room and ask for two slices, a Turk's head and a couple of cloths. Get some cotton waste from him too."

"Yes, sir."

"That's all."

Fearon left the room and made his way to the lamp-trimmer's storeroom.

"Woddyerwant," growled the lamp-trimmer, a Scotchman, as soon as he set eyes on the boy, and Fearon gave him the list of things required. The man mumbled something and gathered the implements together. He handed them out, saying: "Are you the bloody kid they found in the bunker?"

"Yes," said Fearon.

"Oh!"

The door was suddenly slammed in the boy's face. Fearon thought the man a pig and went on deck to no. 3 winch, which the boatswain had told him must be thoroughly cleaned up as the cargo men in Alexandria were very particular about the winches being in good order. Further, he was told that to have a dirty winch and a boy on board would be to incur the fourth engineer's wrath. Fearon had never seen him. Larkin, the fourth, was reputed to be the sourest man sailing the seven seas. Every engineer in the company had heard about him, and it was a commonplace that the men under his charge were continually deserting their ships and endeavouring to sign in any other of the company's ships, excepting the *Hernian*. But the men who had given him this label, and incidentally this special fame, had not seen beneath the sourness of Mr Larkin. It was not contact with man that had brought about this sourness. It was merely a whim of the sea itself. The sea shapes. The sea teaches. And Larkin was trying his best to unlearn all that he had learnt in his twenty-three years of sailing the waters. The sea had twisted something in his nature. From being a kind-hearted and gentle Irishman, he had ended up by being sour and morose, and he was at a loss to understand it. He kept very much to himself, in fact he only spoke when he had to. The men did not like him. Fearon was not the only person hated on the ship.

Kneeling down behind the winch at no. 3 hatch, he soon discovered that the job was even dirtier and more awkward than that of riveting and scaling, with which he had had to familiarize himself much against his desire. Yet he vowed to do everything to the best of his ability. He had promised the Captain that he would work well and he was determined to do so. There were five sailors in the port watch who were at present engaged in painting the funnel. From time to time Fearon stopped for a breather, and would look up at the men busily engaged in recoating the funnel with black paint. It was on a later occasion that he himself was sent up the same funnel, and there he learnt for the first time what a boatswain's chair really was.

A voice hailed him and he looked up. His face and hands were thickly coated with grease. He thought he saw the boatswain smile. Then he shouted out:

"All right! Cut along to your room and get cleaned up. Then go to the galley for food."

Fearon gathered his things together and deposited them in his own room, as he had to return to the same task immediately after dinner. He got the men's dinner, and then quietly retired to his own room until he was called. The call was stentorian and merely one word:

"Boy!"

When he got to the room the men had left it, and were either leaning over the rail or sitting on the hatch talking with each other. The leavings from the meals served as the boy's rations. This went on without any variation. After having his own food he cleaned up.

Then he got his things and returned to his winch. Just then one of the sailors came over to him and asked:

"How are you getting along, sonny?"

"All right," said the boy.

"Are you going to see madam when you get to Alex?"

The boy did not understand what the sailor meant. The sailor laughed, revealing his almost toothless mouth. He continued:

"Come off it! Mean to tell me you don't know what 'madam' means. Ha, ha, ha!"

"I don't," said Fearon, and went on with his work, completely ignoring the sailor.

Later that day the boy happened to be leaving the lavatory when he almost knocked the same sailor down, who said:

"How's your arm?"

9

F EARON WROTE HOME that night:

Dear Father and Mother,

By the time you get this letter I will be in Alexandria. I stowed away in the SS Hernian, *one of the Morrell boats. I thought for a time that I would be landed ashore and put in jail until there was a returning ship that could take me home. Fortunately one of the sailors died of a fit, and the next day the Captain said I was to sign on as an ordinary seaman. I like my work. It is not as dirty as the job I had down at the docks which Dad got me. The food is good and there is plenty of it. I was terribly worried for a long time, wondering what you would be thinking. What you would make out of my disappearance. But I'm glad that in a day or two we will be in port. I feel well in health, although for the first few days I was really very ill, and totally unable either to work or eat. That is all past now and I am happy. Dear Father and Mother, I am not angry with you both because you held me back from the very thing I wanted to do. I did not even wish to go to sea originally. I wanted one thing only. That was to be a chemist. I hated my jobs at home. I was fed up. I am not even angry with Father for nearly killing me that morning. I was however determined to get out of it and make my own road in this world. I have succeeded. The Captain here is rather a nice sort of man and he said that if I worked hard I would have a job in these ships for life. The boatswain is a very rough person, though I am hoping that we will always agree. Of course all these sailors seem to be very rough men. They are kind though. The only man I hate on the ship is the steward. I thought at one* time that the cook was terrible. But perhaps that was because I was so ill and sick. Also I was nearly killed, for I had stowed away in the coal bunkers. It was when one of the trimmers was loading up his barrow that I was found out. I came tumbling down with a great load of coal on top of me. I was taken to the ship's hospital. After I got over that I was sent to see the Captain. He said I was liable to imprisonment for stowing away. I had to do all kinds of odd jobs, because he said the company never thought of giving stowaways a free sea trip. Most of the men were rotten drunk. First few nights I couldn't sleep as men were interfering with me. When one night the cook started to interfere, I reported him to the Chief Officer. He is not a bad man. He had me placed in a room by myself, which used to be the ordinary seaman's room. This company no longer carries these ratings* and everybody tells me I'm very lucky to be signed on at all. By right, they say, I should be in irons until she gets to port, where the Captain generally hands over stowaways and suspicious persons to the civil authorities. Well, Mother and Father, I am now all right. I intend to do my best and to make good. There was a time when I cursed both of you for taking me away from school, as my heart was set on something different from that which you put me to. But now I have thought over it and I see that you could not help it. I know you have both had a hard struggle to live, and I am sorry if I ever did anything to offend you. My one desire now is to earn money to help both of you. I know that Dad cannot always continue at his present job, so I hope that by the time he has to retire, that I myself will be in a good position and able to keep both of you comfortably. There is a man on board this ship who says he knows Dad, as he sailed with him in the old clippers. His name is O'Rourke. Ask Dad whether he can remember the name. O'Rourke has promised to see that I am looked after and come to no harm. The only thing I did not like about him is that on the wall in his room he has photographs of naked women. But he is a good sailor and has promised to teach me splicing and yarning before we return to Liverpool. My wages are three pounds ten per month. When I sign on again I'll be able to leave you an advance note or *an allotment note. I only want to help both of you, because I love you. Also I want to become something in this world. O'Rourke told me the other day that if he had remained steady and kept off the drink he would now have a second officer's certificate. He says that if I learn to steer and study navigation, in three years I'll be able to go up for my ticket. That is my ambition now. Instead of being nothing, I want to be something. Every time I think about it I am glad that I made the move I did. I know you will both be proud of me if I succeed, and that is what I am fully determined on. I must now draw to a close, as I must turn in. I have to be up every morning at a quarter to five, and it is just ringing seven bells, which means that it is a quarter to midnight. I hope that Dad is still working and is in good health. Also yourself. I am always thinking of things for you, plans about the future. I just want to make you feel proud of me. So I have taken a vow that in two years' time I will go up to the board of trade to sit for an examination. O'Rourke says he wishes to be remembered to you, and hopes that he will meet Dad when the ship arrives home. He says it is nineteen years since they sailed together in the* Arama. *The first officer is not bad either. He is a fine swimmer. He is tattooed nearly all over. At present we are having very rough weather and the ship rolls and pitches dreadfully. The boatswain told me that she has no cargo, but merely a sand ballast, so I suppose that's the reason. I forgot to tell you that I was cooped up in the bunkers for nearly three days and it was only after the ship was two hundred miles west of the Fastnet that I was discovered. I remember little about it myself. One of the firemen told me I must have been unconscious for hours and hours. I was very badly bitten on the right leg by rats, but the Chief Steward soon put that right with a little caustic soda and water. I really must close. I'll write again. Will be home soon. Love to you both.*

From Arthur

Fearon read through the letter two or three times. Then he folded it up, addressed an envelope, and placed the letter in and sealed it. Then he put it safely away in a locker. He felt he had achieved something in the writing of it. He looked around his room. It seemed bare and cold. Night after night he had retired there after work was finished and had sat alone. Somehow he could not work up a familiarity with any member of the crew. The first officer had given him a compass chart which he had studied diligently, and he meant to ask to be allowed to learn the wheel on the first opportunity. He still would not establish a friendship with the boatswain or carpenter. They had ceased to complain of his clumsiness, both on deck and off it. He was very reserved and they were quick to notice it. Once or twice the carpenter had pulled off a dirty joke with him. Sometimes he would go out on deck and pace backwards and forwards, sometimes lean over the rail staring far out across the waters, and often he would face about and glue his eyes upon the bridge. He imagined himself there one day, wearing a uniform and walking up and down behind the dodger. He dreamt nightly of his success at the examination in two years' time. He saw himself decked out in blue and gold, showing his proud parents over the ship. Now as he lay in his bunk he began talking to himself.

In the midst of this the door opened and the boatswain called him out and asked him if he would make a cup of coffee. It was nearly one in the morning. The boatswain's watch were busy washing down the decks. When the coffee had been made, he slipped to the room and sat down. Fearon was sitting there too. He was practically falling asleep. The boatswain noticed this and said:

"All right, sonny. You needn't wait any longer. Did you have a cup yourself?"

This was a complete surprise to the boy, who had learnt never to expect civility from one he thought to be the roughest member of the crew aboard.

"I had some, sir," he replied.

"Oh!" drawled the boatswain. "Righto! Clear out!"

As the boy walked slowly down the alloway to his room he heard the boatswain throwing off his heavy leather sea boots. He switched on his light and made up his bed. He turned in without undressing and switched the light off again. He did not sleep. For hours it seemed he listened to the lashing of the waters against the plates, the steady humming of the engines, the roar of the machinery in the after wheelhouse. He had developed a habit of trembling every time the ship dipped her nose. The effect of the incessant grinding in the wheelhouse was to make him sick and to imagine that his whole inside was being churned up. At half-past two a storm rose, the wind sang its crazy song. He could hear the movable objects on deck being lashed from one end of the boat to the other. The ventilators shook with a strange rattle, the ratlines and stays hymned a song of their very own. The boats creaked in their davits, there was a continual pandemonium of falling crockery, and always the horrible grinding noise aft that made him feel sick. He could not sleep, so got up and put on his overcoat. He went out on deck, but not before the heavy wooden door had crashed back on him, marking his face a livid red. For some minutes he stood terrified. He held the door in his two hands, afraid to look either right or left. He could hear nothing now above the wind and wild song of the waters. He held on grimly. The bell in the crow's nest rang a quarter to three and he was still hanging on grimly to the door. The ship lurched, the door freed itself from his small and slender hands and closed with a crash. The boy stood in the dark alloway. He heard a voice exclaiming:

"Jesus Christ! Somebody walking in their bloody sleep, I suppose."

He shook himself, much like a dog, and then started to walk towards the for'ard end of the alloway. He could now see the dim light reflected upon the bulkhead. It came from the galley. The sudden knowledge that the galley actually existed and was only a few feet away made Fearon feel cold. He decided to go there and sit in front of the fire. As he passed the doors of the rooms occupied by the petty officers he paused, listened. But only the heavy snoring of the men greeted his ears, and he continued his walk until he reached the galley. He turned in there. A sickly electric light burned in the dockhead. The huge stove had been cleared of pans excepting for one large tank full of water, which was always left in readiness for the crew's teas in the morning. On the wooden seat where he had curled up, his coat collar drawn up tightly about his neck, lay a loaf and a knife. He felt hungry, so started in on the bread. One of the steel doors was barred and bolted. He now decided to close the other one. He had suddenly become obsessed. He wanted nothing now so much as to shut out the noise. Noise of the engines, howling of the wind, the creaking of furniture, rattle of ventilators, the peculiar hissing sound made by the flapping ratlines and stays. He wondered how on earth the lookout man was going to get down from his perch if the storm had not abated before four in the morning. And sometimes he wondered of other things. Of home and warm fires and comfort. Of companionship. Of safety. Here he resembled a kind of shuttlecock, something being tossed here and there, not at the discretion of the sea herself, but at that of men whose very lives had been fashioned by her, and who now endeavoured to conquer her for ever. He said to himself that the winch job he had had that day was far dirtier and more difficult than any work he had done ashore. He told himself that perhaps the promise he had made the Captain and himself, the promise he had made to his parents, might fade out. He said to himself that perhaps, after all, the whole idea was an illusion. He thought of the boatswain. And when he was asked if he had had a cup of coffee, he had said, "Yes." That was a lie. But he had felt angry with the boatswain. Now that he thought over it in the quietness and warmth of the galley, he realized immediately that no matter how kind and gentle the man became he could never warm to him. He was a man whom he had to hate. There was something in his very nature that would not surrender itself to these men. He saw a quality in them, a hardness, a roughness, a kind of cruelty that he would never allow to dominate him. He said:

"What is the matter with me? Is it because I am feeling ill? Full of fear for my own safety on account of this terrible storm? Why do I hate these men? They do not interfere with me any longer. They have tried to. But I have escaped from that. Why don't I like them? Why don't I?"

His head began to nod. Once he lurched right over and narrowly missed striking his head against the iron range. He thought he heard voices on deck and sat up suddenly. He held his breath. Yes, they were voices all right. The shouts were eaten up by the wind. He could not distinguish one voice from another. He listened again. Then a ton of water crashed over the rail and filled the alloway. He could hear it gurgling in the scuppers. It lapped up against the galley door. There was a terrible roar overhead and he looked up. He jumped to his feet, his face lost colour and he half-moaned, "Good God! I must be going mad all right. Fancy I came in here for quiet and warmth, without realizing it was the worst and most dangerous place in the ship," and he imagined a huge sea crashing down through the skylight and perhaps drowning him. He made towards the door. Lifted the handle. Pushed for all he was worth. The weight of water was against it, and immediately he knew the scuppers in the alloway must have been blocked up. He ran to the other door. Fear seized him. He wanted to scream, but this was useless. His voice was no match for the wind. He pushed again. The door gave. He pushed it right open. A sigh of relief escaped him.

"Good Heavens!" he exclaimed. "I am *really* going crazy. I should have known which was the lee and which was the weather side."

Voices were everywhere now. He recognized one as the boatswain's.

"All hands on deck! All hands on deck there! Show a leg, my hearties!"

Then something was wrong, he told himself. Instinctively he ran in the direction of the boat deck. He could not see in the intense darkness, for all the area for'ard of the bridge was ever in complete darkness. He smashed into a body, heard a muffled curse. Wondered who it was. Then he heard the boatswain's voice once again:

"Starboard boats, lads! Starboard boats!"

"God Almighty!" he murmured, "the damned ship must have sprung a leak."

There was a scurrying of feet behind him. Men were rushing up to the boat deck. He ran up after them. Somebody had switched on a powerful torch. It was the first mate. The men were lining up at their respective boats. He saw the boy and immediately called:

"Here, boy!"

Three o'clock in the morning! He could not understand anything. He was bewildered. Suddenly somebody blew a whistle. It was the boatswain. The men began to disperse. Fearon became even more bewildered. He turned to a sailor:

"Is she sinking?"

The man laughed and turned to descend the ladder.

"Sinking?" He laughed again. "You want to keep your socks pulled up, my boy. No, she isn't sinking. That was only a little emergency boat drill. You'll get used to it in about seven years. Those seven years are always the worst on board a ship." He continued his way down the ladder, laughing heartily. The boy's predicament had opened up his humorous vein. From that night the boy had learnt the importance of being ready. Ready for anything. Food, work, hunger, heat, cold, death. He was slowly learning.

At eleven o'clock the next morning, he was sent with two sailors, Duffy and O'Rourke, to paint the four winches for'ard. Just as they laid down their pots and brushes, the lookout man rang his bell. The boy looked up.

The sailors seemed unconcerned. He heard O'Rourke say casually:

"She'll be in this time tomorrow?"

The other man replied in a drawling sort of way:

"Ay! I guess you'll get the stink, the eastern stink about dawn tomorrow."

The conversation interested the boy immensely. Stink! Ship will be in tomorrow. What was this eastern stink? He quite understood the other matter. He asked O'Rourke when the other man had crossed to the starboard side.

"Well! It's a stink, boy. A stink's a stink. But an eastern one is something more. You'll know all about it sooner or later. How are you getting on? Your dad'll be quite surprised, I'm sure. You must tell him I was asking after him. You will, won't you? Your dad an' me sailed together in the old clippers. Those were the days. A boy had to give up thinking he was a boy. Only men sailed in those days. Why now, well I never saw such a confounded lot of sissies in my lifetime. You'll get on all right. You'll learn. Everybody does. Everybody's not the same, of course. You learn one way, another learns another way, and so on. How'd you like the winch job?"

"It was all right," said the boy. "I can't stand that bloody bosun."

"Why?"

"Don't know."

"You'll get used to people in time. It's a bit strange at first. There are some really nice chaps on board once you get to know them. When I first went to sea…"

Fearon turned the conversation on to another point. He was learning. Already he had heard at first hand the experience of a good many of the crew who seemed to have a flair for switching their memories back to the days of sail. The boy was not unintelligent. He saw a quiet obstinacy in these men. It appeared to him that all men who had shipped under sail were sailing in steam under protest. They could not look ahead. He had gone down one night to the engine room on the bosun's orders. He was instructed to ask the engineer to turn the water on the hydrants in readiness for the washing-down of decks. He met Larkin the fourth engineer for the first time. The man seemed quite an erratic person, though the boy suspected there was a warmth and kindness beneath the apparent sourness and incivility. Larkin had asked him why he had stowed away. The boy, in the few minutes allowed him, had explained why and how.

"Come to my room one evening," Larkin had requested.

And he had gone to his room. Fearon got to like the man. He discovered then that the fourth always dined in his own room, and hardly ever crossed conversation with his brother engineers. It seemed peculiar to the boy. But he learnt the reason one evening when Larkin began to talk quite freely. In his talk he cursed the seven seas and all the men who ever sailed them.

"Boy!" he had said, "When you get back home make up your mind what you are going to do and what you are going to be. It won't take you overlong. There are only two questions to put to yourself. I often wish that I had the sense then that I have now. But I was foolish and harum-scarum and ran away on a fishing schooner. I learnt my engineering at the Edinburgh University. I never wanted to go to sea. Now I have nothing else to do. You're not cut out for the sea, boy. I can see it, in your hands, in your eyes, in your whole make-up and character. Tell me the truth. What do you intend to do?"

The boy was stumped. He felt he was caught between two fires. He had signed as an ordinary seaman. He had vowed to the skipper and to himself that from that opportunity he would fashion his future. And now this man was advising him to keep away from the sea life. Larkin appeared quite genuine. It amazed Fearon, for it was rare indeed when an officer condescended to invite a rating to his room for a friendly chat. It was talked about at the mess table by the other officers, all of whom put one construction upon the affair. Riley, the third officer, said what they were all thinking in their minds, that "Larkin always thought boys better than women".

The fourth took little or no notice of this backchat. He had learnt long since that the only essential thing at sea was to know one's job, and he, as a man from north of the Govan Road,* knew all that there was to know about engines. He had risen from the lower grading of fireman and greaser, and was the only man in that company serving as an engineer on an American ticket. He had been on the lake boats, had studied in New York, and finally had obtained his ticket. In England, such a thing was impossible, for no fireman or greaser could ever sit for his ticket. And if he did the odds were on the theorist from the universities getting the job.

Fearon began to dote on the engineer's advice. The very thought of it seemed to make futile his letter to his parents, his promise to the Captain and mate, and not least to himself. He felt he must decide by the time the ship reached port. Should he or should he not? There was a chance for him if he tried. There was hard work, plenty of it; it meant continual association with men whom in his heart he loathed, for nature had served him differently. He even pulled out the letter from the locker and looked at it hard and long. Then he opened it and reread what he had written. It made him think all the more. It was fine, he thought, to be an officer. One had a nice uniform, a beautiful room, a steward to look after it for you and to wait on you at meals. The salary was ten times more than his own as an ordinary seaman. They were always clean, always had plenty of money and much time to themselves. He wondered why a man like Larkin could offer him such advice. To listen to Larkin was to go back on everything.

O'Rourke called to him: "Hey, Fearon! Take this pot to the lamp room and get it filled up."

The boy jumped. The voice coming in suddenly on the midst of his meditation startled him. He took the pot and filled it with the French grey paint, and returned it to O'Rourke.

"How's Larkin doing?" he asked the boy suddenly.

"Larkin!" How funny he thought, that just when he was thinking of him, O'Rourke should bring his name in.

"All right!" he said. "He's a very nice man indeed. I had a talk with him in his room. He gave me some advice."

"Did he advise you to keep away from tail in Alexandria?"

"Tail?" said Fearon.

"Boy!" exclaimed O'Rourke. "You're stupid. Just stupid. Your dad wasn't much better himself."

Fearon went on with his work. He edged away from the sailor. When he reached the companion ladder near the fo'c'sle head he heaved a sigh of relief. He could not understand why the men in every conversation brought up this argument about boys. He began to hate himself for being a boy. It made him miserable to think that for another three or four years he would still be a boy. What kind of world was it into which he had flung himself? All men sailing at sea seemed to be obsessed with boys. It got on his nerves, made him underestimate himself, perform his work awkwardly. Alone in his room he would review the happenings of the day. Once he burst into tears. He was becoming a failure. He could do nothing right. He was awkward at every kind of work, he was always trembling whenever he had to enter the rooms of the boatswain or carpenter when occupied. The incident of the steward and the cook had got on his mind. He expected every moment to be stripped naked and dragged into some dark corner of the room. Or was it that they were just taunting him, putting him on trial? He wondered about it. One morning he had overslept and the bosun's mate, whose watch happened to be working, had burst into the room, pulled all the clothes from him and dragged him from the bed.

"Where's my bloody coffee? A quarter to six. Where in the name of Jesus do you think you are? In the parlour at home? What the hell are you doing with yourself. Using both hands, eh?"

He had hurriedly dressed and left the room without replying. He could not bear the sight of this little bosun's mate, a hairy individual with lantern jaws, a face almost as white as chalk, and eyes that resembled rat holes in a whitewashed wall. His breath always made the boy feel he wanted to vomit. He would stand watching the man eat his food in the bosun's room. The room itself was afflicted with a most nauseating smell. And when he had remarked upon it to the bosun, that gentleman had said in a drawling way:

"Well, why don't you get down on your knees and clean the blasted room properly? There's all kinds of shit lying under these bunks. You damned worm."

The boy had yet to learn one thing. His nature was so constituted that the learning of it would be slow and tortuous. He must surrender himself as a boy to the habits of men, to the traditions of the sea. He must conquer whatever innate pride he possessed. There was only one place for such as he, as the lamp-trimmer had once remarked to him: "A kindergarten. Or the middy's nest on a destroyer."

The more the boy endeavoured to be himself, the more the something that was alien to his nature fought against it. This something was a kind of growth, inseparable from the forces inherent in the waters of oceans, that stirred men's blood, held them in thrall and bound them fast. Larkin had said:

"You must either give in or break away. In my twenty odd years at sea I have been disarmed and stripped naked by her, a monster I tell you, boy. It eats into the heart, it reduces the brain to a sort of pulp. I am controlled. I no longer control, for I am controlled."

"But…" the boy had protested. That kind of argument was above him. He did not wish to accept the sea as a man accepts a new kind of faith. Not that. He was only a poor boy, son of poor people, who fought with life from the cradle to the grave. He did not want to honour the sea. The sea was nothing to him. It might seem something wonderful, terrifying and magnificent through the painting of a symbolist. The sea was nothing to him. Larkin had listened. He had said to himself: "Well! Well! Here's a bit of a boy can talk with me and even mystify me. There's something locked in that brain of his that must come out." He thought upon it patiently, tirelessly, and he knew that when the ship arrived home again he must say to that boy: "Go away! Do not come back or you are lost. The sea could never have you, and anyhow does not want you. It is not fair. Whoever your people are, whoever put this crazy idea into your head to make a living at sea has done you a wrong, has lied to you. The sea accepts certain kinds of spirits only. You are not one of them."

The boy explained:

"Mr Larkin, I want to make good. I do not want to say to myself: 'Now then, Arthur Fearon, you must try and get on good terms with this sea.'" This ocean, this world of water that sends men towards happiness, that sends men towards damnation and death. The sea that held locked in her bosom the hopes and desires of the spirits whom it had conquered.

A voice called to Fearon:

"Come back! Come back!"

He knew whence that voice came. "Come back to the dirt and dark again."

Finally he told the fourth engineer that he meant only to use the sea and not to be used by it. Mr Larkin smiled and said:

"Who put such ideas into your head, boy? What have you been reading at all? I gamble you are quite a romantic young person so far as the sea is concerned. But, my boy, there is something associated with the sea that you have not yet learnt. The day you learn it you will know the meaning of slavery. That's all the sea ever was. That's all it is. Slavery. Slavery. Take my advice and keep away from the sea. It'll never do you any good. I'm not here because I like it, but because there is nothing else for me and I have to like it."

Fearon could see nothing but well-meant kindness and advice in these little talks. Keep away from the sea. Why should he? Hadn't he told Mr Larkin that he would learn to use the sea, not to be used *by* her? The fourth engineer said:

"You wait! She'll get you like everybody else."

10

THE HERNIAN DREW INTO ALEXANDRIA the following morning at half-past eleven. All the crew were on deck. For'ard Fearon was helping on the fo'c'sle head. He stood behind the windlass, his small hands on the round iron wheel, his attentive eyes upon the second officer, who was standing right for'ard at the railhead, the great collar of his coat almost hiding his face from view. He held a megaphone in his hand, and from time to time roared out orders through it, now to the windlass man, now to the longshoremen on the quay. There was a sudden hitch. The ship was beyond control for a moment and there was imminent danger of her smashing her nose up against the quay. The officer vented his rage upon the Arab longshoremen:

"Damn and blast these black bastards. They never do a thing right, God Almighty's truth they don't!" Suddenly he shouted: "Ease her!" Then louder than before: "Ease her in! For Christ's sake ease her in! Can't you understand English, you…"

Fearon stood there waiting for the order to turn off the steam. On the drumhead of the windlass O'Rourke held the hawser in his powerful hands.

By noon she had tied up and the men trooped back to the fo'c'sle for their meals. Fearon got the petty officers' food from the galley. He laid the folding-up table in the bosun's room, and then quietly returned to his own room until he was called for his own share of the dinner. It was only now that he discovered he had no other clothes but those he stood in, excepting for a pair of dungaree trousers and a jersey, which one of the sailors had given him the night after he was discovered in the bunker. He was ashamed to go ashore in the old clothes. If only he had a coat and trousers and a decent cap.

After dinner he went to the men's fo'c'sle aft. There was only one man there, and he was busy strapping up. The other men had gone out on deck, and onto the quay to look after the wires, as the Captain could never be certain of the efficiency of the agency's men. The man looked up as the boy entered. This man was named Rafferty, a tall fellow with a decided squint and a straggling black moustache. He always looked half-dressed and dirty. Fearon had never spoken to him before. His being in the bosun's mate's watch had prevented his ever coming in contact with him. He now explained his position to this man, who listened in silence.

"No clothes! Hmm! Well, what the bloody hell do you expect I can do for you? Look here, kid, the best thing you can do is to go to the Captain and tell him how you are placed. He's not a bad sort. You try him. He might give you a few shillings and you can always buy a decent pair of trousers ashore, or else you could go on board one of those passenger liners. They have a clothes locker, and the purser might be able to fix you up. Certainly you can't go ashore with those greasy things."

"Thanks," said Fearon, "I'll try that. I never thought of it."

"That's right! Try." The man went on with his work and the boy left the fo'c'sle. He went up to the bridge immediately and knocked at the Captain's door. The steward answered his knock.

"Hell!" he exclaimed. "You again? What the blazes is wrong now?"

"Not much," replied Fearon, who had learnt to measure the man up by this time. "Not much! Want to see Captain Wood. That's all."

"Oh! Well, you bloody little worm, the Captain's not here. He's gone ashore to the office, and won't be back for Christ knows how long. Beat it."

"I'll hang about," said the boy coolly, and began to walk up and down the bridge with his hands in his pockets. The door of the cabin slammed.

"What a rotten crowd," thought the boy. "There's not one among them, excepting that Mr Larkin, who will give you a civil answer." Often he felt it was just part of the general plan to put him on trial, to test his mettle.

The steward came out. The boy watched him lock the cabin door and place the key in his pocket. Just as he neared the ladder the boy ran after him and pulled his arm.

"What's up?" growled the steward.

The boy endeavoured to be as civil as possible. This was the steward who had first tried to do something to him.

"Look here, steward, could you tell me if you have any idea as to the time he'll be back? I was sent up here on spec by one of the sailors. I have no clothes. Not a thing excepting the stuff I'm standing up in. This man said that the old man might give me a few shillings in lieu of the usual tailor."

"Better ask him then," said the steward, placing a foot on the step.

"You don't know when he'll be back?"

"No. I don't." The steward disappeared.

"Stiffen the sod dead," murmured Fearon. "What is wrong with everybody on this boat? God! Once I thought I would triumph over these little things, but already they're getting on my nerves. I suppose if I offered to go to his room with him he would be as nice as pie."

"Fearon! Fearon! Where the hell is that bloody boy?"

"Damn it," exclaimed the boy. "The soddin' bosun calling again." He ran to the ladder, slid down it, and raced along to the alloway. The bosun was standing outside the room door. When he saw Fearon he went up to him, caught one ear in his hand and pulled it. The boy squealed.

"Blast you! How many times am I going to tell you to clear that shit from beneath the bunks? My mate's complaining about the stink."

The boy looked straight at the man.

"I clean beneath the bunks every morning. If your mate does it and then pitches it beneath the bunk, is that my fault? I saw him doing it the other afternoon."

"BOY!"

"That's the truth, sir," said Fearon.

"You'd better tell that to the marines. Get in there, you undersized twim, and clear that muck out bloody quick! Hurry up now. Just wait till my mate comes off the quay. Just wait. He'll kick your bottom for you."

The man laughed as he watched the boy get down on his knees and grope beneath the bunk. There was always a smell there, because water was continually lodging on account of the build of the deck, which was painted a bright red. The bosun bent down and placed his hand on the boy's back. He tickled him. He thumped his behind, saying:

"Boy! You should never have come to sea. You should have joined the brownies. D'you get me?"

Fearon emerged from beneath the bunk. His clothes were wet, his hands clinging with a brownish mud, his face red with exertion. He stood up.

"What were you doing up on that bridge before? Don't you know that it has just been holystoned by the men? Don't you know that a boy must never go up unless he has permission from his PO? I'm your PO, boy. Didn't you know that?"

Before the boy could answer the lamp-trimmer appeared. There was a scowl upon his pockmarked and vicious-looking features. He came straight to the room door.

"Hello, Jack!" said the bosun.

"Hello! Where's that boy? Oh, the bugger's there."

Fearon turned round.

"Come out of it, you friggin' wimp," shouted the lamp-trimmer. "The next time you get issued with a Turk's head brush, or any kind of brush, clean the bloody thing when you've finished with it. Also, those slices you had *trying* to clean the winches the other day. You'd better cut along to the lamp-trimmer and have a look at them."

The boy was now very much afraid. He looked from the bosun to the lamp-trimmer. The latter suddenly leant across, pushed his arm into the room and dragged the boy out by the hair.

"You hard-faced whelp," he said. "Get along there. I suppose the next thing we'll hear from you is that you had a piece of tail in your room."

He followed Fearon to the lamp room. He pulled a big iron key from his pocket and opened the heavy iron door. Then he switched the light on, and pushed the boy inside. He followed himself, closing the door behind him. The offending articles were lying where he had left them a few minutes before. Two slices and a paint brush. He pointed them out to Fearon. The boy picked them up and looked at them.

"Well! Are you going to kiss them or eat them or something? Don't stand there looking at them, you thick bugger. There's the shale oil over there in the steel barrel. There's a bale of waste in the corner behind you. Get going. Take my advice, boy. For the love of Jesus don't come back in this ship. You're the sloppiest kid I ever set eyes on. Anyhow they won't ship you any more. This line has given boys the go-by, and no bleedin' wonder. Of all the nuisances in this world, boys are the limit. The bloody limit."

He walked across and stood behind Fearon, who was busy cleaning the paint brush. He placed his horny hand upon the boy's shoulder, and said:

"Boy! You'd be all right if you did what you were told. If you were obedient, if you were a hard worker, if you were a good mucker-in, if you were willing to learn, if you weren't suspicious of everybody, if you weren't so bloody nesh, if you weren't so much of a bleedin' baby, if you weren't so much afraid of a tool. You soft little bugger. Never mind. You'll learn. You'll learn."

"I am learning," said Fearon.

"What was your daddy when he was your age? Can you remember, sonny? What does he do now for a living?"

The boy suddenly recalled a saying he had heard on the docks, and he said:

"Oh, my father owns a lavatory in New York!"

"Clever! Aren't you now. Come on, get that bloody brush finished and beat it. Hurry up now."

"Here's your brush," said the boy, and handed it to the lamp-trimmer. He left the lamp room. Walked slowly along the deck and turned into the lavatory at the end of the alloway. He was inside before he was aware that somebody else was there. The man turned round and recognizing him said:

"Hello there, boy! What are you doing here?"

"Nothing," said Fearon and fled from the place in a panic.

Inside his room he locked the door. He was white-faced, his lips trembled like those of a person on the verge of a fit, he thought his legs were going to give way, and sat down. Continually he clasped and unclasped his hands. His mind was running riot with all kinds of thoughts. He felt a sickness in the pit of his stomach, a certain pain beneath his heart. He suddenly shouted: "Mother! Mother! Oh, Mother! Father! These men. These terrible men." He commenced to hammer the wooden sides of his bunk with his hands. He continually shouted "Mother!" He imagined that all these men had stolen into his room, that they were crowding round him, taunting and laughing at him, goading him in his misery, cursing him when he endeavoured to do his best. He saw them all. The lamp-trimmer and cook were there. The bosun and leading greaser were there too. "Oh, Christ! Mother take me out of this."

Mr Wood had learnt on his return from the office ashore that the new hand had been looking for him. He enquired for his steward and then told him to go below and bring Fearon up to his room. The steward had been to the room and had returned to the Captain with the news that he had discovered the boy crying on the floor, his hands covered with blood.

"What has he been doing? Didn't you find out? Has he been trying to commit suicide? However, I will go down myself. You may finish now."

The boy was still lying on the floor when the Captain entered the room. The first thing he noticed was that there was a broken water bottle lying on the floor near the boy's head. He thought his steward to be an excellent waiter, but ignorant and devoid of those qualities necessary in an emergency such as this. He lifted the boy up and laid him in the bunk. He could not help but look round, and said to himself that "the room certainly looks bare". There had once been a red settee there, but when the boys were ceased to be carried, most of the furniture had been removed.

"Now where," the Captain asked himself, "could the boy have got the bottle? The bosun never has one in his room, and as far as I know there are only two or three about since that rough weather, when most of the glassware was smashed. Truly this boy has attempted to kill himself."

And even a hardened man like Mr Wood gave a momentary shudder. He gave orders for the boy to be carried to the hospital aft immediately. He would talk with this boy. He would find out what was wrong. There was something good in him, there was some quality in his nature continually fighting against the cruel life of men as it manifested itself in deep waters. There was something in the boy, he told himself, that unless rooted out would wreck him for ever. He fancied the boy still torn between his desire to make good, and that part of himself that would not fit in with all the laws and traditions governing ships and seamen.

"I wonder just why he wanted to see me today?" said the Captain to himself.

He returned to his room and informed the second steward that he was to be called the moment the boy recovered.

The boy recovered. He was ashamed that he had been discovered by the one man he really looked up to, the one man whom he had promised to make good.

At four o'clock that afternoon he felt well enough to leave the hospital. At half-past four he was sitting on a chair in the Captain's room. He had told this man everything. His fear, his hope, his disappointment, his misery, his continual efforts to please everybody under whom he worked. He even told the Captain he had written a letter home promising to make his way in the world. He asked the Captain if he would read it. Mr Wood said no good could result from reading the private and intimate things sacred to a boy. Why had he been looking for him earlier that day?

Fearon saw his chance. He explained his position. Mr Wood gave him a ten-shilling note, told him he must not go ashore by himself, but with one of the sailors, and finally warned him against going to public bars and certain houses in certain streets. He would get one of the men to take him ashore and get rigged up with something like a decent coat and trousers. Fearon thought ten shillings hardly enough, though he did not say anything.

"The old man," remarked a sailor named Donagan, who had been instructed to take Fearon to the "tailor", "is not a bad sort of bloke, excepting that he's a five-to-two,* and you know what I mean by that."

"Sure," replied Fearon. "Learnt all about those fellows in Liverpool."

"His tailor," continued Donagan, "is the biggest robber this side of kingdom come, and I very much doubt whether you'll get a rig-out for ten bob."

"Mr Wood said I could."

"It's a bloody bazaar he had in mind all right," continued Donagan. "I've been in those queer places myself. The Arabs steal these clothes from the ships in port and sell them for a few shillings in their bazaars. I think it would be a good idea if we got into one of those gharries* and let the old Turk take us to the cheapest place in Alex. These old swine know the best places. It only costs a couple of piastres to get to anywhere in town."

"What a horrible smell," remarked Fearon, as they drove along the dock road in the gharry.

"This place is called by all sailors the 'Grand Stink Port' of the world. You can get anything in this place, from measles to chancres. Take care, boy, you keep away from Sister Street. They're bad places. Bad places."

"Well, here we are," he added as the driver pulled up the half-starved-looking pony and got down from his seat. He came over to Donagan.

"Six piastres, Johnny," he said blandly.

"Do you know," exclaimed Donagan, sticking his face almost into the Turk's greasy visage, "do you know where Paddy stuck his nuts?"

"No can. No can," stammered the driver. "No can do."

"Four and a half piastres or nothing, you double-dyed bastard of a Turk."

The driver began waving his hands. Finally Donagan gave him five piastres.

They headed for the bazaar that stood behind a group of disreputable huts.

11

Donagan and Fearon turned out of the bazaar, the former remarking, as he looked the boy up and down, that he hadn't done badly with the ten shillings. "But," he added, "you ought to tell the old man they cost more than that. He's got the dough. I suppose you haven't a red* with you, have you?"

"No," said Fearon.

"Well, what are you going to do?" asked the man. "I'm going up to Sister Street myself. I always meet the same dame each trip. She's not a bad sort. A Frenchy. I suppose that's not in your line?"

Fearon did not understand the trend of his companion's remarks. Donagan continued:

"I tell you what, sonny, you come along with me. I'll see you get a good time all right. I have a few bob to spare myself. You look a bit down in the mouth. What's up? Tell us. Have you swallowed the bloody anchor?"

With this latter phrase the boy was well acquainted. He replied that he had not. That it was his intention to make good on board, as he intended to go in for his ticket in two years' time.

"You what?" exclaimed Donagan. "Say it again, puppy."

"That's what I mean," continued Fearon. "I had a talk with Mr Wood one night. He said he was interested in me. Asked me all about my home life, what my father worked at, how old my mother was. Oh, lots of questions."

"Well?" queried Donagan, beginning to get interested.

"I thought something was up," he remarked. "Hardly ever saw you on the trip across. Stuck in your bloody room night after night. What were you doing there?"

"Nothing much. Sometimes I was studying the compass, sometimes I would just lie in my bunk without a single thought in my head."

"You're a queer youngster," said Donagan. And he said to himself later: "It's the devil. Here's a bit of a kid flying his kite, acting the superior person." He noted how different he looked from other boys he had sailed with. His slender frame, white soft hands like a girl's and satin-like skin, covered about the chin with fine down. Fearon continued talking:

"At first when I decided to stow away I had no other idea in my head than to get away from home. Not the slightest. I had always worked at the docks either in the boilers or hotting rivets for the boiler-makers. For the first few days it was terrible. Awful. I was frightened to death of the men, especially that lousy steward who tried to do me one when I was lying in the hospital aft. Then the bosun started. God! I felt like poisoning him, for he's only a rotten swine. There are only two men on board that ship who took an interest in me. Mr Wood and Mr Larkin."

"Larkin," said Donagan. "Surely you're not thick with that crazy old fool?"

"Didn't see anything crazy about him. He gave me some good advice which I didn't want. He said to keep away from the sea. Was only a dog's life. Said only necessity made him imprison himself in a hot engine room from one year's end to another. But though he meant it well, I had already promised Mr Wood to make good, to work hard and try and make something of myself. I promised myself too that I would study navigation for two years and then try for my ticket."

The pair had now reached the corner of Sister Street. They saw pickets from the naval boats walking up and down the street.

"Ticket! Ticket! So you're another. Boy! Listen to an old sailor talking. Listen to a man who has sailed the seas for over thirty-one years. Chuck it. Stop it, or whatever you like. It's a delusion, all this tripey talk about getting tickets. God damn it, boy, when I get home this time I'll show you my discharge book. You'll see stamped in that, 'Certified as First Officer. Certified as Extra Master.' There you are, boy. Now you know it. And I'm not the only one. Why the bloody fo'c'sles are packed with sailors who have had their tickets, men who have seen better days and better ships than the likes of the damn cork we are floating about in. Get it out of your head, kid. Right away. Be a sailor and nothing else. You don't have to kowtow to any son of a gun. Not a one of them. Well, Christ! Here we are. Tell me, boy, did you ever see a cancan?"

"A cancan?" said Fearon. "What's that?"

"Oh! Surely you know that by now. Well, to put it bluntly, it's just a dame dancing who ought to be ashamed of herself. Come on! I've got the dough. In here. It's only two piastres apiece."

They had stopped outside the door of a large house, whose dilapidated exterior was a sign that it had long since passed into the hands of the destroyer. Its twenty odd rooms were rented off by women and girls of various nationalities. Top floors were mainly the harbours for Arab women, the lower ones were occupied by French and Circassian women. It was to one of these rooms on the ground floor that Donagan wished to take the boy. Fearon stood with one foot on the step, hesitating. The man's hand was upon his shoulder. He whispered into the boy's ear:

"Come, boy! You'll see the finest sight in your lifetime, and if you're going to chuck the sea life, then it's your only chance of telling your mates that you were inside a cancan 'do'." Donagan was fingering the few silver coins.

Just then a young Greek girl appeared in the doorway. She smiled on seeing Donagan and the boy. The man saluted her, and with his forefinger beckoned her to come nearer. She came.

"Ah! Madam. Here is something in your line. How you like him?" and he pointed out the boy to the smiling girl. The gas lamp outside the house cast a reflection and Fearon thought the girl looked terribly ill. Her eyes appeared bloodshot, her skin the colour of mud, her hair dangling over her shoulders resembled matted yarn. Hair without lustre or colour.

"Well!" said Donagan to Fearon, "what d'you say, boy?"

"Oh, all right!" drawled the boy. The two of them entered the house. Strange music came to the boy's ears now. He had never heard anything so weird in his life. He imagined it to be coming from the second room on their right as they walked slowly along the deserted stone passage. Not a single light showed. Fearon suddenly gripped his companion's arm, saying:

"Oh, I don't know. I think I'll go back, Mr Donagan."

"Like hell you will," replied Donagan. "And the fun just commencing… Keep your trousers buttoned up though."

He dragged the boy towards a door. The man knocked. It opened to reveal a fat old woman with a greasy-looking appearance, which made Donagan remark loudly to the boy that "these buggers never wash themselves at all. Still there's a place too that never needs it."

"How much, madam?" he enquired of the woman.

"Two piastres you, two piastres boy," she replied in quite good English.

"Here y'are," he said, and pushed four coins into the greasy palm extended towards his pockets. The woman made way for them and they passed into the room. There were about a dozen people sitting in a circle on the stone floor, among whom both the man and boy recognized sailors from the English ships. They took a place up against the wall. The room was lit by a candle only. In the corner furthest away from the door crouched an old woman, sitting on her haunches and holding a small drum. Upon this she played a weird kind of tune, monotonous and jarring to the ear. But the assembled crowd seemed quite contented, knowing that the real show had yet to commence. Two young Arab girls had come into the room. One of them made for Donagan and sat by him. She tried to catch his hand. Catching sight of the boy, she exclaimed with a chuckle:

"Ah! Piccanin'! Piccanin'!"

"Yes, but my piccanin', not yours!" said Donagan.

The girl sat down by the boy now, whose attention had been attracted by the entrance of a naked Arab girl. Beneath the light her skin resembled beaten gold, her body was as lithe as a young sapling, the feet exquisite, the almond eyes resembled water pools, whilst the lips were ripe and red and full. Her teeth glistened. She would be about nineteen years of age.

For the first time the boy felt a disturbance in his blood, the like of which he could not understand. He imagined it to be the sight of this naked girl, though in reality it was something that in feel and shape was nearer to him than he thought. The girl beside him had placed her hand on his knee, an action which the sharp-eyed Donagan was not slow to notice.

"Here," he whispered to the boy, "see what's crawling on you."

The boy jumped. "Crawling on me. What d'you mean?" and the look he gave his companion was certainly astonishing. But that gentleman laughed.

"Oh me! Oh my! Oh you darling little angel. Did you never hear of the man who had two of these and four of those? Oh Holy jumpin' Jesus! You're the limit." He drew the boy's face to his and said softly in his ear:

"Ssh! She's groping for something. Perhaps she's lost her garter. Eh?"

Fearon now realized that the girl had caught hold of something he possessed. He felt as though somebody had drugged him. A fear arose within him. He tried to turn his thoughts to other things. To recall all that he had told Mr Wood; all that he had told to Mr Larkin. He was so very much afraid of this new drug overpowering him. His blood tingled. It was like having swan's down drawn gently up and down his body. It tickled him.

It was delirious. He shivered a little, but apart from that he never stirred. It was like the force that surrounds a flower and, electrifying the surrounding air, sets up a kind of exotic fever. Fearon felt something similar. He had a great desire to expand, to open and blossom like a flower. An overwhelming desire to undress suddenly seized him, and in that moment he met Donagan's glance, and in the man's eye he sensed both a wink and a leer.

"Piccanin' come with me, eh?" whispered the girl in his ear.

He did not speak. His eyes were focused upon the girl in the centre of the floor who was putting her body through the most amazing contortions. A man had jumped up from the circle, a pretty oldish man with the face and head of a goat. He looked like a goat and nothing else. He had surrendered himself to this shape and movement, and the incessant tap-tap of the old woman's drum drove him almost to distraction. The girl still continued to gyrate. One of his horny hands had touched her body. She stopped moving. She let him caress her from head to toe, his fingers spoilt the geography of her body, lingering here and there, the while his blood whirled. The other men laughed.

"A silly dirty old goat. A dirty old man," said the spectators.

"Piccanin' come with me, eh?" repeated the girl at Fearon's side.

There was something in her voice that to the boy resembled the weirdness and monotony of the drum-beating. "Piccanin' come with me, eh?"

Suddenly Donagan leant over the boy and said to the girl:

"How much for him, how much for the boy?"

She laughed. "Nozzing for boy, eh? Five piastres for you, eh?"

Fearon was helpless. If she had stripped him naked he could not have moved, could not have protested. Even if she had carried him off. Donagan stood up. Pulled the boy to his feet. Looked at the girl and said:

"Sure. All right, baby."

The girl led the man and boy to her room. There was nothing in it save a bed, though Donagan noticed a little religious statue standing on a bracket near the wall. The girl motioned to Donagan. She had sat down on her bed.

"Money," she said. "Money," she repeated laughing, revealing her beautiful teeth, and when the man handed her five piastres, she said again:

"Nozzing for him. Nozzing for piccanin'."

They both laughed in a shrill sort of way. The boy had sat down on a stool by the window, which was covered with a heavy brown curtain. A lamp hung from the ceiling. The whole room spelt dirt, was dirt. The floor of stone was cracked, and here and there the powder had been trailed about by many passing feet. In amazement, Fearon saw the girl undress herself and lie back upon the bed. And then he saw the man partly undress himself and lie on top of her. They did not speak, though once or twice he heard the sound of a kiss, and quite often what appeared to be gurgles, like those of a child suckling. The bed creaked. In three minutes, though to Fearon it seemed hours, the affair was over, and Donagan got off the bed, coming towards him buttoning himself up. He said quite casually:

"Your turn, boy. You get it for nix. A real buckshee one too. Oh my! Go to it, my angel!"

But the boy never stirred. The naked girl had sat up and was beckoning with one of her slender brown fingers. The boy went cold all over. He jumped up and shouted out: "Good God! Let me get out!" and made for the door. But this only made the man seize him and carry him to the bed.

The girl laughed: "Oh my piccanin'. Oh my piccanin'. Piccanin'. Piccanin'."

Between them they had managed to loosen the boy's clothing. He screamed.

"Shut your bloody mouth, you little fool. Oh you soft stupid little bugger. It's only a short time. She won't bite you. She won't eat you. There now, let her sing you to sleep."

The girl had drawn the boy towards her, and by a sudden movement of her body had him on top of her. The boy lay still. He knew she was doing something to him and was powerless to move. Donagan sat watching and grinned. The girl seemed to Fearon to be pushing him up and down. He felt something come in contact with his skin that made him shiver, for it was cold. Then something fell from his coat pocket. Something white that fluttered to the floor. Immediately he knew it was the letter to his mother and father. He began to cry. If they were to see him now, he thought. "Oh Jesus! Jesus!" And that's what the sea was. And that's what the sea was. And he was going to make it his job for life. He was going to work hard and reach the top of the ladder. And so that's what it is. "Oh dear me! Oh Mother! Father! Help me! Save me! Take me away from this, from the sea, from ships and men!"

These thoughts were running through his brain. Then suddenly all his thoughts were cataract. He remembered nothing, saw nothing, felt nothing. He merely lay, still, without sound. The silence in the room was almost sepulchral. Only the breathing of the three out-raged it.

"Come." The voice of Donagan broke upon his ears like a flood of waters. "Come!"

He could not move. The body beneath him was slowly pushing him off. He was helpless, a great weight appeared in his legs and arms. Something was sucking him down. The face of the smiling girl was blotted out. In its stead he saw a kind of spectre, sometimes red, sometimes white. He sobbed. The room was racing round and round. Out of the bed seemed to rise grotesque figures, eyeless, and the features were stamped with a grin, timeless, idiotic, inane, empty. They swam towards him, retreated, swam towards him again. The bed rose and fell like a gigantic wave, and the sound was new. Not a creaking sound, but a hissing one. The ceiling above him appeared to descend upon him threatening to crush him. Fearon rolled off the bed sobbing. Donagan bent over him. Then it was that he saw the clenched hands, the spittle collecting about his mouth and slavering a white froth from his mouth to the floor. Donagan was suddenly afraid, and with this fear there arose a sudden anger.

"God damn the kid!" he growled. "Going into a bloody fit over a short time. S'truth! Him go to sea! God Almighty! Must get him out of this."

He looked round the room. Quite indifferently, the girl was dressing herself. Donagan shouted: "Water! Water!" but the girl did not under-stand nor did she move at all. There was a large basin on the floor beneath the bed. Donagan dashed across and dragged it out. Its liquid contents he splashed in the boy's face, quite unconscious of the fact that it was not water. The white face of Fearon unnerved him. And whilst he looked, the boy's eyes opened.

"Post my letter. Post my letter, Mr Donagan," he said. His eyes closed again. To the man he appeared to be dead, dying, finished.

"Letter? Letter? Oh hell, yes. I remember. Fell out of his pocket. Here it is." He picked the letter up and transferred it to his pocket. Then he lifted the boy in his arms and walked out of the room. At the end of the passage he saw what appeared to be a large though neglected garden. The branch of a tree was the first indication to him that a garden actually lay behind the huge stone house. He walked along the passage, passing two or three women, Arabs and French. Then two Egyptians. Then a Circassian, then a young Turkish girl. One or two stared after the man who carried what appeared to be a dead body in his arms. The man reached the end of the passage and stepped into the garden. It was deserted and it was dark. He laid the boy down beneath a tree. Then he sat down himself and stared at the boy's face, as if the persistent stare might bring back Fearon to life and reality.

"God! I'm sorry about this," he said, and began stroking the boy's hands. "Oh God! I'm terribly sorry about it, I am. Poor kid. Has a mother and a father. Something I've never known in my own lifetime. Mother and father! Well! Well! Had a letter in his pocket all ready to post. The poor kid. Poor little fellow."

He continued stroking the boy's hands, that had now begun to twitch. The eyelids flickered. "Ah!" exclaimed Donagan, "he's coming to. He's coming to." It was then the boy's eyes opened. They were without expression, they had lost their former sparkle. Something in the boy seemed to have died. Something had happened inside him. The man placed a long arm behind the boy's head and gently raised it. He began muttering to himself: "Sorry about this I am. Poor fellow. Poor kid. Shouldn't have done it, I shouldn't. Ah well! I'll see this kid through all right. I'll look after him on the voyage home, I will. I'll see he gets anything he wants, I'll see that the other fellows don't work it on him, I will."

He began stroking the boy's cheeks. The colour was gradually returning to them. The vacant stare still worried Donagan. He spoke to him:

"Hello, kid! Hello, Fearon boy. How's it going?"

"Oh!" exclaimed Fearon. "Where am I?"

Hope returned to Donagan.

"All right! All right!" he exclaimed excitedly. "It's all right! You're all right. We're going back to the ship now. Don't you remember we came to this house to see a dance, then you felt sick, and I carried you out here. Why, boy, you've been lying under this tree for over an hour! How d'you feel now, kid? All right, eh?"

"Did you post my letter?" asked the boy, and the expression and light revealed itself in the brown eyes once more.

"Yes. Yes. I posted it all right. You bet. Nobody ever gives me a letter but I post it right away. They'll have it in Liverpool in six days' time."

"They will?"

"Sure! Sure they'll have it. I hope it was a nice letter you wrote?"

The boy essayed a smile. Perhaps he had been a fool, a little too hasty in his opinion. This man seemed to be kind now. Of course, he had heard people say that everybody had some good as well as some bad in him. And that remark of Donagan's, that he hoped he had written a nice letter home, it loosened something hitherto locked in his bosom, it responded to something that ached in his being. He began talking again, telling the sailor word for word what he had written in his letter to home. Donagan could not help but smile. It was so innocent of the boy to open his heart like that. He felt something of a cur that he had done such a thing. He would make amends in some way, he told himself.

"Well," he said, "they'll have your letter early this week. I suppose you really ran away from home. Tell me the truth, didn't you now?"

"Yes," replied Fearon.

"But why?"

The boy did not reply for some minutes, and then said:

"Because I did not feel happy at home. I liked school best, I wanted to study. I wanted to become a chemist. But my mother took me away before I was fourteen. I went to work at the docks. Didn't like it. Then one morning I threw up my job and went home. My father nearly killed me. So I stowed away on this ship."

"And are you sorry?" asked the sailor.

"No. I'm not sorry. I'm feeling happy now because I have something that interests me. I want to do something. The Captain said that no man or boy was worth his salt until he had justified himself."

"It's worth knowing, I suppose," drawled Donagan. "Are you feeling all right? We must make a move for the ship now," he concluded.

Fearon got upon his feet. "I feel as if I wanted to be sick. Will we get one of those gharries back to the docks?"

"Sure thing, boy. We'll ride back like grand 'uns. Let's get away now." He placed an arm on the boy's shoulder and together they made their way to the long stone passage down which they walked to get to the street.

Halfway down, a room door stood open, and on a chair near the door a young Greek girl was sitting naked. She beckoned to Donagan as he passed:

"Four piastres, eh?"

"Go to hell!" shouted Donagan, and passed on. When they reached the street it was dark. Fearon was conscious of many different smells, and as they passed the cheap cafés, the nauseating one of cheap perfume. He said suddenly:

"The place doesn't half stink. I'll bet there are some queer holes in it."

"Here's our Rolls-Royce," said Donagan, as a gharry drew up to the kerb. He signalled to the driver, who descended and came forwards, saying smilingly:

"Yes. Docks John. Ver' good. Three piastres each, eh?"

"Five for two, you goddamned dirty-looking son of a bitch," said Donagan.

"Five piastres eh? Yes?"

"Yes."

The gharry drove away with the man and boy comfortably seated at the back, the boy with his two hands joined together and resting in his lap, the man with one hand on the side of the car, the other drawn affectionately around Fearon's neck.

In twenty minutes they had reached the quay. Donagan paid the driver and with Fearon walked towards the shed. The *Hernian* was loading a cargo of dates. The gangway for'ard had been shifted aft. The man and boy ascended. At the top the quartermaster said to Donagan:

"Well, boy, how's the old girl this time?" and seeing Fearon with him, added: "Oh Christ! Has he taken you up as a pupil?"

"You mind your own bloody business," said Donagan, and dragged the boy by the arm along the saloon deck. They descended the ladder. Each went their way, the man to the fo'c'sle, the boy to his room.

It was getting late, and as he had to be up at five the following morning, he decided to go to bed. He undressed and climbed in. In the fo'c'sle Donagan had seated himself at the table to make up a game of nap. Most of the men were still ashore. One of the sailors said:

"What the hell were you doing with that kid up the street this evening?"

"Me?" said Donagan, affecting a sort of surprise. "Me! Oh yes. Why the kid asked to go there. What about it? He can mount as good as anybody." He began to laugh as he recalled the boy's predicament. He added suddenly:

"It was bloody amusing. That Russian sissy is there still I see."

Amidships there was a fight going on in the alloway between the carpenter and the boatswain's mate. The two men were struggling with each other outside the boy's room. Both had just come on board drunk, having gone ashore together a few hours previously the best of friends. There was a sudden thud. It woke up Fearon, who jumped out of bed and opened the door. The sight he saw made him feel sorry he had done so. The carpenter was stretched out on the iron deck, his face covered with blood, whilst the bosun's mate was leaning against the bulkhead endeavouring to straighten himself up. But now he saw the boy. And seeing him awoke something in him. He realized that the boy was under him, that he was only the *boy*. He suddenly lurched towards the door.

"Drop 'em, kid. Drop 'em, kid," he blurted, the whilst spittle dribbled from his half-open mouth. "Drop 'em, kid."

There was only one thing that Fearon could do. That was to close and lock the door. But he discovered that one of the bosun's mate's feet had in some way jammed itself. He was afraid to do anything. He did not want to open his mouth at all, and yet he could not close the door. Whilst he stood thinking, the man almost threw himself

134

into the room. He flung himself on the boy, throwing his arms about his neck. He began to rub his chin against the boy's cheeks. Fearon winced. The man had not shaved for nearly a week.

"Nize boy. Nize boy. Oh you darling little innocent nize boy. Nize boy. I like a nize boy I do. Sailed with 'em for years an' years. Drop 'em, nize boy."

Fearon could not speak, for a part of the bosun's arm had stopped up his mouth. He couldn't help it, it had to come, he had been expecting it all night. He suddenly vomited. The man kept pushing him nearer and nearer to the bottom bunk.

"Nize boy. Give me a kiss, nize boy."

They both slipped and fell. A silence filled the room.

"Where's that bloody lad? Where's that undersized hungry-looking rat? Where's that blasted pig of a boy? Hey Fearon! Hey Fearon!"

"Let me go," shouted Fearon, who had now disentangled himself from the bosun's mate. He backed towards the door.

"Who the hell cares about him? Who cares about my bloody mate, eh?"

"Can't you hear him shouting for me?" pleaded the boy. "Can't you hear him?"

"Hear him? Who?"

"Fearon! Where are you, boy? Hey there! Hey there!"

"There he is again!"

The door burst open. The drink-sodden features of the bosun appeared. Fearon began to shiver. He felt returning to him all the old fear, hatred, disgust.

"Well! Are you damned well deaf?" growled the bosun.

"He wouldn't let me go. He wouldn't let me go."

"Tell that to the bloody marines," shouted the bosun, reaching out an arm and grabbing the boy. "Go and make my bloody bed, you dirty little worm. Half doing your work, and then clearing off ashore with the men from the fo'c'sle. Did it taste nice? Did it feel all right? Did it tickle? You little sod. Get out."

As soon as Fearon left the room the bosun entered and began to shake his mate, continually muttering:

"Come! Shake yourself. What's wrong with you? This damned ship's sailing tomorrow for Cairo. Mucking about after a bloomin' boy. Why the devil don't you go ashore and get a woman and be done with it? Come on now. It's late. I don't want my sleep disturbed tonight. Show a leg there, for Christ's sake."

"S'orlright. S'orlright! Fiss off. Go on. Don't be worrying me. Anyhow that kid's all right. You bet. Leave that kid alone. He told me all about you. Chuck it, mate. Chuck it, mate."

"Get to bed, you drunken bastard," growled the boatswain.

He returned to his room.

"Boy," he began, "I hear that you've been ashore to one of those houses. If I catch you going to one of those places I'll tan your backside. See? The likes of it. I have a son turned eighteen on the *Deana*. But he wouldn't go to a dirty filthy place like that. Who put that in your head?"

"I didn't want to go," said Fearon. "When I went ashore I was going to buy some cheap clothes from the 'tailor'. Donagan bumped into me and I asked him where was the best place. I got a coat and a pair of trousers all right. Then he asked me to go along with him. So I went."

"Oh! And did you like it? Did it tickle you? Did it hurt? Did it melt? Did it present arms? Did it get lost? Did it give you a pain? Did it bite you? Did it stand up for itself? You soft little bugger. One of these days you'll regret it. Take my word for it. Why a really decent lad wouldn't go ashore at all in one of these places. My God he wouldn't. No. A decent boy would stay in his room and occupy himself with something better. Study the compass or learn to splice or do something useful. Fine sailor you'll make."

It came as a shock to the boy to find himself lectured by this man, for he had always looked upon him as being the worst person in the ship, a man who by his every word and action revealed himself, and he had done so towards the boy. Here he was poking fun at him, now taunting him, now threatening him. Fearon adopted a stubborn attitude. He vowed he was not going to be controlled outside his working hours by anybody.

"I can go where I like in my leisure hours, can't I? What right have you to order me about?"

The man did not affect to be surprised by this sudden expression of anger on Fearon's part. He merely replied in a slow monotonous tone of voice:

"On board a ship everybody has rights, excepting a boy. Get that, Fearon. In this world everybody has rights and it all comes to a question of experience and age superiority. I have a right to tell you to keep away from such places. I am quite determined about this. I'll make it hot for you if I find you there again. Mind what I say now. Go and make me a cup of coffee."

Fearon had no answer to give. He felt himself disarmed, helpless. He went off quietly to make the coffee. The boy's mind was like a furnace. He returned to the room. He began to question himself:

"After all, what right has anybody to say I will or will not do this and that? I belong to myself. I listened closely to Mr Wood reading out the articles, but I never heard mention of these houses, nor anything about preventing a member of the crew from going where he liked after his day's work was finished. God! Must I always remain a boy? Must I always be at everybody's beck and call? Must I put up with these things for years?"

He felt there was a world conspiracy against boys. Against boys! He had done his work as best he could. Who could complain now? He had tried anyway. And as he studied the men's attitude towards him, he suddenly saw that even Mr Wood and Mr Larkin, the two men for whom he had most respect, even these adopted an attitude towards him, though in a different way. He thought:

"Why, they must be even worse than the others. They obtain power over you in such a subtle, cunning way. The one says work well and work hard and you'll make your way in the world. The other says keep away from the sea. As if I had no mind of my own! I am turned fifteen years old now. Am I to continue on like this? To hell with all of them. I hate them now. Every one of them. Friend. Friend Mr Larkin with his smug lectures to me, his dull sermons. Oh, they're all the same. I'll do what I like, go where I like. I can always look for another ship."

He thought of his letter home, of the promises he had made. Then suddenly everything was blotted out, and in imagination he was back in that house, amidst the riot of thrumming music and flesh, the sights and sounds returned afresh, stirring his blood anew, that between bowels and brain hymned for him the song of the blood-red flower. Slowly actuality was surrendering itself, everything faded away before this nightmare, this delirious memory of a few minutes spent in a world of exotic scents. The feast of the flesh. He remembered the girl now. How she had held on to him, touched him; he had brushed her hair with his mouth, her breast with his hand, and Donagan had watched. Suddenly he said half-aloud:

"I'll go again. I'll go again."

At half-past five the following morning, Fearon was sent for by Mr Wood. Rather shamefacedly he appeared before that gentleman, who roundly lectured him, for it was all over the ship by this time that the boy had been to Sister Street.

"Don't do it again, boy. One day you'll be sorry for yourself."

That was all he said. And Fearon discovered that his surmise was correct. They were all of them right except him. There was nothing they could do wrong. They were all suddenly anxious to protect him. Mr Wood had said: "I've a good mind to stop your shore leave."

Stop his shore leave! He couldn't do a single thing without somebody's interfering. Well, he would go ashore that very evening. He would do what he liked. The ship wasn't sailing that day after all. He would show them. If he needed an excuse for manifesting his feeling of independence it was certainly given him. There was nothing he did that day correctly. Everybody grumbled. The bosun cursed about the bad tea, the muck under the bed. The lamp-trimmer said he'd punch his jaw if he caught him pinching any more cotton waste from the lamp room, the diver in the port watch said he would make it hot for him if ever he found a kink in the hose again. They had been washing down decks and Fearon had had to hold the hose just behind the diver. His thoughts being anywhere but on his job, the hose had buckled two or three times, angering the man who had said something about the boy's hands:

"Keep them in your pocket, why don't you? You'll get them dirty if you hold the bloody thing. You want to care for your hands, sonny, and watch they never stray to strange places."

It was simple to the boy to understand what he was driving at. Then when he had to go down to the engine room to tell the engineer to turn off the water, he had incurred that gentleman's wrath by falling headlong over one of his pet wireless contraptions, Mr Devanny being an amateur wireless enthusiast. Again the remark was the same, his hands came into the light again. The engineer said:

"Boy, people who do things like that generally have a hair on their hands between finger and thumb."

Fearon absent-mindedly looked at the palm of his right hand. The man laughed:

"I thought so," said the engineer. "Go and get a woman, boy, for the love of Jesus and don't go about looking as if you were carrying the bloody world on your back."

The bosun's mate was another. Completely sobered up after his previous night's carousal, he became a tyrant as soon as the boy appeared with the breakfast things.

"What the hell do you call this?" he had asked, pushing away the porridge dish with his hand.

"Porridge," replied the boy quite innocently.

"I call it shit," replied the bosun's mate, "and you can tell that cock-eyed cook who tried to put you in the family way what I said. D'you hear me?"

"But the porridge is all right. All the crew have the same," said Fearon.

"Bastard! You... Don't get giving cheek here, even if you have been with a woman. You dirty young scoundrel. Get out. Those binnacles look lovely this morning. The damned things are almost green. Get your stuff and clean them. Which hand did you use last night? You ought to change alternatively." And as the boy was closing the door behind him, the mate added: "When you get to ninety, change hands."

In the alloway he met the first officer.

"Fearon! Why haven't you cleaned the brass in the officer's alloway?"

The boy stood as though struck. He felt himself on the verge of tears. Here, he thought, is a man who has never interfered all the trip across. A man who got me into that room away from the cook. A man who I hate most in the world to offend. And now he is like the others. He looked at the first officer.

"I'm sorry, sir. I quite forgot about it. I'll do it now. Right away, sir."

"See you do," replied the officer. "The place is a disgrace. The brass almost green. You mustn't go mixing yourself up with these women, or you'll be losing your head."

The mate went off down the alloway without another word. Fearon immediately went to the lamp room for his cloths and oil. The lamp-trimmer was relieving his bladder in a tin bucket, too lazy to go to the proper place.

"Woddyerwant now?" he growled, pulling a face at Fearon, half-turning round as though he had been suddenly seized by a fit of modesty.

"Cleaning tackle."

"Take it, and for Christ's sake don't come back. When you've cleaned the gear take a running jump over the bloody side, you useless bugger."

Ten minutes later Fearon was on the flying bridge diligently applying oil and sand to the green binnacle. It had once been shining brass, but rain and accumulative dirt had sullied its hitherto magnificent appearance. Suddenly the boy sat down, the cloths still in his hands and thought:

"Hell! Why didn't I get smothered in the bunkers and end it all? I never knew such a rotten lousy ship could stick afloat more'n a year. God! What a crew. What a crowd. What a place. Not a single kind word since I came on board. Just a bloody nuisance. That's what I am. Perhaps Dad was right. Perhaps my mother was right. Who knows? But perhaps the bloody lamp man was the most correct of all when he said I should take a running jump over the side. A running jump.

Quick's the word. One jump and it's all over. I don't know whether I'm sorry or not, don't know whether I'm angry or not, don't know whether I'm right or not. Don't know a single bloody thing. I seem to be all upside down, and I have this continual ache somewhere in me. And my hands are always trembling. Christ! That's what it is. I'm a real butterfingers, that's what I am. Well, I'll just go ashore tonight and pass no compliments to anybody. See what they'll do. Can't do a single thing. Say a word. My time's my own. I'll work like hell on the trip home and then I'll ship in a different packet than this. Of all the boats afloat, this wants beating, by jingo it does. Growl, growl, growl. It's in your ears all the time. Men boozing ashore at every port. Bringing women on board, though a boy mustn't do that. Oh no. You're only a bloody boy. Boy or no boy, they won't come it over me after this."

12

THE QUARTERMASTER AT THE GANGWAY saw Fearon coming towards him. It was turned six o'clock. He stopped the boy at the gangway, saying as he gripped him by the shoulder:

"Orders are that you are not to be allowed ashore. The crew are under orders. We may be sailing any time now. Get that, kid?"

"You what?" queried Fearon. "Who said I couldn't go ashore?"

"The first mate, of course. You'd better go and ask him why. I'm sure he'll be nice and tell you." He began to grin and continued: "Just caught you. Just sneaking off to have it rolled, eh? Get back to your room, kid. You don't know what it's like. Honest you don't. Besides, you've never seen a real one. Beat it."

"But I want to go ashore," said the boy. He became pleading in his manner. "Look here," he went on, "you needn't say you saw me. Let's go. Will you?"

"Will you get me a job if I get the bloody sack?" stormed the quartermaster. "Will you? Go on now. Get back to where you came from before I kick your behind and let you have one under the lug too, for your confounded cheek. Go ahead now! Beat it while your boots are good, you two-faced bastard."

So that was it, thought the boy. They had succeeded. They weren't going to allow him ashore for fear he might get into one of those houses in Sister Street. "They must think I'm a proper bloody loon all right. They surely must. I'll beat them. I don't care a damn now. I'll *go* ashore. And I'll get back too and nobody will know anything about it."

Just as quickly he realized that it would be difficult, for until it was properly dark any attempt would be worse than useless. He went back to his room. Lay down. He became excited at the thoughts of getting ashore: visualized all he might see. He had money. Twenty-four piastres. It was so easy to pick up an odd coin here and there. The bosun and his mate were careless with their money. He wasn't going to return any money found in or under the bed, or even in their coat pockets. Hell! I'll go to that same tart. God! I liked the way she did it though. The thought set his mind afire, he became full of an almost agonizing longing to go, to fly there as quick as he could, to find her, this Arab girl, whose skin was like silk, with her gazelle's legs, her perfumed hair, her breasts that hung like pears and which in that mad moment he had caressed with his hand. She had called him piccanin'. He could not understand the word at first. Then it dawned on him. She meant he was a baby. Baby or no baby he wanted to go to this girl now, right away. He seemed to collapse under this last thought. He jumped up and again made his way stealthily towards the gangway. The quartermaster was not in sight. Instantly he put one foot on the step and looked around. He had almost reached the bottom when a voice called him. It was as though somebody had flung a rope that had tightened itself around his neck. The voice robbed him of strength. He stood there, afraid to turn round. He heard somebody walking down behind him. Then he turned. It was the quartermaster. That individual grabbed the boy, turned him roughly round and pushed him up to the top of the gangway again. He still held him. He bent down, looked straight into Fearon's eyes, and said:

"You bugger! You thought you were off that time, now didn't you?"

Fearon did not reply. The blood mounted to his head. He scowled.

"Knew a kid who went ashore in this same place. On the sly too, just like yourself. After a piece of tail before he had wiped his mother's milk from his lips. Tells no one. Goes off ashore. Soft little runt gets lost. Well, what happens? Not much. Firemen saw a body three days later. It was floating in the river. It was only the boy's. Nothing much in that. Except that he had no trousers on. They knew who he was because he was still wearing his jersey with the company's name on it. Funny thing about it though, was the neck of an ale bottle sticking up his behind. Well! What about that too," drawled the quartermaster. "Nothing much. These Arabs are real buggers for boys. But this poor soft stupid little son of a bitch didn't have a hole big enough. That's all. So you see what he got for sneaking off to Sister Street. Same thing'll happen to you. Now go back to your room like a good little lad and go to bed. How'd you like your mother or your dad to find you lying on top of a woman? Huh! I'm old enough to be your grandfather and I tell you I'd sooner lie on top of a wet sack any day. Believe me."

All this time Fearon had not uttered a word. And now he walked back to the room, the words of the quartermaster seeming like knives that hacked about and in his brain. Was all this true, he asked himself? Or was it just one of the impossible yarns? He had heard so many since coming on board. The lamp-trimmer had sworn he saw an Arab do it on a bitch hound right on the quay in front of a ship's crew. Did it for the sake of a loaf of bread from the cook of a French ship. They had all lined the rails to watch a man do it on a dog, then they had pelted him with offal and stale bread. But these yarns were hard to believe. No. The quartermaster was only trying to kid him up. He was *going* to go. He was going to go as soon as it was dark.

With this one thought in his mind he sat contentedly on the edge of the bunk and waited. Nearly the whole of the crew had gone ashore as it was the ship's last night in port. They had meant to get a last drink before she sailed. Only one or two of the officers were in their rooms; the bosun and his mate with the carpenter had gone ashore long ago for a wet.* The lamp-trimmer was sleeping in his room. He never went ashore, vowing that in all the ports he had ever sailed into there was not a single one worth getting excited about. So he passed his time sleeping, with the result that the world saw very little of an interesting personality.

Darkness was gathering. Fearon buttoned up his coat collar. He quietly opened the door and as quietly closed it after him. He undid his boots, tied them together and slung them round his shoulder. Then he ran down the alloway. Not to the gangway, but to the after end of the ship. The peculiar position she was placed in left her bow hard up against the quay and her poop veering at least fifteen feet from it. Fearon could not get ashore for'ard, so he decided to make a swim for it. When he reached the wheelhouse, he went inside and removed his socks. These he placed inside his boots. Then he walked to the bit on which the hawser was secured. He clambered over the rails, grabbed the rope and swung himself clear of the ship's side. Hand over hand he continued for about ten yards. Then he suddenly let go. There was a splash. Fearon was a good swimmer. He swam beneath water until he came to an obstruction which he knew must be the belly of the coal barge against the quay wall. He came up. The water was dirty, a peculiar smell floated about him. He swam vigorously for the heaving line hanging over the side of the barge. This in its turn was lashed to a capstan. He hauled himself slowly on board. His hands smarted, for the heaving line was thin and wet. As soon as he reached the deck he looked all about him. The barge was deserted. He said to himself:

"Hell! It's as easy as winking." He could now see the huge hulk of the *Hernian* looming up out of the darkness, and even discerned the electric cluster hanging above the gangway. He smiled when he thought how easily he had beaten the quartermaster. He put on his socks and boots. He walked along the deck. In the quay wall was fixed an iron hook. But no rope. He suddenly ran back and unlashed the heaving line. Then he returned, made a clumsy bowline and heaved it. It caught. He swung himself and landed heavily against the stone wall. For a moment he was breathless, hanging there limply after the terrible leap. Then his strength returned. He hauled himself onto level ground. As though somebody were at his heels, he began to run, not stopping until he had reached the end of it. He breathed a sigh of relief when he found himself outside the dock gates. His one desire now was to get a gharry, and if possible the one with the same driver as the previous night. Out in the dock road he walked up and down looking into the faces of the various greasy-looking individuals known as licensed gharry drivers. There was one among them, an old man who attracted the boy's attention. He went up to him and said loudly:

"Sister Street. How much, John?"

"Five piastres," replied the old Turk.

This was much more than Donagan or anybody else would have paid, but the boy did not seem to mind, but willingly handed over his five silver coins, got into the gharry and was driven off. In half an hour he had arrived at the street of his longing. He got out and stared about him. He could not see anybody he knew in sight. He must be careful. If he was seen in this street he might be dragged back to the ship right away without any questions being asked. He had not run the gauntlet for nothing, he told himself. Of a sudden he muttered:

"Damn it! I've forgotten which bleedin' house we went into last night. Damn and blast it!"

He began walking in a furtive sort of way up and down the street. At one or two of the doors he saw women and girls sitting on the stone steps, all of them waiting for a prize to come along. He dodged these. It must be this same girl or nobody, he repeated to himself again and again. "Her! Nobody but her. Her! Her! Christ! Where the devil is the house anyhow? If only I could find it. It's a cancan place. That's all I know."

He was seized with a sudden fear that he would not achieve his desire. "Why! Perhaps she doesn't belong there at all. She might have come from anywhere."

"Ah! Piccanin'! Piccanin'!"

Fearon turned round. A young girl was facing him, smiling, revealing her beautiful teeth. The boy's tongue clung to the roof of his mouth. He could not speak, but only continued to stare at this girl. She said:

"Nize boy, eh? Two piastres for nize boy, eh?"

He laughed. There was something thrilling in oneself being sought. There was something of the braggadocio in Fearon. He moved towards her. Said:

"No. No. I look for cancan house, eh?"

"Ah! You cancan, eh? Nize piccanin'! Me cancan for piccanin'."

She leant towards him so that his eyes roved about her dress body.

She lowered her head that he might catch the scent from her hair. Fearon surrendered:

"All right. I watch you cancan, eh?"

She did not reply, but placing her arm in his, led him halfway up the street. As they neared a lamp, the boy shook her roughly, saying:

"Christ! No. No. Not past here."

"No cancan for nize boy, eh?" she crooned.

Fearon allowed himself to be led. He did not want to say anything more. There was nothing more to be said. Only to be seen and felt and experienced. Something to be done. They stopped outside a house, similar in design to that which he had entered with the sailor the previous evening. But when he got inside he found it to be much smaller. She led him up a flight of stairs. They walked along a landing and entered a room. Her room. Here was a bed, two chairs, a small table, on which lay cheap portraits of the girl in various alluring attitudes. The boy was bending over the table looking at these, utterly lost to everything save a something urgent and vital that began to stir like a dark chaos within his bosom. He heard something drop. Looked round. The girl was undressing.

"Nize boy, sit down," she said. He grinned at her.

Suddenly he pointed towards the door, saying: "Door. Savvy? It is locked?"

She laughed: "Nize boy much afraid, eh? S'awlright, eh?"

She was naked now. She called to him. Fearon got up and approached the bed. He sat down by her. For some minutes he sat there bereft of speech, hardly knowing what he must do. Then he placed his hand on her shoulder, saying:

"You dance cancan, eh?"

"Oui! Oui!" she laughed, jumped up and strode into the middle of the room. The boy lay back on the bed and watched her. Her body amazed him. It was like the swaying branch of a tree, weighty with fruit; it turned and twisted, swayed, rolled, now appearing almost like a snake, now like a statue of bronze upon which all the golden fan-wise rays of the sun seemed to have set. She began making peculiar movements with the lower part of her body. She stopped:

148

"Nize boy smoke, eh?"

Fearon felt in his pocket and took out a cheap packet of cigarettes, handing one of them to the girl. As he did so, she caught him, forcing his head with its shock of hair close to her breast, the while one long arm glided down his body until it reached the harbour of all the boy's feeling and desire. There it remained. The boy was kissing her body. He was like a form of lapdog. She felt his hot tongue licking. She looked down at the tiny hands that had cupped themselves to hold one of her breasts. She crushed him to her. And heard him murmur:

"Oh Jesus Christ! Oh! Oh! Oh!"

"Nize boy smoke, eh? Nize boy give nize girl cigarette, eh?"

Suddenly an idea occurred to Fearon. He had one day heard the bosun say that when in Salonica, he had attended a cancan dance, where the girl for a wager had placed a lit cigarette in her philosophic centre. Fearon smiled. He pushed himself away and said to the girl: "You put cigarette there, eh?"

Immediately the girl understood. She watched him light a cigarette. When he handed it to her she placed it where he most desired to see it and again began to dance in the centre of the room. The boy became full and choking with a desire to bury himself in that flesh, to hide away from all that had angered and worried him, all that had humiliated him. There he could hide away from the world of men for ever. He felt in his pockets. Pulled out some coins, almost ran to the girl, grabbed her shoulders, said: "How much? How much? You... me?"

"Ah, well, five piastres."

He handed her the money. In the moment he had done so he was conscious of something. The act of handing it over filled him with a sense of power, of ownership, of mastery, with abandonment and desire like two huge spouts that sucked up all his thoughts. He almost fell with the girl upon the bed. And although he knew something was happening, something was going to happen, he lay still. Closed his eyes. He felt her hands roaming about him, and did not move when she removed his clothes. As though the night itself were pressing him down, as though the phantoms of a mad world were on his back,

149

he suddenly appeared to hurl himself upon that body, to crush it, to hold it, and so doing shut out from his sight and mind the cold reality of everyday urgencies. His eyes remained closed, he heard the girl murmur something and he moved in the bed, he felt her squeeze him until he was almost gasping for breath. Desire, madness, nothingness. He lay. A peculiar silence filled the room. He felt her hot breath upon his face, thought her sleeping, and immediately his hands began to explore, to divine, to receive their sustenance of feeling, to know and to pluck from that moment something that like knowledge was new, and strange and vital to himself. To draw out of that moment of time and bliss and abandonment the richness that in its very essence was a candle flutter, a flame come and gone, a flower opened and closed, a note heard and forgotten, a song sung and ended. Now that the hands had learnt, the feeling withdrew, and all desire in the moment and after was in the eyes. The eyes that searched and looked and harnessed and retained for ever. He whispered:

"Move, eh? Move off, eh? Turn, mademoiselle. Turn, eh? Yes."

He drew himself back, raised himself until he was kneeling now over the reclining figure. And in the agitated movements of his eyes, in the whole trembling of his body the hidden words were revealed, the words unspoken. His brain was full of crazy ideas. He yearned. He wanted to say to her:

"Ugh! Lord Jesus! Look! I want to look at you. To see and stare at you. Turn over this way. Now that. Stretch. Lift this leg. No. Not that way. The other way. Stretch your arms out. Kneel up now. Turn over. Lie still. Swing that breast. Now let it hang. Oh God! Let me place my hand here. Yes there. No. Not that way. Look, move both your feet that way. That's right. Stand up in the bed now. That's it. Ugh! Ugh! Stand straight now. Bend over. Wait. Let me stroke you all over. Turn over the other way now. Christ! I want to bury myself in you, I want to eat you. Oh! Oh!"

All his being was afire, the blood hymned its song of joy. He shouted: "Here I am, eh. Here I am." Commenced to strip all his clothes off and flung himself upon the girl again.

"Finis now," she said quietly, and pushed him off. She looked at his body beneath the light of the lamp, and crooned softly: "Piccanin'! Piccanin'!"

"Finish?" he asked her. A wave of fear overwhelmed him. "Finish?" He did not want to finish. He wanted to go on for ever. No. It must not be. And he shouted in the girl's ear: "Oh no! Oh no! Mademoiselle, look. I have the mon… I have the mon… me give you five piastres again, eh?"

"Finish wiz you," she repeated quietly.

Something in the boy broke. Something collapsed. It was all over. This sense of joy, of full being, of a certain power, the sense of absolute escape from reality. All over. What should he do? That body, the sight of which now set him afire with an all-consuming madness, was lost to him. He was overwhelmed, crushed. Was that all he had paid for? Five minutes of excitement! And was this the famous thing the men aboard ship were always talking about? It only occurred to him then that other men would come along and pay and garner just what he had garnered and nothing more or less than that.

Meanwhile the girl had begun to dress again. She had crossed to the table over which a mirror was hanging. It was whilst looking into this that she saw the boy approach from behind. She felt inclined to laugh at the expression upon his face. It revealed something between laughter and tears. But Fearon was already feeling within himself that this desire had not yet fulfilled itself. He burst into tears, ran sobbing up to the girl and fell upon his knees before her, clinging with his thin white hands to the hem of her skirt.

"Mademoiselle, mademoiselle, look!" and he indicated the handful of silver coins in his hand. "Look! Look! Mademoiselle," he cried out, almost demented.

"Finis wiz nize boy. Finis wiz you," said the girl.

It was not the actual meaning of the words, but the way they were spoken that drove the boy wild. He flung himself upon her and tried to bear her across to the bed. But the girl was much stronger than he, and she succeeded in dragging him to the door of the room. Along the stone passage all was darkness and silence, excepting there being an occasional drumming from some cancan entertainment.

She pushed Fearon out of her room, though he still held on to her dress frantically, as though she were all that was vital, and beautiful and necessary in his life. A thought struck him:

"She's robbed me. Bastard!"

"Finis with nize boy."

The boy suddenly tried to throttle her.

There is a word and the girl said it in that moment. She picked the boy up in her arms, carried him along the stone passage, and flung him down the stairs amongst the filth and rubbish at the bottom.

"Eff you, nize boy," she said.

13

"COME ON! GET UP. What the hell's the matter with you? Are you drunk or what?"

The bosun was standing over the boy's bunk. His face was livid with anger, for he had had to go for his own breakfast to the galley that morning. He began shaking the apparently sleeping boy:

"Hey! You lazy son of a bitch. What's wrong with you? Here! Come out of it, for Christ's sake, you snivelling worm," and he seized the boy's two arms and forcibly dragged him from the bunk. The boy collapsed to the floor. The surprised bosun scratched his head.

"I knew it! Well, there's a cure for buggers like that," and he ran out of the room, to return later with a bucket of salt water, the contents of which he immediately dashed in Fearon's face. But the boy never flinched, never opened his eyes.

"God Almighty!" he exclaimed. "Somebody's been giving this kid booze, or else he's had another fit or something. Holy bloody smoke. What a mess."

He went to his own room where his mate was taking it easy in his bunk.

"I can't understand this lad at all," he said as soon as he entered the room. "I'll swear my bloody life away, but somebody has been filling him full of drink. The bloody kid's practically unconscious. Come and have a look at him. I've just flung a whole bucket of water in his face and he hasn't budged. Not an inch. Something wrong all right. Will you go for the steward? He's the only man aboard who can fathom this mystery."

"Oh all right! Jesus Christ! That kid's been more worry and trouble since he came aboard than anybody I ever sailed with in my life. Damn and blast him!"

When he had gone aft to look for the steward the bosun returned to the boy's room. He was still lying on the floor, but in the interval that had elapsed had turned over on his face. The man could hear him moaning and occasionally a sob came from him.

"Hell! That's what it is all right. Some lousy son of a gun must have given him a bottle of vino. Nice bloody mess this is now."

The bosun's mate returned with the steward, who immediately bent down, turned the boy over roughly, opened one of his eyes with his fingers. Opened his mouth and looked at his tongue. Then he grinned and began to violently shake him.

"Look here!" he exclaimed savagely, turning on the bosun. "What do you mean by sending for me as though somebody was dying of appendicitis or pneumonia? Bloody hell, the kid's only working his jug. Hey!" he shouted into Fearon's ear, "Wake up there! Come on now. You are on the high seas now and bound for Salonica. Hey! Hey!" and once more he began shaking the boy.

"I know a cure for a little sod like that," said the bosun. "Pull his pants down a minute."

He ran out and came back with some white powder in his hand, which he immediately threw on the boy's bare skin. "It'll wake the bugger up, all right. Just you leave him there. There won't be any need to shake or call him at all."

The three men left the room, the steward going aft to carry on with his returns of ship's stores, whilst the bosun and his mate continued talking in the alloway.

"Was he ashore last night? The little sod might have gone to one of those places on his own, you know. By the way, who was on the gangway last night?"

"Summers was on last night," replied the bosun's mate.

"Oh! Just tell him to come to my room, will you. I want to see him right away about a particular matter. You know the old man and the mate warned me about letting this kid ashore alone. That mad Irish bastard Donagan ought to have had more sense."

The bosun went to his room and sat down. He was not worrying about the illness, real or imaginary, of the boy. He was only worrying as to whether the order he had received verbally from the first officer, and which he had transferred verbally to his mate, had been carried out. He had a lot of responsibility on his shoulders, and bosuns' jobs couldn't be picked up easily these times. He didn't give a brass tack about the kid. The kid never worried him at all. Not much of a bosun he would be if he allowed such a thing as a mere boy to worry him. He might have had a joke or two out of the lad, but it had never got beyond a joke and he was glad to recall the one occasion when he had tried to act as father to the boy. So that's what it was, eh? The damned kid was pulling everybody's leg. Pretending he was ill. After all that sudden fit he had in his room coming out might have been only a ruse for an opportunity to kiss the old man's backside. There were sly and cunning kids like that sailing in ships these times. The very thought that such things occurred, that boys had opportunities for going to such places, made him suddenly anxious for the safety of his own son who was a trimmer on a South American passenger liner called the *Desna*. It made one sit up and take notice. Boys! Christ! It took boys to learn the old hands all right. Well, if he discovered that Fearon was really pulling their legs and trying to get a nice soft passage back, well, he'd show him all right. By Jesus he would.

In the midst of this meditation his mate appeared at the door accompanied by the quartermaster Summers. The bosun nodded his head to him as a kind of salute, and said:

"Come in here a minute, Summers, will you? Right."

The man entered the room. The bosun's mate made room for him to sit down on the red plush settee.

"You were on the gangway last night, weren't you?" began the bosun.

"Yes I was. From eight o'clock till midnight."

"I see. Did that boy go ashore during the hours you were on duty?"

"No. He did come along about a quarter past eight, but I turned him back."

"Um! So the little devil did try to get ashore then?"

"Yes," said the quartermaster smiling, "but it didn't come off."

"Who was on after midnight then? I mean, who relieved you?"

Suddenly the bosun's mate interrupted:

"You don't expect the kid went ashore after twelve, do you? Why there's nothing at all doing at that hour. And anyhow he would be bound to make for the one place where he would be discovered. The naval and military patrol there would be sure to ask him what he was doing out that time of night."

"How the hell do we know what he did. How does anybody know?" growled the bosun. "If the old man gets to hear of this there'll be a row for somebody. He gave the mate strict orders that the boy was not to be allowed ashore on any account. The mate passed those orders on to me, and I passed them along. I expect them to be carried out. It doesn't much look like it anyhow."

"Where is this damned kid?" asked the quartermaster. "The whole bloody ship's upset through him. Such a confounded little nuisance I never came across in all my born days. S'truth I haven't. Where is this bloody nuisance?"

"Better go and have a look at him," said the bosun. "The steward just saw him. Only grinned. Says he's acting the bloody goat. How do we know? How the hell does anybody know?"

The bosun again began to scratch his head, for he was certainly bewildered. In his lifetime at sea he had come across a good many malingerers, but if this boy was really pulling their legs, then he felt the kid deserved a medal. "Two days out of this port," he said to himself, "and we'll know all about it. Now I wonder if he *did* go to that damned street? The little ass. He might have got a dose or something. Oh, bugger him anyhow. Why should I start worrying about a boy at my time of life? As if I haven't got a lad of my own, and it takes me all my time to keep the tapes on him. God Almighty! If the old man hears anything about this there'll be hell to pay. There will that."

When the bosun returned to Fearon's room he was surprised to see the boy sitting up, with the quartermaster talking to him and stroking his head.

"Hello!" exclaimed the bosun. "What's wrong with you, eh?"

Fearon did not speak, but lowered his head as though afraid to look the man in the face.

"Have you a bloody tongue in your head, or haven't you?"

Still the boy remained silent. He seemed to be in a state of coma. He was certainly unconscious of his surroundings, his eyes had a glassy stare about them that unnerved the bosun.

"Open your rotten mouth!" he shouted at Fearon, for this continual silence was getting on his nerves, and that dominant thought still held at the back of his mind. The thought that all the blame would be laid on him as the first man amongst the crew. He'd get the sack and probably never run as boatswain again. He rushed at the boy and slapped his knees saying:

"You young sod! Where were you last night, eh? We know all about it." It was a ruse through which he might trap the boy, he thought.

"Come now. What's all this game of yours? There's nothing wrong with you. Out with it now. This minute. Did you disobey orders and dodge the quartermaster last night? If we find out that you did you'll get warmed* for it, boy. Remember that. It's not so bad with a man. A fellow might get a drink too much ashore and miss his ship, but a boy! Good Christ! You'll be ordering the men about just now. Stand up! Stand up there!"

Fearon began to move. He managed to stand up. The two men saw his whole body shake as though from ague. But the bosun was not going to be impressed by these demonstrations. He dragged the boy by the neck and landed him into the alloway. There he began to cuff him, saying excitedly:

"Damn and blast you! Just look at the excitement you're creating. Get along there quick and make yourself bloody useful. Go ahead now! Get those rooms straightened up and that brass cleaned, and those two closets flushed out."

Just at that moment the first officer came down the alloway. He had seen the bosun belabouring Fearon. He went up and spoke to him.

"What is the matter with you this time, boy? What have you been doing now?"

"Nothing, sir. I was really ill, but the men said I was putting it on."

"Where do you feel the pain most?" asked the mate.

"All over," replied Fearon quite innocently, not noticing the sarcasm of the officer's remarks.

"Get along with you," said the mate, and hurried on to confer with the carpenter.

The boy started on his tasks. He was really feeling queer. Something was wrong with him, but what? He felt pain all over. Even waking early that morning he had been itchy all over and thought at first it was the bedbugs. Yet this peculiar aspect of his discomfort was one that he could not reveal to anybody.

"God. They won't believe me. They won't. They won't. I'm not kidding anybody. I'm sick. There's something the matter with me. I feel as weak as a cat. I won't half be glad when this ship docks in the old Mersey. By heck, I won't."

One or two of the crew passed him as he was engaged in polishing the brass steam pipe that ran alongside of the bulkhead from the galley to the engineer's mess room. They passed remarks to each other, remarks which the boy overheard. The *Hernian* had now left Alexandria some hours and was heading for the open sea. Rough weather was expected, and because of this he had not been expected to clean all the brass in the alloway, because the decks were bound to be awash most of the time with such a ship, carrying only a cargo of dates. When he had done the brass he reported to the bosun's room.

"Anything else?" he asked.

He was feeling very tired. He could hardly carry himself about the deck.

"Anything else?" asked the bosun's mate, for the bosun was aft superintending some rope-splicing.

"Anything else?"

"Yes," he said, and spat heavily upon the doormat right in front of the boy. "Pick the bloody bones out of that."

Fearon was not even interested in the joke, if that was what the bosun's mate thought it to be. He asked the man if he could go to his room for a while. He wasn't feeling very well, and wanted to lie down.

"Lie down! I like that. I do indeed. You'd better go and tell the bosun that you feel tired and would like to lie down. Go on. He'll get you a nice feather bed from the chief's room. Go on, you whingin' bastard of a boy. It's certain that the tails in Sister Street have got you down. Down sure and good. You soft little devil. The size of you wanting to go with women… Why if you ever saw a real one, you'd fall into it with fright. And that would be sad, wouldn't it? You'd get lost. That'd be sad too. Go on. Bugger off."

Fearon was turning the door handle of his room when the bosun saw him.

"Hey there!" he shouted. "Have you finished that brass work?"

"Yes!" shouted the boy.

"What you doin' now then?"

"Nothing."

The man ran and almost knocked Fearon down as he bumped into him, saying:

"There are a hundredweight of spuds to be peeled, and the cook is far from well. Go along and start them right away."

Fearon said to himself: "Well, I like that all right. They certainly mean to get their bloody worth out of me, though I suppose there are such things as board of trade rules and they daren't keep me working *all* the time."

"And after that I'll be through for the day," he remarked to the bosun.

But he did not reply with his mouth but with his fist that caught the boy behind the ear. Fearon walked sullenly away towards the galley.

After three hours spent with a bent back over a sack of potatoes, Fearon left the cookhouse and went direct to his room. He stripped off and got into his bunk. He switched off the light. It meant a lot to him, the switching off of the light, though it did not banish the continual throb of the engines and the monotonous roar of the waters. For the second time since he had come on board his thought turned towards home. Somehow he sensed a difference. He seemed not to be able to recall certain facts concerning his home life as easily as he had done on the first occasion. "What is the reason, I wonder? Is it that I am just learning to forget?" He did not want to forget. He wanted it more than anything now, yearned for it. To return to his parents. He was sick of the sea. He had tried so much. Done so much. Worked so hard. And yet nobody had a decent thing to say about him. Nobody ever said a kind word to him. Mr Larkin had been all right, but now he had seen through that man's pious sentiment. They were all the same, he told himself. All the same. Well, he was finished with the sea. For ever and for ever. He had seen things, heard things; he had even made foolish promises, but what were they now? Nothing. Nothing at all. He was going to break away from all this kind of life as soon as the ship touched the quay in the Huskisson Dock. He visualized her docking, his parents waiting at the bottom of the gangway to meet him. His face became wreathed in smiles. "God," he murmured. "It was beautiful then." Yes, it was beautiful. To have a good home. To have a mother and a father. If that wasn't better than this eternal drudgery, hard graft, swearing and cursing. He recalled the lamp-trimmer's advice to him. It made him shiver.

"Take a running jump overboard with yourself," he had said to him. And as he recalled this remark it set up a new train of thought. Perhaps there was a real meaning, a real reason for such a remark, horrible though it was. There was something at the pit of this thought that he could not fathom, could not grasp. It tormented him. It made him almost want to be sick. And he had been sick so many times. The men had laughed at him, made a joke of it. They had tried to do things to him too. He shivered again with fright at the thoughts of what had occurred in the ship's hospital and the cook's room. So that was the sea. That was the great roving and romantic life that they called the sea.

"Ugh! I hate it. I hate it. With all my heart and soul I hate it."

His thoughts turned then to a conversation he had had one evening with Mr Larkin. Recalling it, it suddenly seemed a kind of clue to that other conflicting thought that try as he might would not present itself to him logically. All his thoughts were chaotic. One overrode the other in quick succession. "Mother and Father. Home. Home," he murmured again and again. He began to turn and twist in the bed. He could not lie still. Something was happening to him again. So suddenly. "God! What is the matter with me?" he asked himself again and again. There was this terrible itching all over his body.

"It can't be that itchy cotton they threw on me before. Can't be that. What is it, I wonder? And as soon as this itching comes I feel so terribly weak. Oh Mother! Mother! I wonder what you are doing now. And Father. I wonder what you are doing, Dad, just at this time of night. I wonder if you are thinking of me. Wondering how I am getting along."

The letter came to his mind. That letter full of hopes and promises. And with this in his mind he remembered the circumstances under which it had been posted. Posted from a brothel. If his people knew of that? If they did. If they only realized how anxious he was to restart all over again, to begin a new kind of life, though he would have to climb down from his high perch, he would have to humiliate himself. But it was worth it. "Yes. Yes. Yes," he said half-aloud. "Anything is better than this place. Hell. Hell. That's what it is. Not a minute to yourself. Not a person to whom you can talk without their referring to something which makes you shiver and feel that awful sickness in your stomach. Oh dear me!" he said. What a hopeless mess he had made of everything. So that was what he got through being fed up. His father would say to him: "Well! You've learnt your lesson." And he would be right. Yes, he would be right. His father was always right. And his mother, she would say to him: "Why did you do it? Why did you?"

Yes. Why had he done such a foolish thing? After all, the lads amongst whom he had worked at the docks, they were happy. At the end of the day's work they could always go home to a good meal, and after that there was a football or cricket match, or the pictures. But there was nothing here. Nothing at all. What a fool he had been, what a ridiculous show he had made of himself. Promising himself that one day he would walk the bridge of a ship as her first officer or captain. Why, if his father ever saw him in that position he'd collapse. But now it was his turn to collapse. He had to undo all the things. Begin everything again. Recant. Reveal his vanity and determination for what they were. Ghosts and nothing more.

"I'm a soft bugger all right," he said to himself. "A real noodle as Mother would say. Well, I give in. I give in entirely. I'll go by what they say in the future. Though I did have a lousy rotten time stuck in those bunkers."

14

THE HERNIAN WAS NOW seven days out from Alexandria and had not made port. It seemed as though the seven furies of the sea had gathered together and made for that strip of water wherein she struggled, battered, torn, ever pitching and rolling, ascending and descending into the yawning trough of angry waters. The general appearance of the decks suggested a hurricane, though it had not been so bad as that. But the ship was merely a hulk and nothing more, a kind of weapon with which an order can squeeze the guts out of labour and extract from it just sufficient to keep the average shareholder from getting really low-spirited. Of her eight boats, five were serviceable, the remaining three having felt the crushing and destroying power of tons of water, for the huge seas swept her boat deck like so many charges of horsemen, the chocks were ripped asunder, the boats swung dangerously from their davits that every moment threatened to collapse. The crew had worked like Trojans. And below the engineer had goaded on his men, driven them, jeered at them. Something had to be done. The sea could not act thus without serious reactions. And as one could not chastise her, then the men must be chastised. The men must be made to work harder. The firemen must extract every ounce of energy from her coal, that was not much better than dirt itself. Not a man must wear a look of contentment. Everybody must suffer for the caprices of the sea. The second engineer had said:

"Boys! This ship must make port by tomorrow or else every man jack will get pushed when she gets home. Understand now! Down to it! Down to it! Drive the bitch! Drive her for all you're worth!"

Amidst this chaos, short tempers, angry words, Fearon moved about like one in a dream. There was no doubt about it now, and even the carpenter had had to remark to the bosun:

"That kid looks real ill. Have you asked him what is the matter?"

"Matter!" laughed the bosun. "Wants his behind kicking. That's what he does. Running and telling everybody that a scab has broken out on his bum. The silly little bugger. It's a boil, I suppose." He changed the conversation. "We'll have to have two lifelines run fore and aft, starboard and port, before nightfall. We haven't got out of this bloody squall yet."

"Squall!" exclaimed the carpenter. "I should call it an earthquake, a volcanic eruption and a devil's whirlpool all in one. Never seen anything like it before. Not around these parts."

"I thought you knew little about it," replied the bosun. "Wait till you've done ten years in these waters and you'll know all about it then."

"I'm no chicken myself," said the carpenter, somewhat piqued. "I've seen a bit of rough weather myself."

"That boy," said the bosun's mate, coming up to the two chattering men. "That boy is at his games again. Just brought the grub from the galley. Then lets the whole bloody lot spill over the table. Can't stand on his feet. He's a useless swine. Why the hell didn't the old man have him stuck in the galley anyhow, instead of pushing him on us?"

"I knew he was ill," said the carpenter.

"Ill, my backside," growled the bosun. "Ill! I'll make him feel ill all right," and he rushed off to the room where he discovered the boy mopping up the sticky mess from the deck. He immediately pushed the boy's face down to the floor until it reached the mess, in which he began to rub his nose vigorously, saying as he did so:

"That'll learn yer. That'll learn yer. Now what you going to do, eh? D'you think the blasted cook is going to issue a fresh lot of stuff? You sloppy, shivering, crying little bastard if ever there was one. Get up! Get up out of it and take those tins back to the galley. And don't come back without the grub. D'you hear? Christ! Beat it quick before I kick the guts out of you. A bloody fine dinner gone west."

"What's wrong with you, in the name of Jesus?" shouted the cook. "Well, I haven't any more grub left from the saloon rations. There's only this bit of stew left from the crowd's stuff. Tell me, little boy," he said, grinning. "Tell me, do you roll it or pull it? Which? You're the sloppiest, dirtiest, laziest, thinnest-looking bugger of a lad I ever saw in my life. Go on now. Tell the effin bosun there's only the crew's stuff here now. I hope he gives you a hiding. Sick! Holy Mother, as if the whole ship doesn't know you're sick. Well, you shouldn't go with those women. The size of you. The likes of you. You deserve to be dumped and it's a wonder to me somebody hasn't done it before now. Why don't you sneak along aft some night when it gets dark, and just tumble quietly over the rail? All your troubles will be over then. Sure! That's what I should do."

The ship heaved suddenly, took the half-dreaming and miserable boy off his feet and before he could stop himself, he had lurched right forwards, right into the middle of the galley, almost bringing the cook down with three huge pans that he was going to fill with water.

"Oh!" he roared. "You stupid useless son of your mother! Get out of my sight. Don't come back here. I wouldn't serve you. By hell I wouldn't. Let the bosun or his mate come and get their own grub. Tell 'em I wouldn't serve you. Tell 'em what I said to you. Go on! Go on!"

The boy's heart beat wildly. How long was it going to continue? He couldn't stand it much longer.

"I wish I was dead," he said to himself again and again. "Yes, I honestly wish I was dead. But I'm frightened to do anything. I would walk to the rail. But I'm too frightened to jump. Oh God! If a great wave just came along and washed me out of it altogether!"

He stood outside the galley door, his back turned to the cook, his eyes full of fear, his whole frame shaking violently. He was afraid now. More than ever he was afraid. There was not one among the sailors or firemen who would take his part. Why did they all hate him so? Was it just because he was a boy? Just that. Was he dirty, sloppy, clumsy; was he all those things? And whilst he stood there wondering what he should do, the bosun came out of the room.

"What are you standing there for, you loony? Get that damned grub."

But Fearon did not move. He stood there transfixed, petrified.

"Go on!" repeated the bosun.

"He won't give me any more," the boy managed to stammer out.

"Won't!" roared the bosun. "We'll see about that."

He came running up to the galley door to discover the cook engaged upon his own dinner.

"Hello there!" he said. "What's up here? We sent this kid along for grub. The sloppy little bastard spilt all the other lot."

"And is that my fault?" asked the cook, who was a man who hated to be disturbed during his meal, which meal was something of a ritual with him. "I ask you! Is it my bloody fault? I tell you this. A little bit of advice for you. That kid's getting thin. That kid's going soft in the slate. All for want of somebody to look after him. You ought to tie his hands behind his back before he goes to sleep." The cook grinned at Fearon.

"To hell with that stuff!" said the bosun. "I'm not worrying whether he uses one or both hands. I want my damned dinner and so does my mate." He entered the galley.

The cook said almost affectionately:

"All right boss, old man. Have a look round. There's sure to be something left. You know that kid always makes me feel I've lost a quid. Every time I look at his miserable face. I can't give bits of boys civil answers. I'm not used to that sort of thing."

He went on with his dinner whilst the bosun filled the dish with dry hash.

"What you want to do," said the bosun as he left the galley with the food, "what you want to do is to muck off. Jump over the side. Never let me see your miserable mug again, you useless bastard!"

The boy still stood there shivering, as though the very words of the bosun had rooted him to the spot. Even after the man had entered his room and closed the door, and the cook himself had left by the other door for his customary turn-in, even then Fearon remained standing there.

Then suddenly something snapped in him. And in that moment a great army of voices seemed to descend upon him, a great army of voices that uttered a single word. "Boy! Boy!" Fearon started to run. He went for'ard to the port rails and grabbed them with his hands, and for a minute was lost to sight in a huge cloud of spray. It cleared and he was still standing there, his hands tight upon the rail, his head peering down towards the swirling waters below. He left that position and ran aft. Here he did the same thing; every moment it seemed he must go over and disappear. He was drenched to the skin, the water ran down his white face, his hands shook. Then he began shouting. For a time his voice was drowned in the roar of huge breakers that smashed their way over the after house. Then he could plainly be heard calling:

"MOTHER! Mother! Oh Mother!"

He ceased suddenly, as though in that minute this army of voices speaking in his ears had overwhelmed his own feeble efforts. Again the one word that he could not escape from: "Boy! Boy!" It was an incessant murmur in his ears, an invocation, an incantation, a chant. He began to run now in all directions. Screamed:

"Mother! Mother! Mother!"

Until the first officer coming out of his room discovered Fearon standing by a ventilator, crying, and with his two small fists he was hammering ceaselessly upon it, shouting:

"Stop! Stop! Stop!"

The mate ran to him, grabbing him by the shoulders, saying excitedly:

"What's the matter? What's the matter with you? Come, tell me."

But if there was a suggestive kindness in the officer's voice, it appeared to be useless now.

"Stop! Stop! Oh Mother! Mother!"

The first mate realized something or thought that he did. There was manifesting itself in this weakling of a boy a strength. A terrible strength. It took him all his time to hold him, and he saw with surprise and consternation that Fearon, his eyes brimful of tears, was trying to break away from him; was making frantic efforts to get towards the rails. Then the mate acted. Freeing a hand, he plunged it into his coat pocket, and withdrew his whistle, upon which he proceeded to blow four times for the quartermaster. Four blows upon the whistle was the signal for the quartermaster on duty to appear as soon as possible, which was at once.

Doran, the quartermaster nearest at hand, had just finished brushing his room after the dinner when he heard the whistle. It had interrupted his prospective quiet smoke and he cursed the mate roundly for his trouble.

"Yes, sir," he said, running to where the officer stood with the struggling boy.

"Bosun! Quick!" snapped the mate. "Lend a hand quickly. Something wrong with this boy. Hurry up there."

The amazed bosun came upon the scene almost breathless with the rush of it.

"Hell!" he exclaimed. "Is he at it again?"

"That'll do, bosun," said the officer quietly. "Get this boy to the hospital aft at once," and as the quartermaster and bosun took the boy between them and made their way towards the after house, the mate called after them:

"Tie him down. Yes. Tie him down."

The first mate was alarmed. "The kid is certainly ill," he said to himself. "Looks to me as though he were going potty all right. Wood will have to know about this," and with mention of the Captain the mate recalled a rather troubling fact, the fact that he had not seen the old man out of his room for the past two days. This non-appearance could only be associated with a renewal of his drinking bouts, and of these the mate had witnessed not a few. Some minutes later he was seen coming away from the Captain's cabin, accompanied by the second steward. The latter was carrying on an animated conversation:

"Been like that since we left Alex, sir," he said. "Only this morning I pitched half a dozen empty whisky bottles over the side."

"Yes. Yes. But I didn't think he was helpless and hopeless."

"I don't know, sir," continued the steward, "he seems to have started ever since we put into port."

"Oh well," drawled the mate. "It's hardly any use reporting things to him now," and in his mind's eye he saw again the sprawling and helpless figure of his Captain, stretched upon his bunk, with a four days' growth of beard upon his chin, his face livid and seemingly pockmarked, the eyelids appearing swollen and red. He was like a beast sprawled in its filth. The room stank, the steward had been unable to clean it, for every time he had approached he had been sent away with curses and threats.

"Well, there's something more important, steward," the mate went on. "Something seriously wrong with that boy Fearon. I want you to look at him. I just prevented him jumping over the side a few minutes ago. I'm thinking he's mad."

"If he's mad, I'll soon know it. There's not much I don't know," said the steward, and he seemed to swell with the pride of his knowledge and position, remembering how every man aboard was practically in his hands.

"Where is he? In his room?"

"In the hospital," replied the mate. "The bosun and quartermaster took him there. They're tying him down. I asked them to."

"Ah!" exclaimed the steward, and it was almost like a sigh. He was suddenly silent and meditative. Of all the crew he was the one man with sufficient medical knowledge to be able to treat the usual common ailments with which seafarers are affected. In his time he had performed feats of surgery that would have shocked an ordinary member of the Royal Society of Surgeons. He had extracted teeth with finger and thumb, operated for appendicitis with rum and a penknife, cured blindness, seasickness, coughs, colds and the general run of illnesses current in the quack's catalogue. Also he had been long looked upon as a special authority on venereal diseases, having once cured a dangerous case with caustic soda. But in all his years at sea he had never had to deal with a boy of fifteen years of age, who, as the mate pointed out, seemed to be on the verge of losing his reason.

As he made his way towards the little house beneath the poop, he felt a strange pride stirring within him, like that of a doctor or scientist with a great experiment before him. The steward liked experiments. The first thing he discovered on entering the hospital were the bosun and carpenter, both of whom were standing by the bunk and staring at the white-faced boy lying in it. They had fastened him securely with a heaving line. The moment the steward saw the boy's face he turned and said to the men:

"Take the heaving line off him."

"What for? The mate just told us to tie him up. The kid's gone crazy. You ought to have been here a few minutes ago, you would have seen something to make you open your eyes all right. Take the line off him, eh?"

"Take it off," repeated the steward.

Now a bosun is the last man in the world to take an order from a glassback, as a steward is known in ships' fo'c'sles, but there was an expression upon the steward's face and a look in his eyes that hypnotized the man. He did what he was told.

Fearon lay with eyes closed, his mouth worked convulsively, and to the steward he appeared to be trying to free his hands. He turned and twisted until he felt the rope about him slackening. The steward sat opposite on a stool watching the two men carry out his order in absolute silence. Just as they wondered what to do, for they seemed helpless now under the eye of the steward, he said in a quiet tone of voice:

"All right! Take it away. That'll do. Tell the mate I'll see to him."

He waited until the door closed behind them. Then he went up to the bunk, stood on a stool so that he could get a good view of Fearon, and then began rubbing both the boy's hands vigorously.

"S'only a fit, I suppose."

"Mother! Mother!" shouted Fearon suddenly.

"Ssh! Keep quiet. I want to have a look at you. You're not mad, boy, though I never liked the look of you since we cleared Alexandria. Can you hear what I'm saying to you?"

The boy's eyes opened then.

"Yes," he said in almost a whisper.

Fearon started to scratch himself, his two hands were beneath the clothes.

"Ha!" exclaimed the steward. "Ha! Ha! Now I understand. Well! Well!" And he began to tear off the bedclothes. Then he hurriedly undressed the boy. The lower part of the body appeared to be covered with what looked like blisters to the steward, and some of these had burst, for a smear of pus attracted the man's attention. All the area round this affected part appeared red, tender and much distended. The man scratched his head.

"Jesus Christ Almighty!" he exclaimed. He leant over the bunk. Spoke softly into the boy's ear:

"Boy," he said – then stopped – he was afraid to continue. He must say something. "Boy," he said again. "Listen. Open your eyes and look at me."

Fearon looked up at the steward. A lump seemed to come into the man's throat.

"Boy," he said yet again. "Boy. Tell me the truth. Have you been with any of these women in Alex? You must tell me the truth now."

The boy began to whimper. The steward changed his tactics then. He hated whimperers. He came straight to the point. Lowered his face until it almost touched Fearon's own.

"Well, what's the bloody use of whimperin'? What's the use, boy? You're not the only one. I've seen so many in my time. You've got a dose. That's what you've got. A bloody good dose of syph. Yes. You've got the bloody syph all right." His face touched Fearon's now.

"Ssh! Say nothing. When it's dark just take a header overboard and that's the end of it. I knew a man had it badly in Santos. They put him in hospital there. No use. Couldn't do anything with him. They smothered him in his sleep."

"Mother! Oh Mother!" screamed the boy. "Mother! Save me!"

"Take my advice, boy," said the steward. "You do as I told you."

Fearon continued screaming. A sudden terror had flooded his heart. The words of the steward hummed in his ears. *Syph! Syph! Drown yourself.*

"Keep quiet now," said the man. "I'll be back in a second with something for you. Keep perfectly still."

The steward came back with a glass half-full of a black draught, a great roll of bandages and a jar of ointment.

"I'll do what I can for you," he said in a sympathetic tone of voice. "All I can."

And when he had gone out Fearon began to murmur:

"Will do all he can for me. Will do all he can for me. Kind. Very kind. Got syph. What's syph? Will do all he can for me." Then he suddenly began to cry.

So that was to be the end of his hopes and his endeavours! Again those voices were in his ears. A veritable fury of sound seemed to deluge the room wherein he lay. A powerful wind had sprung up. The ship heaved. The crockery rattled, the ventilators shook. To Fearon all these things had changed. Everything was now a voice in his ears. The ventilators rattled, "BOY. BOY." The wind sang its mad song, "BOY. BOY." The ratlines whistled against the stays, "BOY. BOY." The engine hummed, "BOY. BOY." The boats moved in their chocks, swung in their davits. They sang too, "BOY. BOY." All these things appeared to the boy to have become suddenly humanized. They called for him. His mind wandered. The voices were nearer now. They were speaking low in his ear. He began to ramble wildly.

"Lamp-trimmer saw me coming out of the lavatory. 'How's your arm, boy? BOY. BOY. BOY.' A bloody boy. That's all I am. Made a fine promise to the Captain I did. 'Will do my best. My level best.' Tried. Tried hard. Wrote home. Will work hard for you both, Mother and Father. And now I've got bloody syph. What's syph? All the men keeping away from me now. Must be like scarlet fever or measles. Catching. God! God! This itching. Steward, fancy him saying that: 'Don't say anything. Jump over the side when it's quiet later on.' Bosun cursing, saying I'm only letting on I'm ill. Syph. Syph. Syph. Oh yes. He said he knew a man had it in Santos. Smothered him during night. Oh Mother! Mother! Save me! Save me! Father! Father! Father!"

He sobbed bitterly. The tears welled up into his eyes, pouring down his cheeks like fine rain. Suddenly he shouted:

"Come. Somebody come. Oh God! I'm frightened. Frightened. Everything is roaring and shouting. Everything screaming. BOY. BOY. BOY. Go away! Leave me alone. I've got syph. Let me die."

Long after eight bells had struck he continued moaning, murmuring incoherently. But somebody was thinking of that boy. Somebody on the bridge had him in mind.

Captain Wood, just emerging from his stupor, had managed to raise himself up from his bunk. And as he leant heavily across the table, his half-opened and heavily bloodshot eyes espied a note lying on his table. He rose to his feet, lurched forwards, and grabbed it in his hand. He tore it open, but it was a few minutes before he managed to right it in order to read it. He read very slowly as his mind was somewhat befogged as a result of the five days' carousal. His second in command had written it. He wondered how long it had been lying there. He stared around the room as though unconscious of the fact that it was his own cabin. The bridge had not seen him for a few days. He knew nothing of the position of his ship. His mate was a good man though. He suddenly walked to the door, took his greatcoat off the hook, and put it on. Then with the note still in his hand, he left his cabin and began staggering along the bridge deck. It was quite dark, a high sea was running, and the roaring of the wind drowned all other noise. He half slid, half fell down the companion ladder and went aft. He wandered about for some time, uncertain of the position of the room he was searching for. He had forgotten whether the door was on the port or starboard side.

At last he found it. But he experienced great difficulty with the lock. He stood still. He thought he heard strange sounds coming from within. He braced himself up after a fashion and stood listening. For some time he could not understand a word. A great sea would smash its way over the poop, so that the terrific inrush of water was a hymn of hate in itself, and he had to hang on desperately to the knob of the door to prevent himself being carried along in the swirl of waters to be dashed against the rails and probably hurled to destruction.

For a minute or two the wind died down. The sounds from within the room were audible once more. But as yet Mr Wood was unable to gather what the boy was talking about. And it was so difficult to find the right way of opening the door, especially when one had just risen from a bed after a five-day carousal. The message from his second in command still remained vital and dominant. A huge wave struck the ship astern. The Captain cursed.

"Damn and blast the bloody door!" he said, and tugged again at the lock. At last the door opened and again he had to hang on desperately, for the ship listed. When she righted herself he was flung into the middle of the room. The door crashed to. Darkness. Not a word. The breathing of the boy in the top bunk was drowned by the heavier breathing of the Captain upon the floor.

Damn bloody door! Damn bloody mate! Why didn't he give message sooner? Boy seriously ill. Why wasn't wireless man told? Must be very bad. Must wireless for a doctor. No bloody light in the room.

He shouted out: "BOY! BOY! Where is boy? I am the captain of this ship, I say. Where's boy?"

Fearon suddenly recognized who his visitor was and a great fear overwhelmed him. He must not be seen. No. No. No. He must not be seen naked when the light went up. He had promised the Captain so much. Perhaps he would now be like the rest of the men. Treat him like a real leper. "Oh if only I knew I would be home again in three weeks! Oh Mother! Mother!'

"Wass marrer boy?" The voice was thick.

Fearon remained silent. Perhaps the Captain did not know he was there. He may have stumbled into the room by accident. Like a flash, as though some terrible thing had collapsed within himself, he lost courage and screamed:

"Here! I'm here. Boy. The boy Fearon. Oh sir, please don't switch on the light. Please don't switch on the light."

A moment's silence, then the voice of the Captain broke in suddenly:

"Was marrer with light, eh? Light fused? Where's bloody electrician? Should look after these lights."

The boy heard the movement of the body. The room was flooded with light. For the first time the expression upon the man's face filled Fearon with fear. The man looked positively savage, with his bloated appearance, bloodshot eyes, his growth of beard, his huge frame that towered and filled the room. He staggered across to the bunk. Looked at the boy for a moment:

"Where's clothes, boy, eh? Where's bloody clothes? Was marrer with you?"

"The steward says I am ill with syphilis, sir," said the boy in a gentle voice.

"What? What?" asked the Captain. "You what? You what? Say it again."

"Steward said I had syph, sir. What is syph, sir?" he asked innocently.

"Ah! So you did go ashore then, eh? You disobeyed me then, eh? What's syph? Syph is something that only boys get. Syph is really *for* boys. Boys like you. Boys who tell lies. Boys who do not do as they're told. Boys who try to dodge their work instead of facing it like men. Syph has got you. Syph has got you. The steward has sailed with me in this ship for some years. He is kind. Didn't he tell you anything?"

"Yes sir," said the boy, and he drew his knees up to his chin and embraced them with his thin arms. "Yes, sir. But I'm afraid. Oh Mother! Mother! God! I'm useless. Useless. I did try, sir. I did want to do things. I did want to do things."

Something happened in that moment that made the Captain take off his greatcoat and climb upon the bunk. He looked at the boy. For a long time they stared at each other. Then the body of Fearon moved, lunged, made a frantic effort to get out of the bunk.

"Oh! Mother! Mother! Yes. Steward said do that when it is dark. Jesus save!"

A gentle voice appeared to whisper in the boy's ear: "Boy. Come boy."

The Captain stretched out his arm and switched out the light. Darkness. Outside a single star shone out, a sheaf of clouds suddenly blotted it out. The waters murmured. The voice was in Fearon's ear again: "BOY. COME BOY."

In that instant Captain Wood placed the greatcoat over the face of Fearon, and layed all his weight upon it.

Epilogue

Entry in ship's log SS *Hernian* on the morning of 12th March, 19**:

Ordinary seaman Arthur Fearon reported missing. Ship searched but no trace of him. Put about and cruised in vicinity for one hour. No trace. Search abandoned. Believed washed overboard in middle watch. Heavy ground swells. Resumed voyage. Position: SE 41 by E 39.

G. Wood. Master.

Cable to owners per wireless:

Ordinary seaman Arthur Fearon washed overboard on eleventh and drowned. Search abandoned. Proceeding. Advise. Wood. Master.

Wire from owners to parents of Arthur Fearon, 14th March:

Regret ordinary seaman Arthur Fearon lost at sea. Details later. Horne.

Extract from *The Pilot*, 21st March:

Lost at sea. March 11th. Ordinary seaman Arthur Fearon. Aged fifteen years. RIP.

Note on the Text and Illustrations

The text of the present edition is based on the unexpurgated 1990 André Deutsch edition. The spelling and punctuation have been standardized, modernized and made consistent throughout.

The photograph of the older James Hanley is reproduced courtesy of *The Times*. The remaining pictures, the photograph of the Liverpool docks and the letter by James Hanley are reproduced with kind permission from Liam Hanley.

Notes

p. 4, *Wat Tyler... insurrection*: Wat Tyler was the leader of the Peasants' Revolt of 1381, which was provoked by Richard II's harsh taxation policies.

p. 14, *Junior City*: A scholarship exam taken at the age of twelve.

p. 34, a *meg*: A halfpenny.

p. 53, *fly*: Hughes means a trouser fly.

p. 60, *nesh*: Squeamish, feeble.

p. 75, *the Captain's Tiger*: The captain's steward.

p. 77, *Fastnet*: A small rocky island of the south-western coast of Ireland.

p. 81, *a dose*: A case of venereal disease.

p. 97, *eye splice*: A kind of knot that creates a loop in a rope.

p. 102, *ratings*: Those of lower rank.

p. 110, *the Govan Road*: A road in Glasgow near to a ship-building area.

p. 122, *five-to-two*: Rhyming slang for "Jew".

p. 122, *gharries*: A gharry is a type of small horse-drawn carriage, normally associated with India.

p. 123, *a red*: A coin.

p. 145, *a wet*: A drink.

p. 157, *warmed*: Flogged.

Extra Material

on

James Hanley's

Boy

James Hanley's Life

James Hanley was always vaguely mysterious, especially *Birth and Family* in later life, about his origins and background – probably *Background* because over the years fact and fiction had become so inextricably entwined that he was no longer entirely sure himself. His self-styled "autobiographical excursion", *Broken Water*, published in 1937, is a teasing palimpsest of truth and imagination, written in a light humorous style, in sharp contrast to much of his other writing. It is little more than a series of linked essays, outlining his early life in Dublin and Liverpool, then telling how he left school early to go to sea, describing his time as a seaman and later as a young soldier during the First World War, and finally his long struggle to become a writer, ending with the acceptance of his first novel in 1930.

The book opens on a dramatic note, as Hanley's paternal grandmother angrily recounts how his father had given up a promising career and ruined himself by going off to sea, then makes the young James promise never to do so himself. The rest of the chapter is devoted to a description of a day the family spent picnicking at Howth Head, a famous beauty spot on the coast just outside Dublin, where Hanley finally determines to break his promise and go to sea like his father. This is an extremely effective beginning, and no doubt accurately reflected his grandmother's views, but is also a typical Hanley equivocation, carefully crafted to suggest an Irish background, just as he always intimated he was born in Dublin in September 1901.

Yet, while much about his early life does remain obscure, his origins are relatively well known. Both his father and mother were born and brought up in Ireland, but were well established in Liverpool by 1891. The packed terraces of Kirkdale, the north Liverpool waterfront district where all their twelve children were born between 1892 and 1916, consisted almost entirely of first-generation Irish immigrant families, who had an overwhelming sense of their own cultural hegemony and a yearning expectation of eventually returning to their home country. Meanwhile, they created a strongly homogeneous community centred around the Catholic Church of St Alexander's, with its accompanying presbytery and elementary school, which all the Hanley children attended, only a street or two away from the noisy wharves of the Canada Dock.

James Hanley's father, Edward Hanley, was born in Dublin in 1865 into a respectable though not particularly affluent family. His own father, another Edward, was a successful printer, who became Secretary of the Dublin Typographical Society in 1876 but apparently died young, leaving a widow, Margaret Hanley, and a young family. Edward junior was initially installed in a solicitors' office in Dublin, probably as an articled clerk, but this was not to his taste, and he soon gave it up for the sea. Liverpool, the fastest-growing commercial port in Europe, offered far more attractive opportunities, and it was here that Edward met his future wife, Bridget Roache, from a family of seafarers and ships' pilots in Cobh, a small community at the entrance to Cork harbour. They were married in St Alexander's Church on 10th June 1891, and set up home together in a small terraced house next door to Margaret Hanley.

Kirkdale at the turn of the century was a tough, rough-and-ready working-class community, in which life was hard and frugal. Families crowded together in poor conditions, with only basic amenities such as a shared tap and privy across the yard. Work was largely manual and casual, with men often fighting for jobs on the docks or ships, and steady wages uncertain. Such was the reality facing the young married couple in 1891, and for the next forty years Edward and Bridget Hanley never strayed from the same handful of Kirkdale streets clustered around the Canada Dock, with the River Mersey just beyond. It was a precarious foothold in which to settle and raise a family, but inevitably the children soon began to arrive. Joe was born in 1892, Margaret in 1894, followed by a short lull, suggesting the possibility of a miscarriage, until James himself was born (despite his later protestations of 1901) on 3rd September 1897, to be quickly followed by another boy, William, in March 1899. All four children survived into adulthood, and eight more would arrive over the years. Of these none lived for more than a year or two, except for Frank (born 1911), who initially trained for the priesthood but eventually became a schoolteacher, and the youngest, Gerald (born 1916), who became a writer like his brother James. Throughout this period, Edward Hanley worked mainly as a fireman on local ships sailing out of Liverpool, so would have been regularly away from home, leaving the main care of the children to his wife. However, from 1909 he began a series of shore-based jobs, and apart from occasional voyages remained at home until the end of the war.

The children by turn were christened at St Alexander's *Education* Church and in due course enrolled at the attached Catholic school. Unfortunately, many of the school records were lost during the extensive bombing of Liverpool in 1942, but assuming he followed the general pattern, James would have been enrolled in the Infant School in 1902. What is certain is that he transferred to the Boys' Junior School in August 1905. In school the children would have been taught basic literacy and numeracy skills, together with a good deal of religious education, and some history and geography. Although Bridget and Edward seem to have encouraged their children to do well at school, and make the most of their opportunities, there is no evidence any of them stayed on beyond the normal leaving age of thirteen, in which case James would have left school in the summer of 1910.

There appears to have been some family pressure on all three boys not to take manual jobs like their father and, despite his declared ambition, James did not go to sea for at least another four years, but may have worked instead in an accountants' office. If so, the outbreak of war in August 1914 probably came as a relief to all three brothers, not least as an escape from the inevitable tensions of a large argumentative family of growing children packed into such a tiny space. Joe certainly was amongst the first to volunteer for the newly formed 89th (Liverpool Pals) Brigade of local working men, and served until his death at Loos in September 1916. William also left to go to sea around this time, and was followed by James in early 1915, when he signed up as a seventeen-year-old ordinary seaman on the SS *Nitonian* for a six-week round trip to Galveston in Texas, returning to Liverpool in March 1915.

Life at Sea

For the next two years Hanley remained at sea in a variety of ships, mainly on the North Atlantic run between Liverpool and North America, carrying Canadian soldiers or American supplies for the Western Front, but also on two longer voyages ferrying troops to Salonica in the Mediterranean. Hanley seems to have been a competent seaman and a careful observer of shipboard life, which would stand him in good stead as a writer in later years. By this time, he had already developed into something of a solitary character, a trait which was to become a regular feature of his stories; more an observer, perhaps, than a doer, which may explain why, despite his accumulating experience, he was never promoted to the more regular position of Able Seaman. This lack of promotion was the reason for his gradual disenchantment with life at sea, as he later claimed in *Broken Water*.

Enrolment in the Army and Service at the Front

Whatever the truth of the matter, on 27th April 1917, with two other Liverpool lads, he deserted the troopship *Corsican* in Saint John, New Brunswick, to join the Canadian Expeditionary Force as Private Hanley in the 236th Battalion (New Brunswick Kilties). This was just the first of many occasions on which he would act impulsively. Rather surprisingly, desertion from the Merchant Navy was a fairly regular occurrence during the First World War, largely due to the better wages paid by American and Canadian shipping companies, and appears to have been tacitly ignored by the authorities.

Hanley completed his initial military training in Canada before transferring to Seaford in Sussex in November 1917 for further training, finally arriving in France in May 1918. He saw action at Amiens at the beginning of August, and remained at the front until the end of the month, when he was admitted to hospital in Rouen suffering from chest pains. Shortly afterwards, he was transferred back to Queen Mary's Military Hospital in Lancashire, where he spent the remainder of the war. His symptoms were consistent with minor gas poisoning, probably a result of contact with old or unexploded munitions during the Amiens attack. He celebrated the armistice in November 1918 by going absent without leave to visit his family in Liverpool, but he was not yet through with soldiering, and had to return to Canada at the end of February 1919 to be demobilized in Toronto before finally coming home.

By the end of the war Liverpool was a rather different *Return from the War* place: much of its shipping had been destroyed during the conflict, and the economic slump which followed created massive unemployment as the surviving soldiers and sailors gradually returned home. Hanley was twenty-one and, like so many of his contemporaries, without either a job or many prospects. Life at home was different too: it was a much smaller and more subdued family. Joe and Meg were dead, William had remained at sea and eventually settled in the United States; Frank and Gerald were still at school. Shortly after Hanley's return home, his father was offered an engine-room job on one of the new Cunard liners, and went back to sea again, where he remained until his retirement. Now the eldest, Hanley managed to get a position as a railway porter at Bootle station, only two stops from his home. He now bought a piano and settled down to teach himself music – and become a writer. This was an ambition he seems to have nurtured since his schooldays, and which undoubtedly suited his increasingly solitary and reclusive temperament. He had always been a keen reader, but now started to devour books in earnest, particularly the great nineteenth-century Russians, such as Gogol and Dostoevsky, who were to be major influences on his work, together with Europeans such as Romain Rolland and Émile Zola. His imagination was also captured by emerging dramatists such as Eugene O'Neill, Ibsen and Strindberg, and their plays – which he may actually have seen performed in either Liverpool or Manchester – instilled a life-long dream of becoming a playwright himself.

The deepening economic depression of the mid-1920s was *Early Attempts at Getting* not a good time to be an aspiring writer. But Hanley was *Published* nothing if not determined, and for the next decade words flowed from his pen in an ever-growing torrent. His stories did the rounds of endless London publishers without any apparent success, until even Hanley himself seems to have been close to despair. Little of this early work has survived – he seems to have destroyed much of it himself – but at the end of 1929 his luck suddenly turned, and his novel *Drift* was unexpectedly accepted by Eric Partridge's newly established but short-lived Scholartis Press. The contract was derisory – with Hanley getting just £5 for the first edition, and no royalties – but publication was now more important even than money, and Hanley accepted without question, selling his few remaining books to buy a train ticket to London for the book's publication in March 1930.

Publication of Drift

Drift is a gritty story about a poor young man – rather like Hanley – who tries to break away from his strongly religious family to make a life for himself, grimly determined to shake off the rigid Catholicism that so dominated his own early life. For such a dark book it was surprisingly well reviewed, and to his credit Partridge initially looked after his young protégé, introducing him to a number of influential people and trying to procure him work. It seems likely that it was actually Partridge who began the confusion about Hanley's age – probably in an effort to increase public interest in him – for all previous records have his date of birth more or less correct.

Charles Lahr

One of the more important of these introductions was to Charles Lahr, the exuberant owner of the Progressive Bookshop in Holborn, who gave encouragement and assistance to innumerable writers, artists and poets in his lifetime. His shop was more a literary club than a business, where writers met to argue and plan new projects and borrow a few books – and usually a bob or two from Lahr at the same time. Anarchist and other radical writings from the Continent were always available under the counter, along with copies of Lawrence's *Lady Chatterley's Lover*, which Lahr had arranged to distribute. Hanley soon became a regular at the shop, but social relationships were never his strong point, and he quickly found refuge in Lahr's family home in Muswell Hill, where he helped his wife Esther with their two young daughters, and where he was able to pursue his writing in relative peace. He remained at Muswell Hill throughout the summer of 1930 working on a collection of stories for his new publisher, The Bodley Head. These stories, which included an embryonic version of *Boy*, became the cause of endless friction, as Hanley struggled to express the hard realities of working life, while the publisher in turn constantly tried to tone things down.

Publication of Men in Darkness

So there was a gap of eighteen months before they finally appeared as *Men in Darkness* in the autumn of 1931. In the meantime he was able to publish a number of rather graphic short stories in limited subscriber editions, which at least kept his name in the public eye, and established him as one of the most important new proletarian writers.

Boy by now had gone through endless revisions and increased in size to novel length, but when he sent it back to Bodley Head, together with another new story of Irish family life, *Sheila Moynihan*, both were rejected as being far too graphic for publication. Hanley by this time had moved to Wales, where – having managed to rent a small cottage near Corwen – he could live much more cheaply than in London and have all the seclusion he felt he needed for his work. It was now that he met C.J. Greenwood, whom he may previously have known as a bookseller in Liverpool. Greenwood was setting up Boriswood, a small publishing business in London, and was especially keen to print the new version of *Boy*. Bodley Head raised no objection to this arrangement, so long as Hanley produced a further novel for them – which he eventually did in 1932 with a new story of tough dockside life, *Ebb and Flood*. Greenwood introduced Hanley to T.E. Lawrence, who along with E.M. Forster became a great supporter of Hanley's work. The two met only occasionally, but remained in regular contact until Lawrence's tragic death in 1935.

Rejection of Boy and Meeting with C.J. Greenwood

In Wales Hanley not only had a new cottage and a new publisher – he suddenly found himself a remarkable wife. Until this time he had shown no noticeable interest in women, but seems to have fallen headlong for Dorothy Heathcote, known as Timmy, who was then living in Llandudno. Timmy was a vivacious person with a strong artistic flair, descending from an aristocratic Lincolnshire landowning family and second cousin to the Earl of Ancaster. Her family lost much of their estate in the terrible farming years of the late nineteenth century, and at the end of the war moved to Betws-y-Coed, where things became even worse after the tragic death of Timmy's younger sister. In an attempt to escape, Timmy had married a Llandudno garage proprietor in 1928. The marriage did not work out and, with no money of her own, Timmy had little alternative but to stay in the small coastal town. How Hanley met her is unclear, but she seems to have grasped the opportunity for a new life with enthusiasm. By early 1931, she had moved into Hanley's cottage. Any passion seems to have been short-lived – at least on Hanley's part, for writing was always more important – but the couple developed a loving relationship which would bind them together for the rest of their lives. From this time onwards Hanley earned his living entirely by his writing.

Meeting with Timmy

Publication of Boy   Boriswood finally published *Boy* in September 1931, but even Greenwood lost his nerve in the end, and the book was issued in complete form only as a limited edition for subscribers, with a cheaper trade edition in which words, phrases and even whole sentences had been omitted and replaced by asterisks. Coming from a new small publishing house, it received few reviews, but Hanley's growing reputation was sufficient for it to sell rather well, and two further trade impressions quickly followed, in which the asterisks were replaced by "more acceptable" words and phrases. Equally significant was the fact that the book was accepted by Alfred Knopf in New York, becoming – along with *Men in Darkness* – his first American publication.

Boriswood were confident enough of the author's continuing success for them to agree a weekly allowance to be offset against future royalties. Hanley now settled down to write in earnest, producing two further books in quick succession, and beginning work on the first volume of the Furys sequence, based on his own family life in Liverpool. Things went well for a time, but his books were not selling sufficiently to cover the growing debt from his allowance, and Boriswood began to get anxious. To make matters worse, Timmy became pregnant in the summer of 1932. Given her previous poor health record, in early 1933 they decided to move back to London, where better medical care was available, but the move put yet more pressure on their already small income. This in turn led to growing antagonism with Greenwood, and the relationship finally collapsed when Hanley took legal action to sever his contract. His subsequent move to Chatto & Windus put an end to their immediate financial problems, and they returned to Wales after their son Liam was born in April 1933.

Obscenity Trial   Trying to recoup some of their losses, Boriswood issued a new cheap edition of *Boy* in a particularly lurid dust jacket. This sold steadily until copies were seized by the police in Manchester in November 1934, on the basis of a single complaint, and prosecuted for obscenity. At the initial police court hearing, the Boriswood directors were charged simply with aiding and abetting publication – to which they pleaded guilty on legal advice – and withdrew all remaining copies of the book. By the time the case finally came before a judge the following March, the charges had been substantially increased, but it was then too late for Boriswood to change their plea, and so they were automatically found guilty. They were heavily fined, and copies of the book ordered to be destroyed. Although not implicated in the proceedings himself, Hanley was devastated by the case, which inevitably featured in the Liverpool newspapers. As a result, he briefly became more politically active, joining the British delegation led by E.M. Forster (who famously defended *Boy* as "a serious and painful piece of work, whose moral – if it had one – was definitely on the side of chastity and virtue") to the Writers' Congress in Paris in 1935, and becoming a founder member of the *Left Review*. Shortly afterwards, he visited South Wales and wrote *Grey Children*, to draw attention to the desperate conditions endured by mine-workers and their families.

Fortunately *The Furys*, his first novel for Chatto & Windus, sold well both in Britain and the United States, and for the first time the couple felt sufficiently secure to purchase a large and secluded house in Wales. The next two years saw the publication of the novel *Stoker Bush*, a short-story collection entitled *At Bay* (with Grayson Books) and the second volume of the Furys sequence, *The Secret Journey*. At the end of this prolific spell, Hanley turned his attention to a long troopship novel based on his own Mediterranean experience. He found the writing of this book increasingly difficult, and when he did manage to complete it, it was rejected both by Chatto and his new American publisher Macmillan, who persuaded him to write an autobiography as the last book in his contract. Unfortunately, *Broken Water* did not meet with the degree of success that the publisher had anticipated, and with Chatto's consent he moved back to Bodley Head, who immediately issued a collection of his stories, *Half an Eye*, followed by a revised version of the troopship novel, now retitled *Hollow Sea*.

More Publications and Another Rejection

Although his work remained uniquely individual and realistic, Hanley had now largely thrown off his initial reputation as a proletarian writer and was more firmly established as a literary figure, with increasingly respectful reviews. Unfortunately, sales remained stubbornly low, once again causing serious financial problems. With great unwillingness – particularly with a young child and another war now inevitable – Hanley and his family gave up the house in Wales and moved back to London, hoping to find more opportunities for journalism. After a rather peripatetic couple of years, in which their fortunes declined further, they finally settled in a South

Move to London and Return to Wales

Kensington flat, just as the worst of the Blitz got under way. They were eventually forced back to Wales to a tiny cottage at Llanfechain, in the border country near Oswestry, which would prove to be a sanctuary until the end of the war.

Publication of
The Ocean and
No Directions
After protracted problems over his contract with Bodley Head, Hanley moved to Faber, who published *The Ocean*, a gripping story of endurance in a lifeboat, and shortly afterwards *No Directions*, based on his experiences of the recent Blitz. Both of these short books sold relatively well, and are among his most reprinted volumes.

Like all publishers, Faber suffered badly in the war from paper shortages and production difficulties. This inevitably caused extensive delays and added to Hanley's growing impatience. Somewhat predictably, rather than biding his time he now precipitously left Faber and moved to a smaller publisher, Nicholson & Watson, on the vague promise that they would bring out a standard edition of his works. The new publisher initially issued *Sailor's Song* (1943) – a similar book to *The Ocean*, but showing Hanley's increasing interest in the dramatic use of dialogue – which was followed by reprints of some earlier books, notably *Drift* and *Ebb and Flood*. As well as writing his novels, Hanley contributed to many of the popular literary anthologies which appeared during the war. He also wrote reviews, stories and short articles for a variety of magazines, which just about kept his family going through the lean post-war years. Hanley's initial enthusiasm for Nicholson & Watson – for whom he produced another two short books – gradually evaporated, especially when it became clear the promised standard edition would never materialize, and he was pleased to sign with Phoenix House for publication of *Winter Song*, the fourth volume of the Furys sequence, in 1950. Increasingly concerned that his books consistently failed to make a profit, Hanley wrote *The House in the Valley* for Jonathan Cape under the pseudonym Patric Shone – a name he'd already used for a few of his stories in the USA. Although well reviewed, this novel did no better financially, and the experiment was not repeated (the book was later republished as *Against the Stream* under his own name).

Publication of
The Closed Harbour,
The Welsh Sonata
and Levine
Instead he now moved to Macdonald and produced some of his finest novels: *The Closed Harbour* in 1952, a powerful psychological study of a dispossessed sea captain set in Marseille, and *Levine* – a story about the doomed love of

two lost souls swept together in the aftermath of war – which appeared only in 1956. In between came *The Welsh Sonata*, a haunting evocation of Welsh rural life and a homage to his adopted homeland. In 1958 came the fifth and final volume of the Furys sequence, *An End and a Beginning*, after which Hanley turned away from the novel to focus his attention on work for BBC Radio. By this time the couple had moved to a larger and more substantial cottage, a mile or so outside Llanfechain, where they were to remain until 1963.

After the war, radio broadcasting had developed rapidly, bringing a much wider range of new programmes. Over the years, a number of Hanley's stories had been adapted for radio, but now he began to explore its possibilities more proactively, as the BBC paid much larger fees than he had ever received in the past from publishers. Until this time the Hanleys had continued to live a largely secluded life in Wales, but their son Liam was now grown up and established as a successful London journalist, so they began to spend longer periods at his flat in Bloomsbury – much to Timmy's delight, as she always loved the excitement of city life. Hanley's initial scripts were far too ambitious, but he continued to receive encouragement, and in early 1957 was rewarded by the acceptance of *A Winter Journey*, a simple but effective thirty-minute radio play for two voices. After the programme's success, Hanley soon got into his stride, and over the next few years his plays were regularly broadcast, particularly on the newly established Third Programme, together with an increasing number of his short stories and adaptations of his earlier novels. Among the most important radio plays of this period were *Letter from the Desert* (1958), *Gobbet* (1959), *The Queen of Ireland* (1960), *Say Nothing* (1961) and *A Dream* (1963).

Work for the Radio; Stage and Television Adaptations

Hanley now began to expand his horizons, seeing both the benefits of being able to recycle his material and the growing significance of the television medium. Keen to fulfil his long-cherished ambition to become a stage dramatist, he expanded and readapted many of his early radio plays. *Say Nothing*, for example, reappeared first as a novel in 1962 and was then produced at London's Stratford East Theatre in August of the same year, to generally positive reviews. Although for some time there were talks of a possible West End production, this in the end didn't materialize and, despite Hanley's many efforts, *Say Nothing* was his only play to appear on the British stage. But if his theatre ambitions were thwarted, Hanley had better fortune with television: his TV-play version of *Say Nothing* was screened by the BBC in February 1964, followed by many more readaptations for TV of his earlier radio plays, such as *The Inner World of Miss Vaughan* and a number of original scripts.

Family Trouble   Although Hanley now seemed on course for a more stable and rewarding writing career, he faced problems at home. Timmy had always suffered from poor health, but her condition now deteriorated, with regular periods of illness and bouts of depression. Timmy was finding the isolation of the Welsh countryside more and more difficult to endure. Since Liam had married, she and her husband were no longer able to spend extensive periods in London as in the past. The situation finally came to a head while Liam and his wife Hilary were on holiday in Italy. Timmy in despair declared that she could no longer bear to live in a secluded cottage in Wales, and insisted they move back to London for good. Completely taken aback, Hanley immediately agreed: the cottage was sold and they found a temporary flat to rent in Kentish Town, leaving Liam to oversee the storage of all their furniture on his return from holiday. Hanley mourned for Wales for the rest of his life, devising endless schemes for their return, while Timmy in turn was stricken by the guilt of having caused so much distress and suffered recurring bouts of depression. Eventually the couple moved to a larger flat in Camden Square, and life returned to a more normal pattern once again.

Over the next few years, Hanley continued to work on a variety of new projects for radio, television and the theatre, as well as adaptations of earlier material. He produced a steady stream of work, mostly for the BBC, and collaborated on an English edition of Maxim Gorky's recollections of the great Russian operatic bass, Feodor Chaliapin, which appeared in 1968. But Hanley was now seventy and clearly slowing down, often working at his desk for only an hour or so each day and becoming more and more reclusive. The BBC was also changing: many of the old producers were leaving to be replaced by a younger generation with different ideas, and Hanley's material was becoming less resonant, while he in turn seemed less capable of change. He continued to submit new work with occasional success, but his thoughts were now converging on writing a new novel, especially after a new edition of *The Closed Harbour* was issued in 1971. Over the next few years, in a final resurgence of inspiration, four more novels were published by André Deutsch. Once again he took the opportunity to recycle some previous material: the first three books were all developments of earlier work, but his final novel, *A Kingdom* (1978), set in his beloved Wales, showed his imagination still at full stretch.

Hanley was working on a new novel when Timmy suddenly died from a heart attack in August 1980. This was a devastating blow for him, his editor at the time commenting that "the spring had broken". Hanley moved to a new flat, with Liam and his growing family nearby, but he was now in his twilight years, shuffling the papers on his desk occasionally, in an endless cloud of blue tobacco smoke, enjoying occasional conversation with a few close friends, a glass of whisky at his elbow. He gradually faded away, dying peacefully with his family around him on 11th November 1985, at the age of eighty-eight. A few days later, he was buried in the village of Llanfechain, where he had lived for so many years, surrounded by his beloved Welsh hills. Ironically, in death as in life, he had the last laugh – for the simple slate gravestone gives his dates as 1901–1985. It is a typical Hanley joke, and one he would have particularly enjoyed.

Final Years and Death

James Hanley's Works

James Hanley is generally remembered as a seafaring writer, often bracketed in the same company as Conrad or Melville. Whilst it is true that throughout his career he did regularly produce work of this type, his works actually had a much broader range, covering a widening span of topics, styles and genres. If he is to be categorized at all, it should probably be for his minute exploration of that unbridgeable gap opening up between each individual. In many respects, being more interested in the way characters respond to extreme situations than in the situations themselves, he can be compared to Harold Pinter in his approach. Consequently dialogue often becomes more important to him than narrative, although on occasion he can also be an exciting stylist, vividly describing the experience of a storm at sea or the stokehold of a steamship. But in the end it is the way in which the individual struggles to achieve meaning in life, often in the most desperate circumstances, which remains the central theme of his work.

Themes and Style

193

Hanley was incredibly prolific – and had to be in order to earn a living from his writing. Identifying his full body of work is made even more problematic by Hanley's notoriously cavalier attitude in his choice of publishers. For these reasons it is impossible, in this brief review, to provide more than an outline of the most important of his works.

In the ten years between the ending of the First World War and the acceptance of his first novel in 1929, he produced an incredible amount of work. Unfortunately, very little of this has survived, and can now only be traced through occasional references in publishers' archives. In the main, this early writing was not based on his experiences at sea or in the war, but on the tensions and conflicts of close family life in communities such as those he grew up in. These stories were large sprawling rag-bags, badly in need of being edited into shape, but always showing a rare spark of originality.

Drift   Hanley's first published book was *Drift*, which appeared in 1930, although it had been written at least as early as 1926 and had done the rounds of many London publishers before being accepted by Eric Partridge at the Scholartis Press. *Drift* is a powerful story of a young man's attempt to break out of the religion-dominated confines of his poor working-class family and establish a new life for himself based on his own needs and values. Its early passages owe a good deal to Joyce's *A Portrait of the Artist as a Young Man*, but Hanley soon found his own voice, and the result is undoubtedly a fine depiction of the tensions and conflicts of growing up in a tight-knit family and community. The book received encouraging reviews and went into a second impression before Scholartis Press collapsed. It was subsequently republished in 1932 and again in 1944.

Short Stories   As we have seen above, Hanley had already been working on a new novel and several short stories when he moved to Bodley Head in 1930. He was increasingly keen to produce more realistic depictions of working-class life, but these were delayed as Bodley Head's publisher Allen Lane on the one hand tried to tone them down and Hanley on the other tried to flesh them out. In the meantime he published a number of short stories in relatively expensive signed limited editions, which was a popular way at the time for young writers to make a little money, and also provided a platform for more experimental writing.

The first of these stories was *The German Prisoner*, published by his friend, the bookseller Charles Lahr, in May 1930 (although the book itself says "printed by the author", giving Lahr's Muswell Hill address), with an introduction by the famous imagist poet and war novelist Richard Aldington. The story – no doubt based on Hanley's own wartime experience – describes the atmosphere of chaos and confusion as a battalion moves into the front line to go into action. It graphically portrays the senseless murder of a young German prisoner by two British soldiers who are themselves blown up in the heat of the battle. *The German Prisoner* was followed by *A Passion Before Death*, published by C.J. Greenwood in a small edition of 200 copies in December 1930, a grim story about a war veteran condemned to die for murdering the man who raped his wife, again showing Hanley's imagination at full power. Shortly afterwards came *The Last Voyage*, a memorable story about a steamship fireman being forced to retire after many years with the same company, but still in need of work to support his family. The three stories were originally meant for the collection Hanley was writing for Bodley Head, but were eventually excluded and did not appear in book form until collected together with some other early work in *The Last Voyage and Other Stories* by Harvill Press in 1998. The Bodley Head collection, *Men in Darkness,* finally appeared in September 1931, consisting of five previously unpublished stories, mainly about the sea, with an enthusiastic introduction by John Cowper Powys, which did much to confirm Hanley's growing reputation.

Another story intended for inclusion in *Men in Darkness* was *Boy*, which Hanley continued to rewrite and expand – contrary to his frequently reported claim that the book was written in only ten days – as his dispute with Allen Lane was raging on. In the end, as we have seen above, *Boy* was published by Boriswood in September 1931 in an expensive limited edition of 145 signed copies, followed by a cheaper trade edition in which problematic words, phrases and sentences were replaced by asterisks. The book sold very well and was reprinted the same year, with the asterisks replaced by "more acceptable" words and phrases. A third impression followed early in 1932, and the first US edition of a book by Hanley appeared from Alfred Knopf in April 1932, although with various textual differences to the three British editions.

The only surviving manuscript of *Boy* is the copy Charles Lahr sold to Louis Sterling in 1931, which is a fair copy dated 1930, written on plain paper in Hanley's small but generally readable script, with a note on the front cover: "This is the original MS of *Boy* without any deletions whatever". The final printed version largely follows this manuscript text, although there are innumerable small changes, corrections and stylistic improvements, probably made on the typescript or at proof stage, but there are four specifically deleted pages which relate to the "initiation" ceremony the boy Fearon endures on his first day at work on the docks, which is considerably longer and more explicit in the manuscript, and includes a forced masturbation scene. Much of this material does still appear in the published book, although in a greatly attenuated form, so it seems likely that the original Boriswood limited edition text, from which all more recent editions have been taken, is the best version available.

As we have seen, following Hanley's break with Boriswood in 1934, the publisher issued a new cheap edition with a lurid dust jacket, which led to the obscenity charge and all the remaining copies of the book being withdrawn and destroyed. Despite the heavy fine, and without Hanley's knowledge, it seems that Boriswood immediately sent the plates to the Obelisk Press in Paris, well-known for publishing more risqué British titles, who issued at least two separate editions of the book, one in 1936 and another in 1946, although there may well have been others. Boriswood also ensured that Hanley continued to receive royalties for the book, at least until they went out of business in 1938. Hanley was so upset by the whole case that he set his mind against any further editions, only relenting towards the end of his life, when he began to prepare a new edition. Even then he remained equivocal, and the book was never republished in his lifetime, only appearing in a completely unexpurgated edition from André Deutsch in 1990, some five years after his death, which was followed by a Penguin Modern Classic edition in 1992.

Boy opens with the young protagonist, Arthur Fearon, unable to focus on his lessons as he knows that his parents are soon to withdraw him from school and send him to work in the dockyard. He's temperamentally unsuited to such work, harbouring private ambitions to go to university and become a chemist. On his return home from school, he is beaten by his father. When he starts working at the docks, he detests his job, and decides to stow away on a ship to escape to a better life abroad. Arthur hides in the coal bunker of the SS *Hernian*, and nearly dies before being discovered. By this time it is too late to turn back and return him to land, so the ship's crew keep him onboard and assign him to menial labour. There is also a strong hint that some sailors sexually molest him. However, in time he works his way into a position which makes better use of his natural talents, and the abuse ends as well. When the vessel reaches Alexandria, he is forced into visiting a brothel, where he is traumatized by his meeting with a prostitute. Returning later of his own accord, he has an encounter with another prostitute and contracts a grave sexual disease. The crew fail to recognize the nature of his illness and do not allow him to rest, but when Arthur collapses it becomes apparent that he has syphilis. The ship's captain kills him to spare him from further suffering and throws him overboard.

While the arguments about *Boy* went on, Hanley completed a new novel, *Ebb and Flood* (published by Bodley Head in 1932), a family saga concerning three boyhood friends growing up and starting work on the waterfront. The book contains some brilliant scenes – particularly the one where the boys gamble away their pitiful wages – and was generally well reviewed, appearing in two further editions. Hanley then turned his attention to a rather larger canvas with *Captain Bottell* (issued by Boriswood in 1933), a compelling psychological study of the gradual disintegration and final demise of the eponymous sea captain as he becomes besotted with a young woman passenger on her way to join her army husband in the Middle East. The book became a Book Society Choice and gained him further good reviews. Despite the critical success, his debt to Boriswood continued to mount, and he spent the following year trying to escape from his contractual obligation, before finally being able to sign with Chatto & Windus in 1935. In the meantime, Boriswood issued his early novel *Sheila Moynihan*, which they had been holding for some years, as a limited edition of ninety-nine copies with the somewhat pretentious title *Resurrexit Dominus* ("The Risen Lord"). The story revolves around a hapless young Irish girl caught up in the erotic fantasies of an elderly Catholic priest, and contains all Hanley's bitter antipathy to the Catholic Church, but is poorly structured, probably as it was never properly completed. As T.E. Lawrence

Ebb and Flood, Captain Bottell and Sheila Moynihan

197

wrote in a letter to Hanley: "It is hot writing, like all of yours... and the torrent of idea flows well and brilliantly... But it is unfinished... Work that is not ended is so hard to judge." Most copies of the book were destroyed in the London Blitz, so this has come to be Hanley's rarest title.

The Furys   The move to Chatto came as a great relief, and Hanley quickly settled into an easy relationship when his new novel *The Furys* appeared in 1935. This was the first volume of what eventually became a sequence of five novels about the Fury family, modelled largely on Hanley's own boyhood experience, and somewhat Dickensian in scope, developing each of the characters in some detail as the sequence progresses. The first volume does little more than set the scene for the subsequent fragmentation of the family, largely due to Mrs Fury's single-minded determination that her youngest son Peter become a priest, with the bulk of the family income going to support him in a seminary in Ireland. The novel is set against the turbulent background of the 1911 transport strike, and contains some magnificent set pieces, such as the unprovoked attack on the unarmed demonstrators in the city centre. The novel chimed exactly with the spirit of the times, and did well both in Britain and in the United States, where it was brought out by Macmillan later in 1935, and has been reprinted a number of times since, most recently as a Penguin Twentieth Century Classic edition in 1983.

Stoker Bush and   His next novel for Chatto was *Stoker Bush*, also published
Broken Water   in 1935, a return to seafaring with the story of a young stoker attempting to become reconciled with his unfaithful wife, and the adventures that befall him on the way, including a memorable sea storm. This was followed by *The Secret Journey*, the second – and probably the best – of the Furys sequence, which deals with Mrs Fury's mounting debt to Anna Ragner, a voracious moneylender hovering like a malevolent black spider over the story. As the book reaches its climax, Peter Fury, now home after being expelled from the seminary, eventually resolves the crippling debt by murdering Anna Ragner. The novel appeared in 1936 in both Britain and the USA, but sold fewer copies than *The Furys*, although it received better reviews. Hanley wanted to start the third volume of the sequence, but instead he began a long novel about a troopship during the Gallipoli campaign, which he found extremely difficult to complete. As we have seen, the book was finally

rejected by Chatto, who urged him to write his autobiography. Hanley unwillingly agreed, and *Broken Water* eventually appeared to rather puzzled reviews in 1937.

Leaving Chatto and returning to Bodley Head, Hanley published a revised version of the Gallipoli book, *Hollow Sea*, in 1938, after which he immediately set to work on the third Fury volume. In the meantime, he had spent some time in the depressed mining areas of South Wales, producing a devastating critique of the situation in *Grey Children*, published by Methuen in 1937, with strong echoes of Orwell's *The Road to Wigan Pier*, which was published the same year. His short stories were now regularly appearing in a variety of magazines, helpfully adding to his income, and a good collection of these was published as *Half An Eye* by Bodley Head later the same year. This was followed by a collection of sea anecdotes, with illustrations by Timmy Hanley, entitled *Between the Tides* in 1939, just before the outbreak of war. The third Fury volume eventually appeared from Bodley Head in 1940 under the title *Our Time is Gone*. With Peter Fury now in prison for murder, the book shifts its focus to his elder sister Maureen and the experiences of her estranged husband, Joe Kilkey, as a conscientious objector during the First World War. The book has many particularly compelling scenes, but shows the haste with which it was written, and is less rounded than the previous two volumes.

Hollow Sea,
Grey Children,
Between the Tides,
Our Times is Gone

Despite his unsettled life during the early years of the war, the constant worry about money and the loss of his American publisher, Hanley managed to produce three very powerful short books. *The Ocean*, published by Faber in 1941, and *Sailor's Song*, published by Nicholson & Watson in 1943, both recount the uncertain lives of seamen and their families during times of war. The third book, *No Directions*, also from Faber in 1943, is again about war, but this time the experience of civilians during the London Blitz, showing Hanley at his most jaggedly poignant. The three novels chimed with the prevailing public mood and sold fairly well, despite the wartime paper shortages, becoming the most frequently reprinted of all Hanley's books.

The Ocean, Sailor's Song,
No Directions

Over the next few years, Hanley subsisted largely on the sale of short stories and articles, and published only two slim and rather unmemorable volumes, *What Farrar Saw* (1946) and *Emily* (1948), which were followed in 1950 by the fourth

Winter Song,
The House in the Valley

199

and possibly weakest of the Fury volumes, *Winter Song*, dealing with the old age of Mrs Fury and her husband. It was around this time that Hanley began to turn his attention to writing radio scripts for the BBC, whilst continuing writing new novels.

The first of these, *The House in the Valley*, was published by Jonathan Cape in 1951 under the pseudonym of Patric Shone. Hanley had concluded that he was never going to make any significant impact with the reading public under his own name, and so determined to make a fresh start. Sadly, the book fared no better than the previous ones, getting the usual respectful if non-committal reviews of the average first novel. *The House in the Valley* relates the story of a young boy who, after losing both his parents, is brought up by elderly grandparents in a dilapidated old house on the Welsh borders, where time seems to have stood still. It gives a vivid picture of childhood and the misunderstandings between different generations and social backgrounds. In this form the book is another Hanley rarity, although it appeared again in 1982 as *Against the Stream*, published by André Deutsch.

The Closed Harbour   Reverting to his own name once again, and with yet another publisher, Hanley published his next novel, *The Closed Harbour*, in 1952. Set in Marseille, a city Hanley had visited while at sea in 1917, this is a powerful psychological drama of the mental breakdown of a sea captain who has lost two of his ships and is now ostracized by both the seafaring community and his own family. *The Closed Harbour* went into a second edition the same year, and was also published by a new American publisher, Ben Raeburn's tiny Horizon Press – his first book to appear in the USA since *The Secret Journey* in 1936. This was the start of a long relationship with Raeburn, who published all of Hanley's subsequent work in the United States.

Levine,   Although conceived at the same time as *The Closed*
Collected Stories,   *Harbour,* Hanley's next novel, *Levine,* went through a number
Don Quixote Drowned   of drafts before it finally appeared in 1956. *Levine* is another tense psychological drama, with strong echoes of Conrad's story *Amy Forster*, in which a foreign sailor is washed ashore to a war-devastated Britain, where he lives in an old POW camp and meets up with a young woman as lost as himself. Their basic need for human comfort is contrasted by their mutual incomprehension of one another, and the encounter

inevitably ends in tragedy. The book sold relatively well and was reprinted the same year, and again in a new edition in 1973. Meanwhile, Macdonald issued another Hanley volume, *Collected Stories*, in 1953, containing many of his most noteworthy tales. The same year also saw the publication of *Don Quixote Drowned*, an odd assortment of Hanley pieces, mainly about the sea, but also describing his life as a writer, including the novella-length story 'Anatomy of Llangyllwch' – often said to be the forerunner of Dylan Thomas's radio play *Under Milk Wood*, which was broadcast the following year – exploring Hanley's feelings for his adopted homeland.

Although Hanley now regarded himself more and more as a radio dramatist, with regular pieces for the BBC since the early 1950s, he had not entirely given up on the novel form, and in 1954 produced *The Welsh Sonata*, a further exploration of the meaning and culture of the Welsh and their homeland, showing Hanley's growing interest in the use of dialogue rather than straight narrative for the development of the story. The book was quite successful, and appeared in a number of editions, most recently from André Deutsch in 1978. In 1958 came the fifth and final volume of the Furys sequence, *An End and a Beginning*, in which Peter Fury, now released from prison, travels to Ireland to discover the truth about the death of his parents. During the course of the novel – a suitable conclusion to such an epic endeavour – Peter relives many of the key elements of the drama and the life of his family, through a series of graphic flashbacks and interior monologues.

The Welsh Sonata, An End and a Beginning

By the mid-1950s, the bulk of Hanley's income came from the BBC, initially from dramatized short stories, then short features, and finally major radio dramas. Much of this appeared on the recently launched Third Programme, where he worked with a number of innovative producers who showed great belief in his work and encouraged stylistic experimentation. Apart from his early years with Chatto in the mid-1930s, this proved to be the most fulfilling period of his creative life.

Radio and TV Plays

Hanley's first serious drama was *A Winter Journey* in 1957, a short piece for two voices about an elderly woman living alone. This was followed by a rather more substantial piece of work, *A Letter in the Desert*, which explores the subtle emotional warfare between a couple who have turned their backs on their earlier existence, living together in isolated

201

surroundings and deluding themselves about what is happening to their relationship. When a sudden invitation for the husband to give a radio talk turns out to be a hoax, the careful pattern of their lives is irredeemably shattered. The radio play was repeated a number of times in 1958 and 1959.

October 1959 also saw the broadcast of *Gobbet*, the spine-chilling story of a dwarf used by his father as a ventriloquist's dummy in their joint stage show, in which their mutually dependent relationship gradually disintegrates and the dwarf is killed by the father in front of the spellbound audience. It is one of Hanley's most extreme dramatic situations and, after some tense internal battles at the BBC, it was never repeated. Undeterred, Hanley went on to rewrite *Gobbet* as a stage play. The resulting work, *The Inner Journey* – despite severe casting problems – was performed in Hamburg in 1966 to great success, and again in New York at the Lincoln Centre in 1969. *Gobbet* was followed in 1960 by *The Queen of Ireland* and a little later by *Miss Williams* for the BBC, both stories focusing on the inner life of elderly women as they look back to their youth.

Encouraged by the successful reception of his radio plays, Hanley wrote *Say Nothing*, the deeply disturbing story of Charles Elston, a naive young law student who goes to lodge with the Baines family in a northern town. As the play unfolds, the strange ties between Joshua Baines, his sensuous wife and her reclusive sister gradually become clear to Elston, who tries to help them out of their tangled relationships – realizing too late that they are completely happy with the situation. Deceptively simple in structure, the play operates on many levels, and is one of Hanley's most accomplished achievements.

As mentioned before, over the next few years Hanley continued to write for radio, while adapting many of his earlier dramas for television. The most noteworthy of these productions were *The Inner World of Miss Vaughn* (1964), *A Walk in the Sea* (1966), *One Way Only* (1967), *Mr Ponge* (1965 and 1974) – originally a short story – and *The House in the Valley* (1971). Although many of these radio and TV scripts have survived in the BBC archives, sadly there are no tapes of any of the broadcasts, with the single exception of a 1965 Canadian TV version of *Say Nothing*, shown at the Hanley Centenary Conference at Jesus College, Cambridge in 2001.

Hanley had been toying for some time with the idea of returning to the prose narrative form. After producing a critical study of his friend John Cowper Powys (*A Man in the Corner*) in 1969 and of Herman Melville (*A Man in the Customs House*) in 1971, he began to work seriously on a new novel, which was published – together with the following three – by André Deutsch. These last novels were all very positively received, although they consisted in great part of a rewriting of earlier dramatic work: *Another World* (1972) from the BBC play *The Inner World of Miss Vaughn*; *A Woman in the Sky* (1973), originally *One Way Only*; *Dream Journey* (1976), a book Hanley had long struggled with as a sequel to his war novel *No Directions*; and finally *A Kingdom*, a spare story retailing the meeting of two sisters for their father's funeral in deepest Wales – where he had chosen to live in simple poverty – and the different choices made by the sisters in their lives. It is a deceptively simple book, yet redolent with the unspoken yearnings so characteristic of Hanley's later work.

Critical Work and Last Novels

A Kingdom was to be Hanley's last novel, although he continued to work on a new book for the remaining years of his life (which survives in fragmentary form in the large collection of his material now at the National Library of Wales) and to put together a new book of stories, which eventually appeared as *What Farrar Saw and Other Stories* in 1984, the year before he died.

In the years following Hanley's death, Deutsch not only republished *Boy*, but reissued quality paperback editions of *No Directions* and *An End and a Beginning*, two of Hanley's own favourite novels. This could only encourage another passing glance at Hanley's neglected works and, as none of these editions sold particularly well, Deutsch understandably dropped plans for any further volumes. Since then, the most notable revival of Hanley's work was in 2001 – the supposed year of his centenary – when the BBC aired an effective radio adaptation of the Furys sequence on Radio 4.

Since his death in 1985, Hanley's books have gradually disappeared from public-library shelves and become difficult to find. As yet there has been no biography, although one is in preparation and a valuable review of his work, *James Hanley: Modernism and the Working Class* (2002), has been recently produced by John Fordham.

A revival of James Hanley's work and his contribution to modern literature is now well overdue. Many writers have suffered similar misfortune, but such neglect still reflects sadly upon a life of constant artistic endeavour and quiet dignity. Perhaps the greatest sadness of all is that in truth Hanley himself would have expected nothing less.

– Chris Gostick, 2007

Acknowledgements

The Publisher wishes to thank Chris Gostick for his research and for writing the apparatus, Georgia Glover at David Higham Associates for championing this project and Liam Hanley for his support and for providing visual material.